Her hand was covered with blood. . . .

Suitcases and a garment bag were turned inside out, their linings slashed. A makeup case, its contents oozing into the green carpet, lay on its side, the hinges broken. Peeking out from under the bench were feet shod in pointy rolled-up-toe shoes. It looked as if the remains of the Wicked Witch from *The Wizard of Oz* were crumpled on the trailer floor.

Skye ran over and pushed the bench aside. "Mrs. Gumtree, are you all right?"

There was no answer or movement, but she still couldn't see the whole person, as the head and torso were in the knee-well of the dressing table. She crouched down and reached into the recess, trying to find a pulse, and felt something sticky instead. When she withdrew her hand, it was covered with blood.

* * *

"In Murder of a Small-Town Honey, *Denise Swanson has written a delightful mystery that bounces along with gently wry humor and jaunty twists and turns. School psychologist Skye Denison is the quintessential amateur sleuth: bright, curious, and more than a little nervy. She is an engaging, liberated everywoman who is sure to garner her rightful share of mystery fans."*

—Earlene Fowler, author of the Benni Harper mysteries

"School psychologist Skye Denison finds her old hometown brimming with anger, discontent, and murder, forcing her to nose into all kinds of danger to save her brother from a murder charge."

—Carolyn Hart, author of the *Death on Demand* and *Henrie O* mysteries

Murder of a Small-Town Honey

A Scumble River Mystery

DENISE SWANSON

A SIGNET BOOK

SIGNET
Published by New American Library, a division of
Penguin Putnam Inc., 375 Hudson Street, New York, New York 10014, U.S.A.
Penguin Books Ltd, 27 Wrights Lane, London W8 5TZ, England
Penguin Books Australia Ltd, Ringwood, Victoria, Australia
Penguin Books Canada Ltd, 10 Alcorn Avenue, Toronto, Ontario,
Canada M4V 3B2
Penguin Books (N.Z.) Ltd, 182–190 Wairau Road, Auckland 10, New Zealand

Penguin Books Ltd, Registered Offices: Harmondsworth, Middlesex, England

First published by Signet, an imprint of New American Library,
a division of Penguin Putnam Inc.

First Printing, July 2000
10 9 8 7 6 5 4 3 2 1

Copyright © Denise Swanson Stybr, 2000

PUBLISHER'S NOTE
This is a work of fiction. Names, characters, places, and incidents either are the
product of the author's imagination or are used fictitiously, and any
resemblance to actual persons, living or dead, business establishments, events,
or locales is entirely coincidental.

*To my parents, who always thought I could do anything;
and to my husband, Dave, who convinced me.*

Scumble River is not a real town. The characters and events portrayed in these pages are entirely fictional, and any resemblance to living persons is pure coincidence.

Acknowledgments

I would like to thank the following people: Joyce Flaherty for her unflagging belief in my talent; Ellen Edwards for editorial expertise and understanding; Lucille DeGuile for being the finest English teacher on the planet; Jan Fellers, Nancy Carleton, Alex Matthews, and Carol Houswald for their efforts as the best critique group in the world; Linda Baty for help with those pesky commas and dashes; Lynn Bradley, Kathy Person, Jane Isenberg, and Aileen Schumacher, fellow writers who shared the ups and downs; Monika and Joe Bradley, Robert and Nancy Chidel, Helen Valentinas, Donna Stefan, and Sandy Kral, friends who let me talk endlessly about my ideas and aspirations; Marie and Ernie Swanson, who although surprised to find the book had been written, were supportive; and, finally, my husband, Dave Stybr, who always said yes when I asked him to read just one more revision.

CHAPTER 1

It's Like We Never Said Goodbye

When Skye Denison was forced to return to Scumble River, Illinois, she knew it would be humiliating, but she never dreamed it would be murder. It was embarrassing enough to have been fired from her first full-time position as a school psychologist, but then she'd had to beg for a job in a place she had described as a small town, full of small-minded people, with even smaller intellects. Skye only wished she hadn't said it to the entire population of Scumble River via her high school valedictorian address. Granted, the speech took place twelve years ago, but she had a feeling people would remember.

Nonetheless, she was back, and nothing had changed. Skye had arrived in Scumble River last Sunday afternoon, barely in time for the start of school on Monday. Her plan had been to slip into town unnoticed and remain that way for as long as possible. But it was only Saturday, and she'd already been suckered into participating in one of the community's most hokey events, the Chokeberry Days Festival.

Skye stood behind a huge table made from sawhorses and sheets of plywood. Spread across its surface was a red-and-white-checked cloth on which were lined up hundreds of bright pink bottles of chokeberry jelly. The clashing colors made Skye dizzy, and the idea of actually tasting the contents of all those jars made her nauseous. How had she ever let herself be talked into judging the chokeberry jelly contest?

Before she could make a bolt for freedom, a woman dressed in a magenta-colored polyester pantsuit descended on the booth. "Skye, it's good to see you back home where you belong. Though I do remember you saying something when you left about Scumble River being too *small* for you."

"Aunt Minnie, what can I say?" She could think of lots of things, but none that wouldn't get her in trouble. Minnie was her mother's middle sister, and she would be on the phone griping to Skye's mom in a minute if she felt Skye had been rude.

"Did you hear about what happened Thursday night at the high school band contest?" Minnie was also gossip central for their family. She was better at getting the news out than Dan Rather.

"No, what?" Skye asked warily. Her aunt reminded her of a Venus-flytrap, and Skye was always afraid she was about to become the bug.

"Well, I thought you would've been there, since you got that fancy job working for the schools." Minnie smiled sweetly.

Swallowing the words she wanted to say—fancy job and Scumble River School District did not belong in the same sentence—Skye matched her aunt's smile and said, "Gee, I didn't know you all were impressed by my little job."

After a few moments of silence, Minnie went on as if Skye hadn't spoken. "The problems started when half the kids discovered their music had disappeared and the other half claimed their instruments were missing. Both were later found stashed in the shower stall next to the boys' locker room, but by then it was too late to go on with the contest."

Skye said, "Oh, my, I did hear some teachers talking about that yesterday in the teachers' lounge. There was a fight too, right?"

"Right. The rival band members blamed each other for the missing items, and Scumble River's tuba player ended up with a broken nose. A drummer from Clay Center took home two black eyes."

"How awful. The poor kids had probably practiced for months for the competition." Skye narrowed her eyes. "A prank like that is just plain mean. Do you know if they found out who did it?"

Minnie shook her head.

"I wonder if the band director kicked any kids out of the band recently."

"Not that I heard of. But that's not all that's been happening," Minnie said and fanned herself with her handkerchief. "Yesterday at the catfish dinner, someone replaced all the salt in the kitchen with sugar. Seventy pounds of catfish, potato salad, and baked beans were ruined. The Feedbag was sponsoring the supper, so they're out a pretty penny."

Skye frowned. The Feedbag was Scumble River's only restaurant, other than the fast-food places along the road heading out of town. Like any small business, the Feedbag operated on a shoestring and couldn't afford a big hit in the cash register. "Why would someone do that?" she asked.

Minnie's face grew angelic. "Why, honey, you're the one with the degree in psychology. I'm just one of those people with *small intellects* you told us about in your graduation speech."

Skye felt her face turn the same color as her aunt's suit, and decided the better part of valor lay in switching subjects—quickly. "Chokeberry Days has certainly changed a lot."

"This year is different," Minnie said quietly. "There's a bad feeling in town. Half the people want the festival to grow bigger and bigger."

Skye hazarded a guess. "The ones in town who stand to profit from the crowds, no doubt."

"Yes. And on the other side are all the folks that just see it for a nuisance."

"Who's that?" Skye wrinkled her brow.

Minnie held up her hand and counted on her fingers. "The junior high principal, Lloyd Stark, is the prime instigator of the anti-festival campaign. He hates how it ruins the beginning of school. There are classes for three days, and then Chokeberry Days starts, and half the kids play hooky for the rest of the week."

"I wondered why things were so quiet on Thursday and Friday."

Bending down a second finger, Minnie continued. "The people who live along Basin Street also hate the festival. Their windows get broken, garbage gets thrown in their front yards, and the noise is awful. Mike Young is the head of that group."

"Vince's friend from high school?"

"Yes. At the time we worried when your brother stuck by him, but Mike seems to have straightened up quite a bit since his teenage years."

"Oh, yeah. I remember now. He went to prison for a while for dealing drugs."

"Seems okay now. He owns the local photography shop."

"Nice to hear someone made good." Skye closed her eyes briefly and visualized what her life had been like last year at this time. Living in New Orleans had been a dream come true. Everything was exotic and slightly forbidden. She loved nosing out the mysteries of the city. That is, until one of the secrets turned on her and caused her to be fired . . . and jilted. She shook her head. She had vowed not to think of her ex-fiancé and the pain he had caused her.

"Skye, sweetheart, come give me a kiss."

Skye looked up from her reflections into the faded green eyes of her grandmother, Antonia Leofanti. "Grandma!"

The two women hugged fiercely. Skye noticed how frail her grandmother had become in the eight months since she had last seen her. Antonia's pink scalp peeked through her white hair, and her head barely made it to Skye's chest. It felt as if she was embracing a skeleton.

Antonia backed away first and looked confused for a moment. "Oh, Skye . . . ah, Minnie." Her gaze cleared as she turned toward her daughter. "I almost forgot. They've got a problem at the Altar and Rosary Society's craft tent. Someone switched all the price tags around. Iona Clapp's handmade quilt is now marked twenty-five cents, and little Iris's potholder is going for four hundred dollars."

Minnie gave a shriek and took off at a trot.

Antonia spoke over her shoulder to Skye as she slowly followed Minnie. "Now that you're back in town, you make sure you come visit me. It's time I told someone the family history, and I think you're the best one to hear it."

Skye hurried toward the Port-A-Pots. One of the other judges had finally showed up to take over watching the jellies, and Skye was free for half an hour. When she arrived at the toilets she swore under her breath. The line snaked back past both the Lions' lemonade stand and the Knights of Columbus fishpond grab bag game. As she took her place at the end, she heard a high saccharine voice attempting to tell a children's story while a small child screamed in the background.

By standing with her back to the line, Skye was able to observe the performance currently unfolding on the festival's center stage. A tiny old lady, dressed in a loose white dress over a red-and-white-striped long-sleeved turtleneck and matching tights, was trying to ignore two little boys who were fighting over a stuffed animal. After one particularly loud screech, the woman finally stopped her storytelling and crouched next to the unhappy children. Her dress was so long and she was so tiny, the only thing that showed in this position was the rolled-up tips of her pointy-toed shoes.

The old lady's amplified voice could be heard through-out the food and games area. "Sweetie pies, could you do Mrs. Gumtree a big, big favor? If you stop fighting over that itty-bitty teddy bear, Mrs. Gumtree will get each of you one of her dolls when she finishes the story."

The children were quiet for less than a heartbeat, then a reedy young voice piped up, "Boys don't play with dolls."

Skye watched as the two kids, now united against the enemy, an adult, stood and raced off the stage. It was hard to tell from such a distance, but it looked to Skye as if a fleeting expression of irritation crossed Mrs. Gumtree's features before she turned back and pasted a smile on her face.

As Skye used the facilities, smelly as they were, she shook her head over the way Mrs. Gumtree had handled the children. If she ever ran into the woman, maybe she'd give her a few tips on behavior management.

She still had some time before she was due back to judge the chokeberry jellies, so she decided to walk to the pasture where Cow Chip Bingo was being held.

To play Cow Chip Bingo, a flat piece of ground was di-vided into square-yard plats that were sold for twenty dol-lars each. On the specified day, plat-holders were provided with a barbecue dinner, which they consumed picnic-style on their section of grass. One well-fed cow was allowed to wander the field. The winner was the holder of the plat in which the cow dropped its chips.

Skye heard screams and laughter as she approached the playing area. Hurrying forward, she saw people running in every direction. She was just in time to watch a father, holding his daughter over his head, step in a cow pie and go down as if he were sliding into home base.

Skye asked a man leaning against the gate, "What's going on here?"

He half turned to her, but kept an eye on the field. "Somebody must've slipped something into the cow's feed. It's dropping a load every few feet. They called for the vet." The man tsked. "Worse part is, no winner can be declared, and all the money has to be refunded. This is really going to hurt the 4-H club."

As he was talking, a middle-aged woman in a go-to-meeting dress and high-heeled pumps ran directly into a large pile of cow chips and went down. When she yelled, "Shit!" the crowd roared and agreed that was what she had stepped in.

Skye watched for a moment longer before turning back to her duties. With all the pranks being played, she didn't want to leave the jellies unguarded.

The crowd inside the corrugated-metal building where all the domestic goods were to be judged was buzzing when Skye returned.

Her fellow jelly judge was bursting with news. "Did you hear what happened at the go-cart races?"

"No." Skye felt her stomach tighten. She had always been afraid someone would kill themselves on the Go-Kart track. "What happened?"

"Someone poured water in all the gas tanks. All the karts are ruined." The woman's face was so red from the excitement, Skye was afraid she was going to have a stroke.

"How awful. I just came from Cow Chip Bingo and it was spoiled too."

After Skye gave her the details, the woman excused herself. "It's only quarter to. I'll be back by three and we can get the judging going. I've got to find my sister and tell her the latest."

*   *   *

The judging of the chokeberry jelly contest was one of the main events of the Chokeberry Days Festival. With only a few minutes before the official start, the building was crammed with people. Skye heard snatches of conversation, mostly discussions of the various pranks and why Chokeberry Days should or shouldn't continue.

Skye looked at her watch, wondering where Mayor Clapp was. They couldn't start the judging without him. As time passed and the judging did not commence, the crowd grew restless. They had already divided themselves into two groups—those for Chokeberry Days and those against. As the heat rose in the metal building, tempers flared. Skye gnawed on her lower lip. Five more minutes and she was starting without the mayor.

Gradually she realized that one voice was making itself heard above the crowd. "These pranks have got to stop. People are getting hurt. Mayor Clapp needs to do something."

Skye scanned the throng, trying to see who was speaking. Instead she spotted Lloyd Stark, the junior high principal, who was chanting, "Cancel Chokeberry Days!"

When the opposition heard him, they began to accuse Lloyd of pulling the pranks. Faces turned red and fists were raised. One man brandished a hammer.

Turning to her co-judge, Skye said, "We'd better do something. That mob's reaching the point of accusing Lloyd of assassinating John F. Kennedy and kidnapping the Lindbergh baby."

Before the other woman could reply, Skye's grandmother, Antonia, who had been standing with Minnie on the sidelines, walked over to Skye's table, grabbed the biggest jar of chokeberry jelly, and smashed it on the floor.

The roar was abruptly silenced at the sound of the breaking glass. Into the stillness Antonia asked, "Can any of you really imagine Lloyd messing with a cow or crawling in the dirt around the Go-Karts?"

Although the silence continued, tension still throbbed, until Minnie snickered and everyone else started laughing.

Lloyd looked around the sea of faces and perhaps not seeing a friendly one, marched out the door in a huff.

The crowd remained quiet until one man dressed in a suit started preaching about the sins of Chokeberry Days. He talked about the property damage, the people injured, and the trash scattered everywhere.

Skye whispered to her fellow judge, "Who's that guy?"

"Mike Young. Nice-looking, isn't he?"

Before Skye could think of a response, the name-calling started again, this time led by the owner of the liquor store, and was quickly picked up by other merchants.

Chokeberry Days was to Scumble River what Mardi Gras was to New Orleans. It brought in so much money that retailers could afford to run their businesses at half profits for the rest of the year. They tripled their rates and sold souvenirs, overpriced crafts, and soda at two dollars a can. The liquor store stayed open twenty-four hours, and the town's restaurant actually required reservations.

Even the farmers made a profit selling "antiques" from their barns and attics, and the last of the vegetables from their gardens. Their wives sold quilts, afghans, and home-made preserves.

Anyone who threatened Chokeberry Days threatened these people's pocketbooks. And they were mighty protective of their cash flow.

Skye's attention was drawn back to Mike Young, who was shouting, "The only reason the mayor allows this whole debauchery is because he gets to pose with a celebrity and gets his picture in the paper."

Skye was still eyeing the crowd when a young boy with flaming red hair ran through the open door screaming, "The mayor's dead! The mayor's dead!"

The crowd was silent for a moment, then a babble of voices erupted. It grew louder and more angry. Skye slipped out from behind the jelly display, grabbed her aunt and grandmother, and ran for the door. She was afraid Scumble River was about to experience its first riot, and she didn't want to be around to see it.

CHAPTER 2

Don't Rain on My Parade

Skye stood trapped on the telephone in her kitchen. She was still dressed in the perspiration-soaked clothes she had worn to attend Mass that Sunday morning. No air-conditioning for Saint Francis Church. Let the Protestants have their creature comforts, the Catholics sweated for Jesus.

The mayor's "death" and miraculous recovery had been the talk of the congregation. The official story was that he had seen someone messing around the beer tent and gone to check things out. When he tried to tap one of the kegs, he received an electrical shock. An open current had been rigged to the metal handle. Although Mayor Clapp had briefly stopped breathing, he appeared to be fully rejuvenated today. Some people wondered out loud why he had been trying to open the beer—one of the most vocal had been the owner of the liquor store.

But Skye's caller wasn't interested in Mayor Clapp's health. Easing her grip on the telephone receiver, she tried to keep the exasperation out of her voice. "Yes, Uncle Charlie. Mom dropped off the T-shirt, but I told you I'm not doing it."

Charlie Patukas wasn't really her uncle, but he was a close friend of the family, and godfather to both her and her brother, Vince. More important, he was grand marshal of Scumble River's Chokeberry Days parade and a man not used to being argued with, as his irritated tone clearly indicated. "I'm counting on you, Skye. The whole town is counting on you."

"I did my duty yesterday. Judging the chokeberry jelly contest was awful enough." She twisted her arm behind her back, trying to reach her zipper, and listened to the silence emanating from the receiver. "Isn't there anyone else who can do it?"

His tone grew silky. "There's no one that I trust, or that owes me her brand-new job."

"You know how grateful I am. Thank you again for making sure they didn't look too deeply into my employment history. Insubordination is hard to explain." She mopped the sweat from her forehead with a paper towel. Having a godfather who was president of the school board had its uses.

"Good. Saying 'thank you' is nice. *Showing* your appreciation is nicer." Charlie's satisfied grin could be detected over the phone lines.

"Okay, I give up. You got me. I'll be there in half an hour." In the past year Skye had become good at admitting defeat.

Hanging up the phone, she stomped into the bathroom. The humidity had turned her long chestnut hair into a mass of unmanageable curls, which she swept into an elastic band. She jammed a baseball cap on her head and flipped her newly created ponytail out the back opening.

The Weather Channel had predicted temperatures in excess of ninety degrees, and by the way the sunlight had shimmered on the parked cars when she'd driven home from church, she guessed it was already well over that mark. The heat did not improve her mood, and as she changed into navy shorts, she berated herself for promising to help Charlie baby-sit the parade participants.

For some reason she'd been having trouble saying no to people since she'd moved back to Scumble River. Did she feel guilty for all the nasty things she'd said about the town as a teenager, or was she just tired of fighting the system?

Skye put on a freshly washed and ironed white cotton blouse. As she began to button it, her glance strayed to the fashion monstrosity thrown across her bed. Sighing, she reluctantly shrugged out of the top and donned the official Chokeberry Days T-shirt. The front of the shirt featured a picture of Mrs. Gumtree, star of *Mrs. Gumtree's Gumdrop Lane,* a children's TV show produced in Chicago. Printed on the back was:

SCUMBLE RIVER CHOKEBERRY DAYS
High School Band Competition—Thursday, August 27
August 28, 29 & 30
Cow Chip Bingo
Fish Fry
Carnival
Arts & Crafts
Beer Tent
Go-Kart Racing

Only people wearing this shirt were to be allowed "backstage" at the parade, but it was a hideous pink, supposedly the same shade as chokeberry juice, and Skye felt ridiculous in it. Small comfort that the men forced to wear the shirt would feel even more ludicrous.

Skye had barely buckled her seat belt and turned on the car radio before she arrived at the parade's staging area. Nothing in Scumble River was farther than a five-minute drive. It was a small farming community grouped around a downtown that lacked adequate parking space. Most of the larger businesses had long since moved to the outskirts in search of asphalt. The floats, bands, and official cars were meeting in the block-long parking lot shared by McDonald's, Walters' Supermarket, and the Ace Hardware store at the edge of the city limits.

The parade's route was all of a mile and a half long, following the two main streets that bisected Scumble River. Its finish line was at the other side of town near the railroad tracks and the river, where another large parking lot could hold all the participants.

Skye pulled her car into a narrow spot between a battered brown truck with a wire hanger stuck into the space where an antenna should have been and a bright red motorcycle. After maneuvering her way out of the tight space between her door and the other vehicle, she began to look for Charlie.

Squeezing between vehicles and people, she came to a float representing the high school's football team, the Scumble River Scorpions. It was done all in red with a huge black scorpion crouched in the center. A blood-like substance dripped from its stinger onto the prostrate dummy dressed in a rival football team's uniform. Several football players and cheerleaders were adding finishing touches to the gore, but there was no sign of Charlie.

An equestrian group was gathered off to the side, the riders grooming their massive mounts. The horses' coats gleamed brightly: black, white, brown, and roan. The people themselves sparkled with rhinestones and glitter.

Her next stop was a white convertible on loan from the Scumble River Lincoln-Mercury dealership. Apparently Mayor Clapp, the owner of that business, was taking no chances on anyone forgetting that his company had provided the car, as it had huge placards on both front doors. Mrs. Gumtree would ride in solitary splendor in the backseat.

Close by, a large motor coach acted as the TV star's dressing room. It was on loan from Clay Center's RV dealer, as its large billboard pointed out.

Another sign, this one hand-lettered, stated:

DO NOT DISTURB
NO AUTOGRAPHS
ABSOLUTELY NO ONE ADMITTED
THIS MEANS YOU!

Skye smiled to herself as she continued her search for Charlie. She hoped the trailer had good soundproofing and a sturdy lock because no sissy sign would keep out the citizenry of Scumble River if they took it into their heads to visit Mrs. Gumtree before the parade.

After wending her way past the high school band, a troop of clowns, and the Lions Club float, Skye's T-shirt was sticking to her back and her feet were beginning to burn. She could smell the aroma of hamburgers coming from the nearby McDonald's. Her stomach growled, reminding her that she hadn't had anything to eat since dinner the night before. *I've had it. If I don't find Charlie in the next ten seconds, I'm going back to my car and he can find me if he wants my help so badly.*

Taking a left at the next float, Skye began to head back toward the parking area. She heard Charlie before she spotted him. He was yelling at Fayanne Emerick, the owner of the liquor store across the street from his motor court.

Today Fayanne was dressed in the official Chokeberry Days T-shirt, two sizes too small, and red stretch pants. To Skye, she looked like a raw sausage oozing out of its casing. Fayanne's mouth was puckered tighter than the shrink wrap on a package of meat and her X-ray eyes looked as if they could bore a hole into Charlie's skull. Fayanne was poking him in the chest with her right index finger.

Skye hesitated, not wanting to get involved in whatever trouble Fayanne was trying to stir up, but also not wanting to forsake Charlie in his hour of need. Before she could settle on a course of action, Fayanne stalked off.

Charlie spotted Skye and motioned for her to come over. At close to six feet and three hundred pounds, Charlie

Patukas was not easily ignored, nor his wishes disregarded. He wore his standard uniform of gray twill pants, limp white shirt, and red suspenders. His expression implied he'd seen it all—twice—during his seventy years. He began talking before she could ask what was up with Fayanne. "Skye, you look beautiful. I'm so glad you finally put some meat on your bones."

"Thanks, Uncle Charlie. What a sweet thing to say." At least someone, besides herself, was happy with the new curvier Skye.

Charlie went on smoothly, "I'm glad you're here. I need a woman's touch."

"For what?" Skye backed up, prepared for flight.

"I need to talk to Mrs. Gumtree, to tell her what to do in the parade, but she doesn't answer her door."

"I saw her dressing room while I was looking for you. If the sign on the door is any indication, she doesn't want any company."

Charlie took out his handkerchief and wiped his face. "I'm not company. I'm the grand marshal, and I need to give her some instructions. I'll bet she wouldn't pull this shit if the director from her TV show wanted to talk to her. For crying out loud! It's less than an hour 'til show time and I haven't even met the woman yet. No one has. Except for the storytelling yesterday, she hasn't come out of her trailer."

"I'm sure she's afraid she'll get mobbed by kids wanting her autograph."

He held up one hand and clutched his throat with the other. "I've pounded on that trailer door 'til I bruised my hand, and I yelled until I was hoarse. She knows it's not kids wanting her autograph, she's just being a pain in the—"

Skye interrupted before he could get into a full-blown description of his true feelings on this matter. "So, you want me to go injure my hand and lose my voice too, right?"

"Yep. I figure you can psychoanalyze her out of her trailer."

Giving him a dirty look, she turned to go. "What am I supposed to say if I do get her to open the door? Maybe you should come with me."

"I've got to go talk to Wally about who he's assigned for the parade's police escort. I'll check on you in ten minutes or so."

Skye stood on the top step of the motor coach's metal stairs and knocked. There was no response—not that she expected any. If Mrs. Gumtree could ignore Charlie's banging, it was a sure bet she wouldn't be motivated to open the door by Skye's puny efforts.

Next she called, "Uh, Mrs. Gumtree." She felt asinine calling a grown woman "Mrs. Gumtree," especially through a closed trailer door.

No reply. She raised her voice and tried again. "Mrs. Gumtree, I'm not a fan." Skye realized how bad that sounded as soon as it left her mouth.

She was beginning to feel desperate, which prompted her to yell as loudly as she could, "Look, Mrs. Gumtree, I'm from the parade committee. Mr. Patukas, the grand marshal, needs to speak to you right now."

Nothing. Skye grabbed the knob, intending to rattle the door, but on her first shake it swung open. She braced herself and stuck her head into the room. To the left was the kitchen area. A divider blocked her view to the right. She called out again. Silence.

Stepping inside, she stopped for a moment to allow her eyes to adjust to the darkness. As she edged past the panel, she could see the section of the trailer previously hidden by the room partition. It contained an immense dressing table with a mirror surrounded by lights and a padded bench, turned on its side. All the drawers of the dressing table had been pulled out and their contents scattered on the floor.

Suitcases and a garment bag were turned inside out, their linings slashed. A makeup case, its contents oozing into the green carpet, lay on its side, the hinges broken. Peeking out from under the bench were feet shod in pointy rolled-up-toe shoes. It looked as if the remains of the Wicked Witch from *The Wizard of Oz* were crumpled on the trailer floor.

Skye ran over and pushed the bench aside. "Mrs. Gumtree, are you all right?"

There was no answer or movement, but she still couldn't see the whole person, as the head and torso were in the knee-well of the dressing table. She crouched down and reached into the recess, trying to find a pulse, and felt something sticky instead. When she withdrew her hand, it was covered with blood.

Pressure, Skye thought, fighting to stay calm. *I should apply pressure to the wound. But I can't see where it is. Should I drag her out of there? No. You aren't supposed to move people who are injured.*

Stop it, she commanded herself. *You can do this. You've been trained to remain detached. You've got to distance yourself.*

This isn't grad school. This is an actual emergency. Do something constructive. Skye sank to her knees. The sour taste of bile surfaced in her mouth.

She tried to disconnect her emotions. *Is she alive? Find out.*

Skye crawled forward and steeled herself to reach back into the blackness. Stretching as far as she was able, not wanting to slip and land on the woman, she pressed her fingers into the bloody neck. *No pulse.*

Before she could make a decision about her next move, someone started pounding on the door.

Things were happening too fast for her mind to process. Skye reacted instinctively. "Who is it?"

"Goddamn it, Skye, who do you think it is? Santa? Let me in." Charlie's voice was unmistakable.

She stood up, mindful to touch nothing—all those years of watching *Dragnet* reruns were paying off at last.

She walked to the door, gathering her thoughts before speaking. "Charlie, listen carefully. Something has happened in here and you can't come in. I don't want to touch the knob on this side of the door, but since it isn't locked you can open it. Don't come in, just open the door and then step aside, so I can come out."

The door swung open and Charlie plunged into the room. Skye grabbed him by the arms and propelled him back out. He tripped on the top step, stumbled down the remaining stairs, and landed in a sitting position on the ground.

He looked up at Skye, who was closing the trailer door as if it were made of eggshells. "What the hell was that about?"

Skye tried to speak but felt tears clogging her throat. *I will not cry.* Instead, she held out her right hand, still covered in blood.

"Did you cut yourself?" Charlie looked confused.

"I think Mrs. Gumtree has been murdered." Skye leaned against the closed door.

When Charlie didn't speak, Skye asked, "Did you find Chief Boyd?"

Charlie got up from the asphalt and dusted off the seat of his pants while still staring at the blood on Skye's hand. "Yeah, he's over by the Vintage Cars."

Taking a deep breath, Skye descended the stairs and sat down on the bottom step. She found a tissue in her pocket and tried to clean up her hand. "Why don't you go get him? I'll sit here and make sure no one goes inside." Skye saw that her knees were shaking, and she thought she might vomit.

Charlie started to walk away, but turned back before he had taken more than a few steps. "What if the murderer is still in there?"

Looking around, she spotted one of her many cousins heading their way. "Kenny, Kenny Denison. I need some help over here."

He waved, trotted over, and sat next to her. "What's up?"

When Charlie still didn't move, Skye touched Kenny's bulging forearm and asked her uncle, "Do you think anyone will mess with me while Kenny is here?"

Charlie took a good look at the nineteen-year-old and turned away. "Fine. I'll get Wally."

A camouflage-green T-shirt with the message IF YOU ABSOLUTELY NEED IT DESTROYED WITHOUT QUESTION BY TOMORROW, YOU NEED THE UNITED STATES MARINE CORPS was stretched taut across Kenny's muscular chest.

"Who's messing with you? Why's Charlie got blood on his sleeve? Why's he getting Chief Boyd? You don't need the police. I'll take care of whoever's bothering you." Kenny stood and balled his hands into fists.

Skye reached out to Kenny with her left hand, pulling him back down onto the step, careful to keep her right hand concealed behind her back. "Thanks, Kenny. I know you'd help me, but I'm okay. Someone else is in trouble."

"Who? What's going on?"

"Mrs. Gumtree, the TV star who was going to be in the parade, seems to be dead."

"That tiny little old lady on the kids' program? What happened? Did she have a heart attack?"

Skye considered saying yes, but could think of no reason to answer dishonestly. "No. It looks like she was murdered."

"What?" Kenny bellowed.

"Charlie asked me to get her. She wasn't answering her door. When I tried, the door was unlocked, the place was ransacked, and she was on the floor. Charlie is afraid the murderer might still be in the trailer, so he didn't want me to wait here alone. Please, let's just wait for the chief. I'm going to start crying if I talk any more."

Kenny leaped to his feet once again and faced the door. He asked over his shoulder, "Is there another way out? What makes you think the perp is still in there?"

She shuddered. "I don't know that he is. When I was inside I didn't see or hear anyone. Of course, I wasn't paying much attention at the time. He could have been hiding in the bathroom, I suppose. There probably isn't another door, but there are plenty of windows."

"We'd better get some people over here to secure the perimeter." Kenny trotted off, calling over his shoulder, "I'll go find your brother and the cousins."

Skye sat still for a moment, catching her breath. It was quiet. The trailer was fairly isolated, and the crowds had moved to the parking lot in anticipation of the parade's start. Closing her eyes, she said a prayer for Mrs. Gumtree's soul. Suddenly a loud bang reverberated through the air. Skye jumped off the step and turned to look at the door. It was open and swinging back and forth on its hinges.

I'm sure I closed that door. Didn't I feel it catch? Skye tried to make sense of what she was seeing. *Oh, my God, the murderer must have still been in there.*

Before she could react, a heavy hand descended on her shoulder, and she screamed.

CHAPTER 3

Send in the Clowns

Skye sat alone in the squad car watching police officers go in and out of the trailer. She was still a little embarrassed about having screamed at the chief when he first arrived at the scene and put his hand on her shoulder. Especially since he convinced her that the door had been blown open by the wind.

Charlie and Kenny, along with everyone else in the area, were banished behind the yellow crime scene tape draped around the parking lot's border. Two harried officers tried to get people's names and addresses before the crowd dispersed. Three more were busy keeping folks behind the tape.

The townspeople had been drinking steadily from their coolers since they began to gather for the parade at eleven o'clock. They were angry when its cancellation was announced, and seeing the police made them curious. Fights were already breaking out among the more well lubricated of the group.

When Chief Boyd first arrived and saw the body, he questioned Skye about her movements inside the trailer. Upon learning that she hadn't touched anything except the outer doorknob, the vanity stool, and the corpse, he ordered her to sit in his squad car and talk to no one.

Since that time it seemed to Skye as if every Scumble River police officer and Stanley County deputy there was had arrived. She was up to thirty when she lost count. People, mostly men, in blue or khaki uniforms swarmed over the crime scene like ants over a piece of candy. One was taking photographs, another was videotaping, and yet another appeared to be drawing a picture of the site.

Around one o'clock a hearse arrived. The man driving it walked straight into the trailer without looking at either the throngs of onlookers or the police. Skye couldn't see who it was from where she was seated, but he carried a doctor's bag.

She was staring out the window without seeing anything when the opposite door was abruptly yanked open. Startled, she let out a yelp. She didn't recognize the man sliding in next to her, and he wasn't wearing a uniform. Acting on instinct, Skye flung open her door and stumbled out of the car.

As she ran toward the trailer, Skye hoped to find Chief Boyd, but instead a Stanley County deputy she didn't know grabbed her by the upper arms and spun her around. "Whoa there, Missy, where you goin' in such a hurry?"

Looking over her shoulder, Skye struggled to free herself from his grip. The stranger had emerged from the squad car and was now leaning against the trunk. When he saw her looking at him, he waved.

The officer holding her had a name tag on his tan shirt that read "Deputy McCabe." He was not the type of person Skye would have picked for protection. Not only did Deputy McCabe strike her as missing a few buttons on his remote control, but physically he reminded her of Barney Fife on *The Andy Griffith Show.* She would have preferred Marshal Dillon from *Gunsmoke.* All those years of watching reruns as a child had left an indelible impression on her.

Skye pointed to the man by the squad car. "See that guy over there?"

Barney Fife didn't answer.

"Is he a suspect? He got into the police car with me."

Still no response from the deputy.

"Did you guys forget you told me to wait there in the squad car?"

Deputy McCabe took his time before speaking, examining the man by the car who was now engrossed in writing something in a pocket-size notebook. "Why, that there is the coroner, Mr. Simon Reid."

She frowned. "Doesn't the coroner have to be a doctor?"

"Well, Miss, I don't know about places like Chicago or New York, but around here the coroner has always been the owner of the funeral parlor."

Shaking her head in disbelief, Skye thought, *Being back in Scumble River is worse than I imagined. Things here truly are fifty years behind the times.* Before she could pursue that line of thought, Chief Boyd emerged from the trailer and joined them.

"Why, Skye, honey, what are you doing standing here in the hot sun? We don't want you passing out on us. You were white as your mama's sheets when I first got here. I told you to wait in the squad. That's why I left the air-condition running."

Skye blushed. When Chief Boyd had first come to town as a twenty-three-year-old patrolman, she'd been convinced she was in love with him. Back then Walter Boyd was a handsome young man who filled out his crisply starched police uniform superbly. He had warm brown eyes, curly black hair, and a gorgeous year-round tan. But his most attractive feature was his kind and generous nature.

The summer she was fifteen, Skye discovered his work schedule and managed to turn up wherever he took a break or stopped for a meal. He was always a perfect gentleman, never mocking her or taking advantage of the situation. Nevertheless, she was embarrassed to remember how lovesick she had acted, and she now found it difficult to look him in the eye. She also had a hard time calling him anything but Chief Boyd.

Time had been kind to him. His uniform still fit exceptionally well, revealing only a hint of thickening at his
waist. The silver in his hair made him look, if anything,
more distinguished.

"Sorry, I didn't know Mr. Reid was the coroner, and he
frightened me when he got into the car without any warning."

Deputy McCabe gestured toward her with his thumb.
"Yeah, she thought he was the murderer. She shot outta that
squad like a bat outta hell."

"What do you find so amusing, Deputy?" Chief Boyd
asked. "That seems a sensible precaution, considering we
don't have any idea who the killer is and he might think
Miss Denison saw more than she did."

Skye shivered. She hadn't considered that the murderer
might think she was a witness.

Chief Boyd turned to her. "Why don't you go back and
introduce yourself to Simon? He has some questions he
wants to ask you. I think he moved to town after you left.
His uncle, Quentin Reid, up and died about eight years ago.
Quent never married, and he didn't have any kids, so
Simon inherited the funeral home. Simon is Quent's
brother's boy."

She nodded to the chief, understanding his reasons for
the genealogy lesson. In Scumble River you were an out-
sider, and not to be trusted, unless you could prove your
connection to someone from town.

Gritting her teeth, she walked over to Simon and held
out her hand. "I'm Skye Denison. Chief Boyd said you
wanted to speak to me?" It was hard having to face a person you had just run away from.

Simon straightened and took her hand in a firm but not
crushing grip. "It's nice to meet you. I'm Simon Reid, the
coroner."

Raising her eyes to his, Skye discovered that he was
well over six feet tall and very attractive in a Gary Cooper

sort of way. The silence lengthened, and she realized that she had been staring at him for several minutes. Blushing, she looked away.

He did not seem the least bit uncomfortable with her inspection. Instead, he leaned back against the fender and crossed one long leg over the other. His next statement surprised her. "Miss Denison, tell me about the blood you had on your hand."

For some reason his self-confident attitude irritated her. "I prefer *Ms.* Denison. Why do you need to know about the blood, Mr. Reid?"

"Do you know what a coroner does, Ms. Denison?"

"No, Mr. Reid, I do not know what a coroner does. Something with dead bodies, I presume."

His slight smile did not reach his eyes. "To save a lot of time explaining why I'm asking the questions I'm asking, I'm going to explain the duties of a coroner to you, Ms. Denison."

Nodding, she waited for him to continue.

"The number one duty of the coroner is to conduct the inquest, but at the crime scene we take vital signs, draw blood—directly from the heart if possible—and take urine samples from the bladder."

"You don't perform the autopsy?" Skye shifted from one foot to the other. This was getting a little more graphic than she liked.

"No, we need a licensed medical examiner for that. We hire a guy from the county hospital to do the actual cutting. He uses the specimens I've collected at the scene to run toxicology screens and lab tests."

"So, what do you want to know? I was in the trailer all of five minutes, so I didn't see much. I can't even tell you what the victim looked like."

"I'm most interested in your description of the blood. Wally mentioned that you had quite a bit on your hand when he arrived." Simon moved closer.

"Yes, I must have stuck my fingers right next to the wound while I was trying to find a pulse, but I couldn't see what I was doing because the body was under the vanity. I know you're not supposed to move injured people, so I didn't want to drag her out from the knee-well." Skye explained all this in one breath, still feeling as if she should have done more.

"All I want you to do is to picture the blood on your hand right after you first saw it."

Skye closed her eyes and tried to think about the earliest instant she looked at the blood on her hand. After a long pause she said, "It was bright red. At first I thought I'd cut myself."

"Good. It looked like new blood. What was its consistency?"

She tried to reconstruct the scene in her head. "It was runny, more like chocolate syrup than molasses but not as thin as oil."

"Great. That's exactly what I needed to know."

"Why?"

"It will help pinpoint the time of death," Simon said, then added, "I hope."

"I don't understand why it took you so long to get here. It was over an hour and a half since I found the body and reported it to Chief Boyd."

"The police have to take all their pictures and gather their evidence before they call me to take the body. I've tried to convince them that they should notify me immediately and let me examine the scene, but we have so few homicides I haven't been successful."

"How many murders have you handled as coroner?"

For the first time Simon looked uncomfortable. He cleared his throat before answering. "This is the first murder, but I've done suicides and accidental deaths."

Skye raised one eyebrow. "That's not quite the same thing. You must be feeling somewhat anxious. There have been so many cases lost in court due to the evidence being spoiled at the scene. I read an article in *Time* magazine a few years back that said something like sixty-five hundred murderers each year go free, most because of coroners who were not well trained. I didn't realize at the time that many were not physicians."

"The only thing I'm nervous about is you. We didn't get off to a very good start." His golden-hazel eyes sparkled. "The reason the funeral director in small towns is usually also the coroner is simple. We own the hearse and we have a place to store the body."

He was attractive, and as everyone kept pointing out, there were not many appropriate men Skye's age in Scumble River. She surreptitiously glanced at his left hand. He wore no wedding band. Of course, that didn't prove anything. One strike against Simon was that he reminded Skye of her ex-fiancé. It had been only a few months since they broke up, and the pain was as sharp as ever.

She smiled. "I'm sure you didn't mean to scare me earlier, and I am sorry for screaming and running away when you got into the car."

He waved away her apology with a gesture of his hand. "No problem. After what you've been through, I'm sure most girls would have been frightened."

Girls! Biting her tongue, Skye managed a thin smile in response to his chauvinism and decided to change the subject before she was forced to tell him what she thought about that remark.

The shock of finding a body had worn off, and her natural curiosity was beginning to take over. Tilting her head to the side, Skye looked up at Simon through her eyelashes. "Why, how gallant of you to be concerned for my feelings."

She wondered what he was honestly thinking as they smiled at each other. She would bet money he couldn't figure out her real thoughts.

After a few minutes of silence, Skye opened the door of the cruiser. She sat sideways, with her feet still outside the car. "How did Mrs. Gumtree die? Is there any way it could have been an accident? I realize the trailer was trashed, but could she have done it herself, then fallen somehow?"

"I don't see how it could be anything but murder. She was stabbed in the jugular vein. That's why there was so much blood."

Skye paled slightly, but her inquisitiveness won out. "Was she robbed?"

"They don't think so. It looks more like a search than a burglary."

"Isn't that odd? What would anyone be looking for? Who around here would even know what she had with her?" Skye leaned forward, intent on the puzzle.

"That's not all that's odd. When we finally got her out from under that dressing table, she turned out to be in her thirties, not her sixties."

"Are you sure it's Mrs. Gumtree? When I saw her performing yesterday, she looked like Granny from *The Beverly Hillbillies,* only shorter."

"It's her, all right. We found the wig and makeup she used to make herself look old. Also, she was wearing the costume." Simon took a small notebook from his pocket.

"Do you know her real name?" Skye stretched her neck, trying to get a look at the pad from which he was reading.

"No. We asked Charlie, and he said there was no formal contract for her appearance today since she wasn't getting paid. So, they have no idea who she really is. The only thing we know for sure is she isn't in her sixties."

"I guess they'll have to get in touch with her agent."

Simon continued almost to himself. "She was really a very tiny person. I haven't measured her yet, but I'd guess she wasn't even five feet tall and couldn't have weighed ninety pounds."

"Then almost anyone could have killed her," Skye said.

CHAPTER 4

Call Me Up

Around five, the police finally allowed Skye to leave. Even though she was hungry, she did not want to see anyone she knew or answer any more questions. This narrowed her options to driving to Kankakee, which would take almost an hour, or returning home and hoping she could find something in her fridge.

As soon as she reached her cottage, Skye showered and changed into a pair of old denim shorts and an orange University of Illinois T-shirt. She slipped her feet into rubber thongs and went to explore the food situation. A chunk of cheese, a few slices of salami, and half a box of crackers tossed onto a tray made up her meal. She added a glass of Caffeine-Free Diet Coke and walked out to her deck. After placing her dinner on a side table, she settled into a cushioned lounge chair and tried to forget the past eight hours by gazing at the river and allowing her mind to go blank.

As she felt the muscles in her neck and back relax, she thought how lucky she'd been to get this cottage. Discovering it was the only good thing that had happened to her since she'd found out she would have to move back to Scumble River. She'd rented it sight unseen through a newspaper ad and had been relieved that it was even better in real life than the picture and description promised.

The owners were from Chicago. Before their messy divorce they had used the cottage as a weekend hideaway.

Neither was willing to sell it, give it up, or share it, so until they could come to some compromise they were renting it. Skye hoped they wouldn't achieve any common ground until after she could figure out a way to leave Scumble River.

She loved the unusual octagonal shape of the house. And the deck reaching from the left of the front door, around the side and all along the back, made her feel almost like she was living in a tree house. The small center cupola acted as a skylight, drawing extra sunshine into the high-ceilinged rooms.

The cottage's location among the weeping willows and the elms along the riverbank allowed for the privacy Skye had missed since she'd left her family's farm. There were few other houses on the road, and all were obscured by thick foliage.

Skye tried to focus on the house, but her thoughts kept returning to the murder. After a few minutes she gave up and went to phone her mom. She needed to talk things over with someone, and since she'd been gone from Scumble River for over twelve years, her choices were limited.

May answered on the first ring.

"Mom, it's me." Skye pictured her mother standing in her green-and-white kitchen, looking out the big picture window at the backyard. May's salt-and-pepper hair was cut very short to take advantage of its natural waves, and her emerald-green eyes matched Skye's own. She would be wearing denim shorts and a T-shirt, probably one with the insignia of her beloved Cubs baseball team printed on the front.

"Oh, thank God. I was so worried. I've been calling over and over ever since I heard about the murder. Are you okay?"

"I'm fine. Charlie's fine. Everyone we know is fine." Skye took a seat on a kitchen chair. This was going to be a long conversation. "Mrs. Gumtree, that children's TV star, was the one killed."

May sighed. "That's a relief. So, the person who was killed was from Chicago—nothing to do with us."

Skye thought about explaining that people who didn't live in Scumble River were still worthy of their concern, but took a deep breath and instead broached the subject she had called about. "Mom, do you know any of the teachers at the high school?"

"No. Not offhand. Why?"

"Well, I spent Friday there visiting classrooms and observing students. I took a break around ten that morning, and Chokeberry Days was the hot topic of conversation in the teachers' lounge."

"There has been a lot of fighting this year about the festival. People really took sides," May said.

Skye stretched the phone cord to its limit and grabbed a cookie from the jar on the counter. "Yeah, I saw that at the chokeberry jelly judging yesterday. I thought there was going to be a brawl right then and there, especially after the mayor's death was prematurely announced."

"Wasn't that awful? But I hear Eldon's fine today—not that he didn't get what he deserved."

"Huh? What's happened to Chokeberry Days? When I was little, the whole festival started Saturday afternoon with the judging of the jams and jellies. There was a carnival that night and a parade Sunday. How did all these extra activities get started?" Skye took a bite of her Oreo.

May's voice indicated her disapproval. "Things really got out of hand this year. Our beloved mayor is trying to put Scumble River on the map. Every year Chokeberry Days gets bigger and more extravagant. And ends up causing more trouble. A couple of years ago, he had the bright idea of having a Harley-Davidson exhibition, so now we get hundreds of bikers tearing up the town during the festival."

"Let me guess—you really can't say anything against the whole thing because of Uncle Charlie."

"Chokeberry Days is his baby," May admitted.

"True, and we all know what happens to people who aren't nice to other people's children." Skye put the rest of the cookie in her mouth and crunched.

CHAPTER 5

The Sounds of Silence

Monday morning, heading toward her meeting with the junior high principal, Skye felt a lump of dread settle in her stomach. Since she'd started her job a week ago, things had not been going according to plan, and she felt the whole situation slipping out of her control. The principals of both the high school and the elementary school had made it clear the week before that they had no time to talk to Skye about her duties or answer her questions.

No one seemed very interested in having her around or even sure what to do with her. Finding out where she was supposed to work and locating the supplies she would need made her feel about as popular as a Christmas fruitcake.

She had just met with the superintendent, who after several telephone calls between his secretary and those at the various schools, promised her an office in the junior high. If she was still employed next year, the elementary would take a turn housing her, and if the unheard-of occurred and she stayed a third year, the high school would ante up a space.

When Skye entered his office, the junior high principal, Lloyd Stark, glanced pointedly at his watch and scowled.

"Oh, gee, sorry to be late. The superintendent kept me longer than I expected."

He nodded, but his impatient expression was easy to read. He gestured to the pair of straight-back vinyl chairs across from his desk without speaking.

Skye felt her temper push its way to the surface. In order to regain control, she let her gaze sweep the small room. It was painted a dull beige. The walls were decorated with engraved plaques and citations. No posters or paintings were present to reveal the taste of the occupant. The furniture was utilitarian—nothing stuffed or upholstered that might invite the occupant to get comfortable or stay longer than was strictly necessary. Flat brown carpet suggested that it, too, had been selected for thrift rather than style. And the only light glared from the ceiling fixture's fluorescent bulb.

As she sat, Skye slowly arranged her purse and briefcase by her feet and allowed herself to examine the man behind the desk. Lloyd looked more like a used-car salesman than an educator. She had heard that he had been the principal of Scumble River Junior High School for nine years. Before that, he was a P.E. teacher and coach at the high school for ten years. She guessed that although Lloyd was not originally from Scumble River, over his nineteen-year tenure he would have become well acquainted with its foibles, especially nepotism.

One of her Denison cousins worked as a custodian at the high school and had told her that Lloyd and the other principals had held a private conference after the July school board meeting, the meeting at which it was decided to hire Skye as the new psychologist without even a token interview or reference check.

According to Kenny, none of the principals was happy about hiring her, but all agreed they would reserve judgment and not hold her relationship with the school board president, Charlie Patukas, against her.

Skye continued to study Lloyd. He did not match his cheaply furnished office. Dressed in an expensive blue pin-striped suit, monogrammed white broadcloth shirt, hand-made silk necktie, and highly polished black tasseled kilties, he wore no wedding band, but there was a large pic-

ture on his desk, framed in heavy gold leaf, of a drab
woman and three ordinary-looking children.

Finally, since it appeared that Lloyd was not about to
begin their meeting, Skye leaned forward and extended her
hand. "Hello, I'm Skye Denison, the new psychologist."

"Yes, I had figured that out." Lloyd held her hand for a
fraction of a second too long, and then they sat without saying anything further. His flat black eyes exactly matched
his slicked-back black hair, which was such an unvarying
color that it had to be dyed.

As the silence lengthened and Lloyd showed no indication of talking, Skye sat back in the chair and crossed her
legs. Although she had been taught to wait, because often
the most interesting revelations came when people grew
uncomfortable with silence, waiting was still extremely difficult for her.

Lloyd rearranged the objects on the desktop, aligning the
blotter carefully with the edge of the desk. Turning to a
fresh page on his legal pad and selecting the most perfectly
sharpened of his pencils, he finally looked at Skye. "I do
not run a democracy. We do not vote on issues. I solicit
opinions, but make the final decisions myself. Do you have
a problem with that?"

Skye struggled to remain composed, while allowing herself the time she needed to formulate a suitable response.
"So you're saying it's important to you to feel in control of
the school you are responsible for?"

A puzzled look crossed Lloyd's face. "Well, yes, I guess
that's what I am saying."

Skye found herself able to read Lloyd's thoughts as he
realized that this discussion was not progressing in the
manner he had envisioned. He began to feel uncomfortable,
and she saw him struggle to regain control of the conversation, floundering as he persisted, "Is that a situation you can
live with?"

Concentrating on not losing her cool, Skye leaned forward. "You want to know if I'm going to respect your authority, right?"

"Well, yes, that's one way of putting it. Are you?" he insisted.

"Of course, I will back you in any matter that is not against my professional ethics." Skye gave him an insincere, yet dazzling smile. "But I'm sure you would never suggest anything less."

Lloyd seemed flustered, and sat silently for some time before continuing. "Let me give you a brief summary of my school. We have one special education teacher, and she has two assistants. There is a school nurse and speech pathologist whom we share with the rest of the district. We do not currently have a social worker, so with the addition of you, me, and an occasional visit from the representative from our co-op, that pretty much makes up our PPS Team."

"When does the Pupil Personnel Services Team meet?"

"Every other Tuesday, starting tomorrow, at eleven-thirty."

"What special education cooperative are we with?"

"StanCoCo."

"And that stands for . . . ?"

"Stanley County Cooperative. Any more questions?" Lloyd's tone made it clear that he found her queries tiresome.

Ignoring this, Skye proceeded, taking out a pad and pencil. "How do we handle fulfilling the components of a case study evaluation without a social worker to do the social history? How does all the counseling get done?"

"We don't need a social worker to do a social history. What we've done in the past is have the nurse address the medical segments and the psychologist deal with the adaptive behavior, family structure, and so forth."

Skye frowned, thinking, *I will definitely have to take a look at the Illinois rules and regulations to see if this is legal. I'd also better check with the Illinois School Psychol-*

ogists Association as to whether it's ethical. And, if it is, I'd better brush up on taking social histories really soon.

Lloyd was looking at Skye as if he expected to be praised for his resourcefulness. "Oh, how clever," she said. "Maybe we can talk more about this later."

Without warning Lloyd changed the subject. "You were the one who found that body yesterday, right?"

Nodding, Skye sat straighter, wondering where this was leading.

"It must have been extremely frightening. You probably didn't have a chance to notice much . . ." Lloyd's voice trailed off, encouraging her to fill in the details.

She knew he wanted something, but she couldn't imagine what. "No, I was in and out in a couple of minutes. Why do you ask?"

"No reason. Just curious. I didn't even know the woman, for heaven's sake."

"Oh, you sounded like maybe you had a specific question in mind."

He stood abruptly and walked to the door without commenting. "Why don't I take you to meet some of the team?"

He was halfway through the main office before Skye could gather her belongings and follow him. Keeping an eye on his retreating figure, she hurried after him. Lloyd was of medium height and build, but he moved as if his legs were as long as a basketball player's. Skye didn't catch up until he was already most of the way down the central hall.

Skye was wearing the coolest professional clothes she owned, a short-sleeved lilac linen shirtdress with matching high-heeled pumps. Midwestern style valued matching accessories, but after trying, without success, to keep up with Lloyd's quick pace on the highly polished and slippery linoleum, she immediately resolved to buy lower-heeled shoes—no matter what the color.

She rounded a corner in time to see Lloyd enter a classroom near the back of the building. Judging from its location, she knew without asking that it was the special education room. Such classrooms were usually as far away from the front door as the structure of the school allowed.

Upon entering, Skye spotted Lloyd with a woman in her thirties. She was much taller than average and cadaverously thin. When she held out her hand for Skye to shake, her nails were bitten so short they looked raw. Her grip was listless.

The room was painted bile-green and held only a blackboard, a teacher's desk, and twelve student work stations, the type where the chair and table area are welded together. It was obvious that they had interrupted the teacher as she was attempting to liven up the room by putting various posters and pictures on the walls.

Lloyd introduced them. "Darleen, this is our new psychologist, Skye Denison. Skye, this is our special education teacher, Darleen Boyd. She's married to the police chief."

Skye checked Darleen's reaction to Lloyd's having gratuitously announced her husband's occupation. Even by Scumble River standards his remark had been a bit sexist. Darleen remained impassive. Her short baby-doll dress revealed twiglike arms and legs. No one spoke.

Searching for something polite to say, Skye settled at last on, "How nice. My mom works as a police dispatcher."

Before Darleen could reply, Lloyd broke in. "Where are your assistants?"

"They're with the kids in their mainstream classes. Remember, last year the PPS team decided to put the aides in regular classes to help the special ed kids?" She nervously smoothed her hair, which was a dull brown and cut as if a bowl had been placed on her head for a pattern.

"How about the nurse and the speech therapist? Surely they're not in the classrooms too? They should be around." Lloyd scanned the room as if the people he sought might be hiding behind the desks.

"Abby's in the health room, but I haven't seen Belle. She's probably at the elementary school." Darleen studied the poster she had just hung on the wall, not meeting Lloyd's eyes.

Turning to Skye, Lloyd asked in an affronted tone, "Did you meet Belle Whitney, the speech and language therapist, at the elementary school when you were there earlier?"

"Why, no, I spoke with the principal on Thursday, and she gave me a list of meetings. She ran out of time before she had a chance to show me around the school or introduce any of the faculty or staff."

Lloyd nodded in satisfaction. "Let's press on, then. At least I can introduce you to the nurse."

"Could you show me where my office is, too?"

"It's on the way." A line appeared between Lloyd's eyebrows.

Skye moved closer to Darleen. "It was nice meeting you. Would it be convenient for me to come back this afternoon so we could discuss your program and how my services might fit in with it?"

Looking uneasily at Lloyd, Darleen's hazel eyes bulged alarmingly. "Sure. I'll be here until four. We can talk then. We don't want to keep Mr. Stark waiting."

As Skye followed Lloyd back toward the front of the school, she pondered Darleen's attitude. She appeared much more subservient, even fearful, than other special education teachers Skye had met.

Skye was convinced that the room Lloyd indicated as her office had started life as a janitor's closet. Its windowless walls were painted an egg-yolk yellow, and the smell of ammonia made her sneeze when she pushed open the door. A battered desk and a single metal folding chair crowded the small room.

Turning to Lloyd, who was hovering outside the doorway, Skye said, "I don't see any secure area for confidential files. I'll need a locking file cabinet."

He scowled. "I suppose you'll have a whole list of things you absolutely have to have. Just remember we aren't a rich district like the one you came from."

Nodding, Skye said, "I understand, but I do need a place where files can be kept locked up." She aimed the next suggestion at his ego. "Maybe we could put them in your office. Of course, I'll need a key."

"My office is not a storage facility. I'll make sure you get a cabinet." Lloyd took a handkerchief from his pocket and wiped away the sweat that had suddenly appeared on his brow.

The health room was located beside the main office, but with a separate entrance. It was very small, with just enough room for a brown vinyl cot, a locked cabinet, a desk, and a chair.

Lloyd was standing in the doorway tapping his foot when Skye caught up to him. He moved to one side and gestured for her to go in. "Abby, this is Skye Denison, our new school psychologist. Skye, this is Abby Fleming, our district's school nurse."

With that statement Lloyd walked away, saying over his shoulder, "You two talk, I'll see you both at the PPS meeting tomorrow."

"Wait—we haven't even discussed my duties yet." Before Skye could follow, Lloyd closed his office door.

His voice came from behind the glass panel. "Talk to my secretary. She'll give you a schedule. I'll be busy the rest of the day."

Skye stared after him as if she were waking from a nightmare, and then turned to Abby, hoping for a friendly reaction. "Tell me this is unusual for him. He's under a lot of pressure, right?"

Abby looked Skye over before indicating that she should take a seat on the cot. "No, I'm afraid he's always like that."

Skye examined Abby carefully. She was everything Skye would like to be—five feet ten and built like an athlete. Her white skirt showed off her tanned, muscular legs to advantage and was paired with a tucked-in navy polo shirt and spotless white tennis shoes. More striking than pretty, she was the kind of woman who would fit in better at a health club than a cocktail party. Skye knew her brother had been going out with Abby, and now she understood why—Vince always had been attracted to physical perfection.

As silence once again threatened to engulf her, Skye wondered if everyone in this school was the quiet type. Scrambling for a topic of conversation, she searched the bare walls for inspiration. Finding none, she remarked, "So, you're dating my brother?"

Hearing no response, Skye leaned forward. "Vince, Vince Denison is my brother."

"Yes, I know." Abby tucked a strand of long white-blond hair behind her tortoiseshell headband.

Rearranging her skirt and smoothing her own hair, Skye waited for Abby to continue. When she didn't speak, and gave no indication that she intended to, Skye scooted toward the end of the cot. "Have you worked here long?"

Abby nodded. Set against the fairness of her brows and lashes, her large aquamarine eyes dominated her face.

Smiling her encouragement, Skye waited, although Abby's persistent silence was beginning to get on her nerves. Abby did not look up; instead she began filing her nails.

Skye waited a while longer, then stood up. "It is obvious to me, that despite Lloyd's suggestion that we *talk,* that we have very little to say to each other. I think it would be best if I left you to your busy schedule." At this Skye stared significantly at the empty desktop.

She paused with her hand on the knob. "Sorry to have taken up so much of your time."

Abruptly, Abby burst out laughing. Skye was sure this was going to be her first nutcase at her new job and was frantically trying to recall how to react to hysteria.

Before Skye could act, Abby regained her composure. "Boy, Vince really has you pegged."

"Pardon me?" Skye responded stiffly.

"Chill. Sit back down. Relax. Vince told me nothing would drive you crazier than for me not to talk to you." Abby got up and tried to take Skye by the arm.

"What?" She shook off Abby's hand.

"Vince said that ever since you were children everyone has always confided in you. He claimed even strangers come up and spill their guts."

"So?"

"When he asked me to test out his theory, I figured, What the heck? What would you do if I didn't respond as you're used to having people respond? If someone you were expecting to be friendly wasn't? Vince knew you'd either get angry or cry. He thought you'd get angry; I voted for cry."

"You're telling me you were willing to make me cry just to test out my brother's silly theory? That's a pretty sadistic thing to do to someone you don't even know. I've always suspected that nurses enjoyed giving those painful injections." Skye held her temper with great difficulty.

Abby patted Skye's knee. "You're right, of course. It was a mean joke, and I apologize. I guess I wasn't thinking about it from your point of view. I'm not very good about putting myself in other people's shoes. But do you realize how hard it is on Vince, being the brother of Miss Perfect?"

"Now what are you talking about?" Skye's head was beginning to ache.

"Don't be modest. You were a straight-A student, never got into any trouble. You not only went to college but also to graduate school, not to mention your noble sacrifice when you joined the Peace Corps. Let's face it—you are everyone's darling, and now you've moved back home. How would you like to be the older, less successful sibling?"

Skye shook her head. It felt odd to be described as successful. True, she had done well at the University of Illinois—only a hundred miles away from Scumble River, but light-years from it in terms of lifestyle.

But her stint in the Peace Corps was not the noble sacrifice that Abby described. Instead it had been a place to hide when she couldn't face coming home to Scumble River and found there were no jobs for someone with a bachelor's degree in psychology. And graduate school had been two years of being made to feel never quite good enough.

This was followed by a year of internship—something akin to being an indentured servant. Not to mention being fired from her first job for insubordination and being jilted shortly afterward by a fiancé who was more in love with his own social standing than with her.

"My brother thinks of himself as unsuccessful?" Skye allowed herself to be led back to the cot. "I had no idea. I'm sure a great psychologist," she said sarcastically. "I don't even know what my own brother is thinking."

"Vince is hard to read. He turns on the charm if he thinks you're getting too close. Besides, how often have you seen him since you moved away?"

"You're right. A lot of things seem to have changed in the twelve years I've been gone. Maybe it's a good thing I came back after all."

CHAPTER 6

Suspicious Minds

Later that afternoon, the door to Skye's office banged open and Lloyd entered the room. "Well, you certainly have managed to make yourself comfortable. I suppose you'll want a couch and your own coffee machine next." He examined the desk, chair, and file cabinet closely. "None of our other psychologists had an office to themselves. They took whatever room wasn't in use when they stopped by."

Skye bit her tongue, counted to twenty, and breathed deeply—all the while trying to refrain from explaining that perhaps that was one of the reasons they had such trouble keeping support staff, such as social workers and psychologists.

Instead she made herself smile. "Yes, I want to thank you for all your help. The other schools seemed unable to assist me." She was very proud of herself when no trace of sarcasm leaked out.

Lloyd puffed out his chest. "I'm the one to see in this district if you need something. Those other two principals don't have the influence I have. The superintendent and I are fishing buddies, you know." He completely disregarded the fact that he had done nothing. The secretaries had arranged everything.

Once Lloyd left, Skye spent some time organizing the confidential special education files she had found. The search had turned out to be more like a scavenger hunt than the simple task she was expecting. After being directed to at least ten different locations, she finally located the folders in the basement next to the cleaning supplies. They were moist and smelled like a mixture of mold, pine scent, and lemon.

Taking the records from their damp cardboard boxes, Skye put them into her *new* file cabinet, stopping now and then to separate pages that were sticking together. They completely filled one drawer and part of the second. She didn't attempt to read them, but was content with putting them into some recognizable order . . . like alphabetical.

After an hour of sorting out the records of the students currently enrolled in the Scumble River Junior High special education program, she looked at her watch and realized she hadn't been back to talk to Darleen. She stuffed the remaining folders into the cabinet, locked it, and hurried to the special ed room. She arrived just in time to find Darleen locking the door.

Skye apologized, and they made another appointment, for the next day during Darleen's planning period. Darleen seemed relieved that she didn't have to talk to Skye that day after all.

It was nearly five that afternoon, and Skye had finished up at school only half an hour ago. She rested her hip casually against the registration desk of the Up A Lazy River Motor Court and scanned the small office, noting that little had changed in the years she'd been away. The walls were still painted a drab brown, the desktop was still scarred and in need of refinishing, and the only chair remained occupied by her honorary *Uncle* Charlie, who was busy barking orders into the phone.

When she had first arrived, Charlie's gray color and rapid breathing had scared her. He'd just been ending a telephone call when Skye walked through the door, and she heard something about paying someone some money by

Friday. She had tried to ask what was going on, but the phone rang again, and Charlie had been on one call or another ever since.

At least his color was better and he seemed more like his usual self—aggravated, headed toward infuriated, possibly not stopping until he hit fully enraged. "We are not refunding the parade entrants' fees. Check the contract the carnival people signed. No refunds for an act of God." He listened for a few seconds. "And I say murder is covered under that clause."

The window air conditioner labored in an attempt to keep the tiny room cool. When Skye had driven past the Scumble River First National Bank, the thermometer read ninety-one degrees. The humidity hung like used plastic wrap.

Skye dug into her purse until she found a coated rubber band. She gathered her hair into a thick ponytail and narrowed her green eyes against the smoke from Charlie's cigar. Tapping her fingernails on the counter, she waited for him to hang up.

He pounded on the desk and yelled, "Then check with your goddamn lawyer! Why in the hell did you call me in the first place?"

Charlie banged down the phone and ran sausagelike fingers through his thick white hair, then heaved himself out of the battered wooden swivel chair and swooped Skye into a bear hug.

Intense blue eyes under bushy white brows scrutinized her face. "Are you okay with what happened yesterday? Everyone treating you right? Anyone bothering you, just let me know, and I'll take care of them. Nobody better mess with my goddaughter."

She was breathless, but returned his hug. "Uncle Charlie, you haven't changed a bit. I'm fine. They're all being nice to me. I just wanted to thank you again. I don't know what I'd have done without this job."

Releasing her, he settled back down into the creaking chair. "We should thank you. We've been trying to hire a school psychologist since the middle of last year. The last one we had up and quit in November. Said we weren't paying enough for the amount of problems he had to deal with. And you know we've never been able to keep a social worker—they say we're too primitive."

Skye frowned. "What kind of problems was he referring to?"

"We never could figure that out. Sure, we've got our share of troubles. Usually at least one suicide or drowning a year, child abuse, family feuds . . . but that goes on everywhere, right?"

Her one year of experience had ended with her being fired, so she was hardly an expert on what was usual. Not wanting to talk about her last job, Skye answered evasively, "Guess I'll find out soon enough. Maybe being from town will help."

Sighing, she leaned her forearms against the desk. "So, tell me all the gossip. What's this about Mrs. Gumtree really being only in her thirties?"

"Everybody is sure talking about this murder, but no one is saying anything. It was a terrible thing, you finding her like that. We don't want anyone thinking that you're a witness or anything, so you make sure everyone knows you didn't see a thing when you were in that trailer. You didn't see anything, right?"

"Nope. But everyone sure is interested in what I didn't see."

"Good. You make sure you tell everyone you didn't see anything and you don't know anything." Charlie shook his finger in her face.

"Sure." Skye shrugged. "What do you know about her? I never heard of Mrs. Gumtree before all this happened."

"She was just a character actress on a children's television show."

"Funny, I haven't heard about her from the kids."

"Her show, *Mrs. Gumtree's Gumdrop Lane,* is only on in the Chicago area." Charlie finished his cigar and stubbed it out in the overflowing ashtray at his elbow. "But I did hear there was talk of syndication."

Skye shrugged, losing interest. "Do they have any idea who killed her?"

"The police chief is still trying to get in touch with her agent or someone from that TV station. It seems they all went away for the weekend."

She reached for the motor court's register. "Gee, I wonder if any of them weekended in Scumble River."

"Mike Young says it's gotta be someone from Chicago, like her publicist or personal manager. He says all those show business people are sinners and abominations in the eyes of God." Charlie slid the ledger out of her grasp and into his desk drawer.

"When did he become God's messenger? The week before I left town, he was sent to prison for dealing drugs. Now he dresses like a lawyer and talks like a TV evangelist."

"You're way behind. Mike only spent eighteen months in prison. He's been out over ten years. He's hardworking and God-fearing now." Charlie sat back, thinking out loud. "Why, Mike's active in his church and makes a good living. That other stuff was just wild oats when he was a teenager."

"I really don't remember him very well. He was a friend of Vince's from high school, but they were four years ahead of me. Do you know anything about his jail time, or was it kept a secret?"

"Skye, honey, you been away too long if you think there isn't a person in Scumble River who doesn't know every last detail. There are no secrets here."

"Except for the murderer's identity," Skye said quietly. Moving closer to Charlie, she asked, "Who do you think killed her?"

"Well, now that you mention it, I thought I saw the principal of the junior high, Lloyd Stark, hanging around her dressing room yesterday. I only saw him from the back, so I didn't get a good look. Of course, I'm probably not a very good judge because I just plain don't like him." Charlie put his arm around her.

"Wonderful. That should make my job easy, since he knows you were behind my getting hired."

"He won't give you any trouble. He knows I won't put up with any bull. In fact, you could do me a little favor."

"What?" Skye crossed her arms and backed away.

"Hey, don't be like that. I get the feeling all is not right with Lloyd. He's hiding something from the school board. I want you to nose around and let me know if you hear or see anything suspicious."

She rolled her eyes. "Charlie, you're skeptical of anyone who has a different opinion than yours. I can't spy on my new principal."

"Don't think of it as spying. Think of it as being a good listener and an intense observer. Kind of like the job description of a psychologist, isn't it?" Charlie walked her to the door.

Skye's smile was sickly. She had forgotten how convoluted small-town politics could get.

Even for the end of August in Illinois, it was sweltering. During the day the sun had beat mercilessly on the blacktop of the motor court's parking lot, turning the asphalt into glue. Skye's T-shirt stuck to her back. She felt her sandals being sucked almost off her feet with each step as she walked across the empty lot toward her blue Chevy Impala with patchwork fenders and a crumpled hood. God, she hated that car—ugliest thing in three counties.

Skye noticed that the Brown Bag Liquor Store across Maryland Street was enjoying a brisk business. It hunkered on the river embankment like a malevolent toadstool.

In high school her classmates had often dared each other to go in and try to convince its owner, creepy old Fayanne Emerick, that they were old enough to buy beer. Skye never made the attempt, preferring even then not to take chances. She was still faintly uneasy about entering that building, always having pictured underage teens tied to medieval torture devices in the back room.

The car's black interior was blistering hot. Before gingerly sliding behind the wheel, Skye pulled the legs of her shorts down as far as they would go, in order to cover the backs of her thighs, while making sure the bottom of her plain white T-shirt extended past the waistband. As always, the car started smoothly and idled perfectly. She rolled down all the windows—it had no air-conditioning—and put the transmission into drive.

I wish the damn thing would die so I wouldn't feel like it was such a waste of money to buy a new one, Skye thought as she turned left on Maryland. Her brother's hair salon, Great Expectations, was the second building to the right after the bridge. This was the first time Skye had seen Vince since Christmas. He'd been out of town when she arrived last week, and with the Chokeberry Days excitement she hadn't been able to catch up with him over the weekend.

As Skye turned into the gravel lot, she saw two children hurling stones at the glass sign in front of the building. She got out of the car and strolled toward them.

They did not acknowledge her presence or stop their rock throwing. The boy looked to be about eight and the girl a year or so younger. Both were wearing grimy shorts, dirty tank tops, and sullen expressions.

She squatted between them. "Hi. It's pretty boring around here, isn't it?"

Glancing at her as if she were something he'd scraped off the bottom of his shoe, the boy selected the biggest stone from his pile and threw it as hard as he could. Skye heard the sound of glass cracking but could see no damage . . . yet.

She tried again. "You know, my brother owns this place, and I'll bet he has some toys inside you could play with while you're waiting for your mom or dad."

This time the girl was the one to hurl a rock after giving Skye a defiant look.

Skye examined them carefully and thought of what her favorite professor always said: *Understanding works with some kids, but most need structure and consequences.*

Determining that these children were of the latter variety, Skye said, "Stop throwing those stones right now. You're going to break that sign, and your parents will have to pay for it."

They both looked at her contemptuously and threw a fistful of rocks.

Without another word, she took each by an arm and marched them into the building, undisturbed by their squirming protests.

The door of the salon opened into a waiting area. A woman sprawled in an upholstered wicker chair, her dirty feet propped up on the glass table in front of her. She held a grocery store tabloid inches from her nose.

An archway revealed the styling area, where another woman sat in an elevated chair, shrouded in a plastic cape. Skye quickly sized them up and guided the children toward the one reading the paper.

This woman was in her late twenties and looked like many of Scumble River's young mothers. She had do-it-yourself dyed-blond hair and watery brown eyes. Ignoring the children, she glared at Skye. "Yeah? What d'ya want?"

"Are these your children?" Skye met her stare with a neutral look.

"Yeah. You got a problem with that?" The woman's voice became more strident, and she stuck out her chin.

In response, Skye made her speech more formal. "They were throwing rocks at the glass sign outside. I'm sure you do not want to incur the cost of replacing it. I believe the price to be nearly two thousand dollars."

"You blaming my kids?" She shot out of her chair and put her face within inches of Skye's.

Skye took a step back. "No. I'm blaming *you* for how you're raising them."

The woman's eyes darted rapidly around the room. "Who do you think you are? The police?"

"Simply a concerned citizen." Skye paused for effect. "But I'd be happy to call the police if you prefer to deal with them."

The woman swept her belongings into a large, discolored straw purse and slid her feet into rubber thongs. Her face wore an ill-tempered expression. "I don't have to take this. I'm telling Vince."

Skye smiled and crossed her arms. "Please do. I'm sure my brother will be interested to hear why you allow your children to damage his property."

Huffing and puffing like the Big Bad Wolf, the woman appeared to see the children for the first time. She snatched them away from Skye and jerked them toward the door. "Junior, Bambi, get away from her." Tugging at the crotch of her denim shorts, her halter top exposing a large expanse of chalk-white skin, she spun back toward Skye. "You keep your hands off my kids."

Skye lifted both hands, palms forward. "My pleasure."

As the woman scuttled out, dragging the children behind her, the little boy looked back at Skye. His smile appeared victorious, and she realized that he had gotten exactly what he wanted: his mother's attention.

The banging of the door brought Vince hurrying from the shampoo area. His long butterscotch-blond hair was tied in a ponytail, and there were beads of sweat above his emerald-green eyes. Through the window in the door he saw his customer's retreating form. "What did you do to Glenda Doozier?"

"Told her the truth."

Skye marveled at how out-of-place Vince looked for Scumble River. Dressed in chinos, a blue chambray shirt, and boat shoes without socks, he could have just stepped off a movie set.

In contrast, she'd summed up the town years ago by explaining that there are white-collar communities and blue-collar communities, but Scumble River is a no-collar community. Consequently, the rednecks could be identified without obstruction.

Brother and sister stared at each other for a few seconds before Vince made the first move, as he always had since they were children, gathering her into a hug. "What have you done to yourself?"

Feeling uncomfortable, Skye plucked at her shorts and shirt. "What do you mean? I know I need a trim. That's one of the reasons I stopped by."

He shook his head. "No, I mean your weight. How much have you gained?"

"A few pounds, but it's no one's business but my own. I admit I'm calorically challenged, but I've decided to exit from the diet roller coaster."

Vince held her at arm's length and examined her. "But, Skye, you have such a pretty face. You can't let yourself go like that."

Skye stood tall. "Let's get this straight once and for all. The decision has been made. I am tired of eating less than eight hundred calories a day. This is my natural weight. I stopped dieting right after Christmas and have been where I am since April. This is what they call my set point."

"Does this have anything to do with breaking up with your fiancé?" Vince questioned.

"No. And I've told you I don't want to talk about him— ever."

"Look, I know keeping thin hasn't been easy for you, but what will people say?"

"I can't believe you would care what people say, Vince. Haven't I always accepted you for yourself? Who has always defended you to Mom and Dad? I've never asked you to get a more *masculine* job so people won't talk. How can you do less for me?"

Vince had the grace to look chagrined. "You're right, Sis. It was just such a surprise. I guess you still look pretty good. At least you filled out in most of the right places."

"Thanks a lot. I know some people won't think I look good unless I become anorexic, but I'm finished obsessing about my weight. End of discussion."

"Okay, okay. Since I seem to have an unexpected cancellation, I can cut your hair as soon as I finish with Iona." Vince gestured toward the woman in the styling chair, who had been following their conversation with great interest.

She waved.

"Great. I'll wash it myself while I wait." Skye started in the direction of the shampoo bowls but turned back. "By the way, why are you working alone?"

"Things have been kind of slow, so I had to let the receptionist and the other stylist go."

Skye emerged from the shampoo area with her hair in a towel and plopped herself into the chair, still warm from Iona's recent occupation. Vince whipped off the towel and started to comb out her tangles.

She squirmed and frowned at his image in the mirror. "Don't cut off too much. Only any inch or so, to get the split ends."

"Why don't you let me try something different? Maybe a shoulder-length pageboy."

Skye gave her brother a forbidding look. "No! No! No! I like it long and one length so I can tie it back or put it up."

"You're no fun."

"Last time you had *fun* with my hair I ended up looking like a Navy recruit."

"Fine. If that's how you feel, I'll just trim it." Vince grabbed a section of hair and held it straight up from her head.

They both turned to look as the front door opened. A UPS deliveryman held out a small package and a clipboard. "Hi. Sign right here, please."

Vince grinned and reached for the pen. "Thanks." He scribbled his name, grabbed the box, and tore it open. "I've been going crazy without these."

After the UPS man left, Skye asked, "What was that all about?"

"I misplaced my styling shears last Saturday. I've had to make do with an old pair until these got here. The other ones just aren't as sharp."

Vince continued talking as he started to cut her hair. "I'm glad you stopped by. I wanted to ask you about double-dating with Abby and me on Wednesday."

"I don't know. She and I didn't get off to a very good start."

"Oh, I forgot. Did she give you the silent treatment?" Vince began snipping off pieces of hair.

"Yes. Why didn't you just tell me how you felt? I never knew you thought of me as Miss Perfect, until Abby explained about you feeling unsuccessful around me."

"It's not a big deal."

Skye looked him in the eye via the mirror. "It sure seemed like one to me. Can't we talk about it?"

Shrugging, Vince looked away. "There's nothing to talk about."

She sighed and changed the subject. "This is the longest you've dated anyone since that awful girl in high school. What was her name?"

"I don't remember."

"Are you serious about Abby?"

"Maybe, if other things work out." Vince finished cutting and took out the blow-dryer.

"I'm really happy for you. I'd sure like to start over with Abby, but who would make up the fourth in this little outing?" Skye gazed up at him warily.

"For crying out loud! It's only dinner and a movie in Joliet, not a lifetime commitment."

"True, but I still would like to know who I'll be sharing a backseat with."

"He's a good friend of mine. You probably remember him. Mike Young."

"I saw him at the chokeberry jelly judging last Saturday. He sure hates Chokeberry Days." Skye raised an eyebrow.

"Well, he's pretty religious now. Chokeberry Days probably reminds him of his wild youth."

She narrowed her eyes. "How interesting. He's your age, right?"

Vince nodded.

"Has he ever been married?"

Shaking his head, he switched off the dryer and picked up the curling iron.

Skye pounced. "What's wrong with him?"

"Nothing. Boy, try to do you a favor and this is the thanks I get." Vince shook his head in disgust. "You have such a suspicious mind."

"That's one drawback of being a psychologist," Skye conceded. "You're always looking for what's beneath the surface."

"So, are you going out with us or not?"

"Against my better judgment, I'll say yes. I've learned that anything or anyone that sounds too good to be true usually is."

"Mike's a great guy. He's good-looking, and he has his own business." Vince attempted to sound straightforward but failed.

"Look, I said I'd go out with him." Skye hesitated as an unwelcome thought occurred to her. "Have you asked him yet if he wants to go out with me?"

"Yep, it's all set. We'll swing by and pick up Mike first, then be at your place about six. That should give you plenty of time. You school people get off work around three, right?"

"Yeah, right," she said sarcastically. "I finally found all the files today. It looks like no one has done anything since the last psychologist left a year ago November. I'll be lucky to get out by five."

He finished curling Skye's hair, brushed her off, and folded the cape.

She jumped out of the chair and walked over to the nail polish display. "You should get a manicurist in here. I'd love to get my nails done."

"Not everyone can afford to indulge all their whims like you."

"Would I still be driving the Impala-from-Hell if I indulged my every whim?"

Vince busied himself sweeping up the curls of hair on the floor.

Skye made her selection, Springtime Lilac, and walked to the counter. "How much?"

Vince folded his arms. "I can't charge my sister."

"I won't come here if you don't let me pay. Besides, I cost you a customer."

He balked, then reluctantly keyed the cash register. "Nineteen ninety-eight."

Skye dug her wallet out of the bottom of her canvas tote. She gave him a twenty and joked, "Keep the change."

With a flourish Vince took two pennies from the cash register and put them in his pants pocket. "Gee, Sis, you're too generous."

"Any time. When's your next appointment?"

"In about five minutes. I try to book them as close together as possible without making people wait too long."

Skye paused with her hand on the door. "Is there anything wrong, Vince? I mean, I'm surprised you had to let the receptionist and stylist go. I thought you did a pretty good business."

"There is something else I wanted to talk to you about, if you have a couple of minutes."

"Sure, let's sit down. You must be on your feet all day." She headed to the waiting area.

"Let's sit in the back by the shampoo bowls. It's kind of personal."

After they settled themselves, Vince hesitated.

In her best counselor mode, Skye leaned forward with her hands held loosely on her lap. "You can tell me anything. It won't go any farther than this room."

"I'm short on money this month. Some extra expenses came up that I wasn't expecting, and I'm not going to be able to make the mortgage. Could you lend me fifteen hundred dollars? I won't be able to pay it back for a while." Vince didn't pause for breath.

Before she could reply, Vince interrupted her thoughts. "You probably don't have much money right now, but I can't ask Mom and Dad. You know the answer I'd get from them."

She nodded. "How about Uncle Charlie?"

"He doesn't have the cash either. This hasn't been a good year for the motor court."

"That's odd. Even if the motor court isn't doing too well, I always had the impression that Uncle Charlie had money from other investments."

"Me, too. But when I asked, he said he couldn't help me, he didn't have that kind of cash. What was I going to do—call him a liar?" He slumped back in his chair.

"Gee, I'm sorry, Vince, but I'm broke. My salary last year barely covered my living expenses. Would I be back in Scumble River if I had any cash?"

They sat in silence for a while, each trying to figure a way to get the money.

Finally Skye stood up. "I have an idea, but I don't know if it will work and I really hate to do it."

Vince looked at her imploringly. "I'm going to lose the shop if I can't meet the mortgage."

"Well, the only thing I have that's really worth anything is Grandma Leofanti's emerald ring. I could try to get a loan with it as collateral."

He buried his head in his hands. His heavily muscled chest heaved as he took a deep breath. "I'm quite a big brother, aren't I? Maybe next time I'll try stealing candy from a baby."

"Don't ever be ashamed to ask for help," Skye rushed to reassure him. "I only wish I had it to give. I'll try to find out by Wednesday if I can get a loan. Will that be too late?"

"If the answer is yes, it will be just in time. If the answer is no, time doesn't matter."

CHAPTER 7

If You Could
Read My Mind

It was nearly six that evening when Skye walked out of Vince's salon and headed toward her parents' house. She drove back down Maryland Street, and as she approached the Basin Street crossroad the signal turned red.

"The only stoplight in town, and I never manage to catch it on green," Skye grumbled to herself.

Looking down Scumble River's main drag, Skye noted an unfamiliar sign, Young at Heart Photography. She figured it must be Mike Young's studio—the one her aunt had mentioned Saturday.

Up and down the street were banners promoting the now-passed Chokeberry Days, but something had been added since they were originally hung. Each pennant had been hand-painted with a red circle and a line bisecting it, the international sign for *no*.

The light changed and she drove on, easing around the sharp curve after Webster Drive. She turned right onto County Line Road. Her parents' farm was about a mile east off the paved road.

Skye could hardly believe she was back. She had spent her whole adult life putting distance between herself and Scumble River. She went so far as to join the Peace Corps after graduating from college, and spent four years in Dominica, a tiny island in the Caribbean. But a single stubborn decision and all her plans were wiped out. It had taken only one long, emotional call home to get her reestablished here in town. Mothers sometimes worked in mysterious ways.

Smiling ruefully, she mused, *I was certainly eager enough to come home this time. Well, ready or not, I'm back where I started. At least my parents are happy I'm here.*

The tires crunching the white pea gravel on her parents' well-tended lane interrupted her thoughts. Her father, Jed, was on his riding mower finishing up their acre of grass. When he spotted Skye he took off his blue-and-white polka-dotted cap and waved it in the air, revealing a steel-gray crew cut, faded brown eyes, and a tanned, leathery face.

On the step near the back patio, she noticed her mother's concrete goose dressed in a bikini with sunglasses perched on its beak and a bow on top of its head. It was usually attired in holiday garb, but with the Fourth of July long past and Halloween nearly two months away, this must have been the best her mom could do. Skye quickly checked out the trio of plaster deer to make sure they weren't similarly costumed.

Returning her father's wave, she went in the back door of the red-brick ranch-style house. The large kitchen was bisected by a counter edged with two stools. Its pristine celery-colored walls looked as if they'd been painted just that morning, and the matching linoleum glistened with a fresh coat of wax.

Her mother, May, stood at the sink, cleaning sweet corn. First she tore off the outer husks, then scrubbed the corn silk away with a vegetable brush. Despite her fifty-five years and short stature, May's athletic build reminded Skye of the cheerleader her mother once was. The few pounds she had gained since high school did not detract from this image.

The first words out of her mother's mouth were, "Hope you're hungry. Supper's almost ready." To May, food equaled love, and no further words of affection needed to be spoken.

Skye noted the time on the green-and-white-flowered wall clock—five minutes after six. "Isn't it a little late for you guys to be eating dinner?"

"Dad's been up since five-thirty. He's already cut Grandma Leofanti's grass, put new seat covers on the pickup, and will be finishing our lawn in a few minutes. I dispatched from eleven to seven last night at the police station, then walked my three miles with Hester and Maggie, cleaned up the house, put up twelve quarts of corn, and slept this afternoon. You know we're busy in the summer. We hardly have time to eat."

Skye knew better than to prolong this conversation. She'd had the same one too many times before. If it went any farther, her mom would start asking what Skye had accomplished that day—merely going to work would not have met with approval.

Instead, Skye started to set the table. The plates, glasses, and flatware were in the same place they had been for as long as she could remember. She moved the salt and pepper shakers and the napkin holder from the counter to the table.

"What are we having?" Skye asked, peering into the refrigerator.

"Fried chicken, corn on the cob—it's the last of the season—Grandma Denison's rolls, mashed potatoes, and stewed tomatoes."

Skye grimaced. *Stewed tomatoes, the soul food of Scumble River.* "It's hard to believe Grandma is still making rolls from scratch at eighty-one. I stopped over there last Friday after school and she was making pies for the Lions Club to sell at Chokeberry Days."

May stopped stirring long enough to give Skye a sharp look. "Hard work keeps us all going."

Seeing that Skye was holding a brown plastic tub, she added, "Make sure you put out the real butter for Dad. He

won't touch that Country Crock stuff I use for my choles-
terol." May paused and gave Skye another sharp look. "You
better use the Country Crock too, since you're still carrying
around all that weight you gained last year."

Before Skye could respond, the back door slammed. Jed
detoured into the tiny half bath off the utility room in order
to wash his hands, and came out still carrying the towel.
His jeans hung low, accommodating his belly, and his navy
T-shirt was sweat-soaked and torn, evidence of his hard day
of work.

"Ma, I think this one's had it. You can see right through
it, and it won't dry my hands no more."

Jed held the threadbare towel up to the light.

"Maybe Vince could use it at his shop. I hate to just
throw it away." May walked over and examined the towel
critically.

"How many times do I have to tell you? We aren't giving him a thing 'til he gets over this notion of being a hairdresser. No son of mine is going to do ladies' hair for a
living. I've got three hundred acres to farm, and my son
won't even help me."

May started to reply but seemed to think better of it and
turned back to the stove to remove ears of sweet corn from
boiling water. Jed stomped to his chair. Skye finished
putting the food out and joined him at the table. May, carrying an enormous platter of chicken, was the last to sit.

They ate silently. Skye brooded, upset because her father
still hadn't accepted her brother's choice of occupation and
her mother was still nagging her about her weight. It was
no use trying to change their minds, and she was tired of ar-
guing with them.

Near the end of the meal, Skye's thoughts turned to the
murder. "So, Mom, any news at the police station about
Mrs. Gumtree?"

Nodding, May took a sip of her iced tea. "Yeah, but
they're all acting really secretive. I tried to pump Roy last

night, and he just said the chief would have his hide if he blabbed anything."

"Maybe what they're trying to hide is that they're clueless. That new coroner didn't seem too impressive."

"Sounds like you and Simon didn't hit it off," Jed said as he slathered butter on his third roll.

"He seems a little arrogant and conceited." Skye studied her plate and carefully speared a tiny bit of stewed tomato.

May tilted her head. "Seems to me that's the pot calling the kettle black."

Skye pushed back her plate. "What? Are you saying you think I'm arrogant and conceited?"

"I wouldn't say arrogant and conceited exactly." May jumped up and brought over strawberry shortcake, dishing it out without asking who wanted some. Refusing food was not an option in May's kitchen. It never seemed to occur to May that she sent mixed messages—lose weight, but be sure to clear your plate first.

Skye's mother continued, "But you are a little snobbish and sort of vain. I mean, look at what you said in your valedictorian speech at school."

Skye pushed her dessert plate away. One mistake, twelve years ago, and not even her own mother ever let her forget. "You just don't understand the difference between self-esteem and egotism," Skye said.

"Maybe not." May finished her cake and began to collect the dirty dishes. "But I do know what the Bible says: 'Pride goeth before destruction, and a haughty spirit before a fall.'"

No one spoke as the two women finished clearing the table.

Finally Jed got up and headed toward the back door. "So how's the car running?"

Skye faked a smile. "Fine. It never breaks down, that's for sure."

"That car will last forever if you take care of it the right way. If you're going to be here a while, how about I change the oil?"

Skye hid her true feelings about the car. "That would be great, Dad. I'm going to help Mom with the dishes, so you'll have plenty of time." She went to the sink and shook out the dishcloth. "If you get a chance, take a look and see if you can figure out why the seat belt on the passenger side won't unfasten."

"Will do. I'll probably need to order some parts," Jed said as he left for the garage.

May took the dishcloth out of Skye's hands and replaced it with a towel. "Why don't you talk to Vince? Maybe if he helped in the field, your dad could forget the other." Obviously May had decided the subject of Skye's pride was closed.

Skye carefully dried the dish she was holding and tried to form an acceptable answer. Finally she equivocated, "Remember, I'm Vince's little sister. I'd be the last one he'd go to for advice."

"He'd listen to you if you explained about Dad." May rinsed the soap off the plate Skye was about to dry.

"Vince has had the shop for almost ten years now. He has real talent. He's happy doing what he's doing. He hated farming. He hated the hours, the uncertainty, and the dirt. It's time for Dad to give it up."

May stopped scrubbing the big black cast-iron frying pan that Skye's grandmother had also used to fry chicken when May was a little girl. "Maybe if you married someone who would help your dad in the fields . . ."

"Mom, that isn't going to happen either. You and Dad have already tried to fix me up with every guy whose father owns land anywhere near ours." She twirled a lock of her hair. "Let's see, there were the two pig farmers to the south, the four Piket brothers to the west, Zeke Zadock to the north, and the triplets to the east. Presumably at least some of those *eligible* bachelors are married by now."

"What did we do wrong? It's not natural that neither of my children is married. What about our marriage scared you so much?"

Skye muttered, "You don't really want to know. Maybe I should tell you just for spite."

Her mother was a social butterfly, wanting to be out doing something or going somewhere all the time. Her dad, on the other hand, was a homebody, content to putter in his yard and garage. It seemed to Skye that her parents rarely agreed on anything.

Withdrawing her head and upper torso from the cupboard, where she'd been putting pans away, May gave Skye a hard look. "What's that? What did you say?"

"Nothing, Mother, talking to myself. How do you like dispatching? I was surprised at Christmas when you told me you were taking a job—especially that one."

"A little extra money is always good. Besides, it's been pretty lonely here with you gone and your brother on his own." May looked sideways at Skye. "So, I took the first job Charlie could get me."

"Did Charlie help Vince too? It looks as if everyone but Dad owes Charlie their job."

"Well, in a way. You can never tell your dad this, but he co-signed Vince's loan for the shop."

"Mmmm, I always wondered how Vince got the money. I knew Dad didn't give it to him, so I thought maybe you had managed to slip it to him somehow."

"Your dad and I don't have that kind of money, you know that. Besides, I'd never go behind your father's back." May snapped the towel out of Skye's hands and folded it across the rack.

"Are you working tonight?" Skye asked.

"Yes. I've got the eleven-to-seven shift again. Things are really crazy with that Gumtree woman getting herself killed and all."

Skye checked her watch and discovered it was already

past eight o'clock. "Time to get going. There's still a lot of unpacking I've got to get done. I don't know where the past week has gone."

"Why couldn't you live here? Your room is ready for you, and you could save all that money you're paying for rent. How much are you paying?"

"I'm used to having my own space. You'd be as uncomfortable with me back home as I would be living here." Skye avoided revealing exactly how much her rent was.

"Well, why didn't you at least move back sooner? I could have taken some time off and helped you unpack and get settled."

"Don't you remember me telling you I needed to finish some cases after school got out? There were several meetings scheduled that I had to attend."

May pouted. "We didn't even have time to go shopping for school clothes."

"Mo-o-ther." Skye drew out the single word to show her extreme displeasure.

"Okay, okay. I hope you wore something nice for your first day."

"Yes, Mother. I wore clean underwear, too."

At first May scowled at the impertinent retort, but seeing Skye's grin she wavered, and then started to giggle.

They were both laughing at that oft-repeated line by the time they walked out the back door and watched Jed finish with the Impala.

He wiped his hands on the rag sticking out of his back pocket. "I'll have to order a part for your seat belt. I got it undone, but don't let anyone use it. It'll probably take a couple weeks to get the new buckle. With the age of this car, parts are hard to find."

Skye nodded and looked around for the family's pet Labrador retriever. "Where's Chocolate?"

"I had to put him in the pen. He wouldn't leave me alone."

"Chocolate's only a puppy, Dad. You've got to train him. I'll give you some books on behavior management. It's like what I do with kids. If he does what you ask, you reward him. When he does something inappropriate, you give him consequences."

"The only thing that dog understands is a kick in the ass."

"Da-ad."

Feeling besieged by both parents' attitudes, Skye thanked her father for the oil change and her mother for supper, all the while sliding into her car and anticipating her escape down the lane.

CHAPTER 8

You've Got a Friend

Skye didn't realize she was holding her breath until she felt herself exhale. What was it about her parents that impaired her verbal abilities and made her react like a twelve-year-old? Although they were wonderful, down-to-earth people, they could not accept either of their children making adult decisions. She loved them dearly, but they drove her crazy.

She relaxed against the car seat and retraced her route as far as the stoplight on Basin Street. Here she turned left and headed toward her cottage. This six-block area of Scumble River's business district contained Stybr's Florist, from which Skye had received her first corsage; the Strike and Spare Bowling Alley, where she went on her first date; and Oakes Real Estate, from whom she rented her cottage. Mike Young's studio, the bank, and the dry cleaner were also situated on that modest stretch of road.

She sighed. Scumble River was so much the same as when she'd left, it was hard to remember she wasn't eighteen anymore.

Upon reaching home, Skye put a load of laundry in the machine and started to unpack a carton of books. She stopped to admire the built-in bookshelves lining the great room's outer walls between the sliding glass doors.

Working steadily, she stopped only to put wet clothes in the dryer, soiled clothes in the washer, or clean clothes in drawers and closets. She had lost track of the time when the phone rang but glanced at the microwave's clock before she answered it. Its digital readout glowed 11:06 P.M., too late by Scumble River's standards for a social chat.

"Hello?"

There was no answer, and Skye was beginning to think she was the victim of an obscene call when she heard someone crying.

"Hello, who is this?"

Another pause, then finally a voice said, "It's Mom. Hold on."

Skye's heart stopped. If her mother was calling this late and crying, it could mean only one thing. Someone in the family had died.

After a few minutes, May continued, "Skye, it's your brother."

Her eyes began to tear, and she sank suddenly to the floor. "Vince? What happened to Vince?"

"He's been arrested for the murder of that Gumtree woman."

"What?"

"They have him at the police station right now. They were just bringing him in when I got to work. Wally wanted me to go home, but I said I'd go on and work my shift." May's voice sounded more steady as she told the story.

"Does he have a lawyer?"

"No, there's no one here but Vince, Wally, and a few other officers."

Skye's thoughts were coming fast and furious. "Okay, Mom, do exactly as I say. I don't have time to argue or explain. Put the phone down and go tell Vince to say absolutely nothing until I get there with an attorney. If they try to stop you from seeing him, push your way in. They certainly aren't going to risk hurting you. Make sure Vince understands not to say anything. Not one word. Put your hand over his mouth if you have to. Do it right now."

The sound of the dial tone surprised her. Skye had been

sure she'd have to argue with her mother to get her to do anything that rude.

Now the problem was to find a good lawyer with experience in criminal law. Skye flipped through her address book, trying to remember which of her sorority sisters had become the hotshot attorney in Chicago. When she'd joined the Peace Corps, she'd lost touch with most of her college friends, although she was always conscientious about keeping her address book up to date. Finally spotting the name, she punched the numbers into the phone so hard she broke her fingernail.

As the phone rang and rang, Skye chewed on the nail's jagged tip and chanted in her head, *Be home. Come on, be home.*

On the tenth ring the phone was picked up and a groggy voice answered, "Yes?"

"Hi, this is Skye Denison, from Alpha Sigma Alpha. Is this Loretta Steiner?"

"Yes. Who did you say you were? Is this a sorority fund-raising drive?" the voice asked in a bewildered tone.

"No. Look, you were a senior the year I pledged. During second semester I lived two doors down from you in the house. My mom made those special thumbprint cookies everyone loved." Skye hurried to explain before Loretta hung up the phone.

"Yeah, I remember you. You had the most striking green eyes I'd ever seen. What's up?"

"I'm sorry to bother you, but if memory serves, you became a lawyer and you practice criminal law. I think I've seen you in the *Trib*?" Skye clutched the receiver.

Loretta answered cautiously, "Yes, I'm an attorney and my practice does include criminal cases. Are you in trouble with the law?"

"No, not me, but the police have just arrested my brother for murder. Will you represent him? Can you come right now?" Skye's voice cracked.

"Where do you live again? Scrambled Eggs or something quaint like that?"

"Scumble River. It's seventy-five miles south of Chicago, off of I-55. Take the Scumble River exit and follow that route until you come to Coal Mine Road. Turn left. You'll go over some railroad tracks—Scumble River's version of a speed bump—and a bridge, then turn left again on Maryland Street. The police station is on the corner of Maryland and Kinsman."

Loretta's tone became sober. "Okay, it will take me about an hour and a half to get down to you. Are you at the police station?"

"No."

"All right. Give me your number, the number at the police station, and your cell phone. When we hang up, go immediately to the station and tell them you've retained me. Don't let your brother answer any questions."

"I don't have a cell phone." Skye slipped on her shoes.

"That's okay. Just give me the other numbers and get to the station as quick as you can."

"Thank you. Thank you so much." Stretching the cord as far as possible, Skye was able to grab her keys from the table in the foyer.

"Don't thank me yet. I have two questions, then we both need to get going. What's your brother's name and did he do it?"

Skye took a deep breath. "His name is Vince Denison and no, he did not do it."

Scumble River's police department was housed in a two-story red-brick building bisected by a massive double-deep three-door garage.

Accessible from both streets, the police department occupied half the main floor, with the jail and interrogation room on top. Offices of the city hall were on the other side of the building, and the town library was on the second floor of that half.

When Skye arrived, shortly after midnight, the city hall/library part of the building was dark. Her mother's white Oldsmobile and her father's old Ford pickup were the only vehicles in the parking lot. To add to her feeling that she was the last person left alive on Earth, Skye saw an empty squad car in the open garage.

There was no one behind the counter when she walked through the frosted-glass door, and the phone was ringing. Standing on tiptoe, she reached over and felt for the lock-release button located under the counter's lip.

Upon foiling these elaborate security measures, Skye let herself in to the dispatch area. The telephone continued to ring.

"Mom?" Skye called.

Silence except for the ringing phone.

She tried again. "Is anyone here? Should I answer the phone?"

Afraid it was Loretta trying to reach her, Skye picked up the receiver. "Scumble River Police Department. May I help you?"

"May, is that you?" Mayor Clapp's distinguishing whine came through the handset.

"No, sir, it's her daughter. May's not feeling well at the moment," Skye said. *I'm sure Mom really is sick. I know I feel like throwing up.*

"Uh, well, uh, you tell whoever's on duty that dog is back in my yard raising a ruckus. I want them to drop what they're doing and get over here right now. Do you hear me, girl?"

"Certainly, sir. I'll relay your message. Have a good night."

Walking into the hall and to the bottom of a flight of stairs, Skye yelled as loud as she could, "Mom, Dad, where are you?"

Chief Boyd came hurrying down the stairs. "Boy, I'm glad to see you, Skye."

She interrupted him. "Why have you arrested my brother?"

"He's not under arrest. We just brought him in for questioning."

"At this time of night? What's he got to do with Mrs. Gumtree's murder?"

He moved closer. "Look, I can't discuss this with you. Could you just come up here and convince May that she doesn't have to sit with Vince? Really, I'm not trying to railroad him. I just want to ask him some questions. The rest of the men have gone home."

"Sorry, Chief, I was the one who told her to do what she's doing. His attorney should be here soon, and she'll straighten things out."

"Well, at least tell your dad he doesn't have to wait. He keeps dozing off. I'm afraid he's going to fall off his chair. "

"Fine, I'll get Dad to go home. Don't you try anything funny with Vince." As she climbed the stairs, Skye added over her shoulder, "By the way, Mayor Clapp called to request your services. It seems there's some dog that's keeping him from getting his beauty sleep, and he'd like your assistance in removing it, ASAP."

Sitting at the dispatcher's station, Skye waited for Loretta to arrive. The chair was armless and covered in shiny green vinyl. She thought it served more to keep the dispatchers alert during the long stretches of time when nothing was happening than to make them comfortable.

Although she'd persuaded her father to go home and rest, she decided that May was the best protection Vince could have, next to a lawyer. Skye had been waiting there for over an hour, and now she expected the attorney at any minute. In the meantime, she had been instructed by May to answer the phone. So far, that wasn't a problem. It hadn't rung.

Chief Boyd had called one of his men at home and ordered him to take care of the mayor's dog problem. He'd been less successful in finding a substitute for May.

The Scumble River Police, Fire, and Emergency Departments shared a common dispatcher. Four middle-aged women each worked thirty-two hours a week, rotating between the afternoon and midnight shifts. One woman worked straight days during the week. They covered the phones and radios, as well as doing paperwork for the officers. None was willing to climb out of bed at midnight and come down to the station, although all wanted to know what was wrong with May.

Despite the uncomfortable chair, Skye was starting to doze off when the buzzer on the police station door sounded and Loretta Steiner marched in. Six feet tall and well muscled, she was even more impressive than Skye remembered. Everything about her was genuine, from her coal-black hair to her dark-brown skin.

Loretta didn't bother with preliminaries. "Where's my client?"

Matching the lawyer's demeanor, Skye opened the door between them and motioned Loretta through. "He's in the interrogation room at the top of the stairs. My mother and the chief of police are with him."

"What's your mother doing there?"

"Seeing that the chief doesn't question him. She was the best protection I could think of until you got here." Skye led her toward the stairs.

"Where's everyone else?" Loretta looked around the empty room.

"This is a small town. There's not much personnel available at any one time. My mom's the dispatcher on this shift, and Chief Boyd couldn't get anyone else to come in, so I'm answering phones. By the way, when you get up there, tell my mom to come down and take over."

Striding past Skye and up the stairs, Loretta muttered about small towns and not liking to leave Chicago. Halfway up the stairs she turned and called down, "Skye, they ever see a black woman lawyer here before?"

Skye smiled for the first time since her mother's phone call. "No. There are no blacks in town, and there sure aren't any women lawyers."

Loretta whooped. "Well, we're going to have us a good time tonight."

CHAPTER 9

Maybe Baby

Six o'clock Tuesday morning came too early for Skye. She had never enjoyed rising at the crack of dawn, and having had less than four hours of sleep did not improve her disposition. Her first thought when the alarm went off was to wonder if she could get away with calling in sick. After a brief consideration, she decided that doing so might be frowned upon after having worked only six days.

At almost the same moment, the idea that maybe she'd better save her personal and emergency days for Vince's trial popped into her head. She firmly shoved that thought back down into her subconscious, refusing to even contemplate Vince's being treated as a criminal.

Sitting on the side of her bed with her head in her hands, Skye tried to gather the energy required to take the next step and get into the shower.

Abruptly the hypnotizing music coming over her clock radio was interrupted by the WCCQ weather announcer's voice. "Well, folks, you'd better sit yourself down in a big tub of ice, because we're going to break all records for heat and humidity set on this day in history."

Groaning, she began to search her mind for something to wear. Some of the rooms at school were air-conditioned and some were not. It depended on when that particular addition had been added and how much money had been in the budget at the time.

Following a quick shower and a cup of Earl Grey tea,

she dressed in a short-sleeved empire-waist cotton-knit dress. Remembering the problem she'd had keeping up with Lloyd Stark on Thursday, Skye chose to wear white flats instead of the heels that matched the dress. She hoped the Midwest fashion police would forgive her lapse. She was undecided about panty hose, so she stuffed a pair in her white canvas tote, just in case there was some school rule about bare legs. But since her dress's hemline reached almost to her ankles, she hoped no one would even notice. At the last instant she wove her hair into a French braid to keep it out of her face.

It was tough knowing what to wear on any given day. In the morning she might be sitting on the floor with the kindergartners, and the afternoon could find her at a meeting with the superintendent. Her wardrobe had to be more versatile than a one-man band playing Tchaikovsky's *1812 Overture*.

The drive to Scumble River Junior High took less than five minutes, allowing Skye to be in her makeshift office by seven-thirty. With her first Pupil Personnel Services meeting not until eleven-thirty, she would have plenty of time to prepare a list for the PPS team of students who needed reevaluations or counseling.

She worked steadily until her door burst open and Ursula Nelson, the school secretary, flew in. "Come on. Mr. Stark wants to see you."

"Okay, I'll be there in a minute." She started to put the folders she was working on back together.

Ursula's beetle-brown eyes bored into Skye. "Mr. Stark does not like to be kept waiting."

"I'll come to the office as soon as I've secured these files."

Ursula turned without another word and rushed out of the room.

Skye inserted the loose papers back into the various records and placed them in the file cabinet. She then conscientiously pushed in the metal bolt and made sure the drawer was locked. Smoothing her hair and dress, she grabbed paper and a pen and set off for the principal's office.

Lloyd was pacing in front of the doorway when she arrived. Without saying a word, he hurried inside, apparently expecting her to follow. Once they were both past the threshold, he shut the door. "We have a problem."

"Yes?"

"One of our students, Travis Idell, an eighth grader, spent the summer having parties while both his parents were at work."

So far Skye was unimpressed. "Yes?"

"They were pretty wild parties." Lloyd seemed to think Skye should understand without him having to go into detail.

"And this is our problem in what way . . ."

"The other kids were all from this school or the elementary." Lloyd clarified, "They were mostly eleven and twelve, but some were only ten."

Skye was starting to have a bad feeling about where this was leading. "What did they do at these parties, get drunk?"

"I wish it were as simple as that. They did disgusting things."

"Like what?"

Lloyd turned red and muttered, "They played games, sex games."

She took a few steps and sat. Lloyd must have thought this was a good idea because he sank into the adjoining chair.

"This is terrible, of course, and I'm sure many of those kids will need to see a counselor, but I'm still not clear on how this relates to school." Skye crossed her legs. "You're aware that the school is required to provide counseling services only if the emotional problem directly impacts a child's ability to learn?"

He sighed. "Yes, I know, and so far it hasn't impaired their learning, if we strictly interpret the law. On the other hand, word has gotten out about this, and since school has started, Travis has been beaten up every day by angry brothers and cousins of the girls involved."

"Let me see if I have a correct picture of what's been occurring." Skye jotted a few notes on her pad. "Travis's parents no doubt are denying that anything took place this summer, while demanding we do something to protect their poor innocent baby boy. Right?"

Lloyd nodded.

"Calls are coming in from the other parents wanting to know why we haven't expelled this demon from hell." Skye looked at Lloyd for confirmation.

He nodded once again.

"So—we need to think of something that will satisfy both sides."

"Precisely. What do you suggest?"

"Has DCFS been called? We have to report any suspicion of abuse or neglect, and it sounds as if Travis may have abused the other children or the Idells may be guilty of neglect by not having provided adequate supervision for Travis. Although, I must admit, I've never quite understood what criteria the Department of Children and Family Services uses. Regardless, we are mandated to report."

"The parents of one of the girls involved called DCFS a couple of days ago. Her mother got suspicious when the girl cried every time she was made to undress. Her parents finally got her to tell them what was wrong. That's how this all got started. Once the DCFS started interviewing the various kids, everyone in town knew something was up. News around here spreads like a heat rash in summer." Lloyd's leg jiggled like a Slinky.

Skye considered their options until Lloyd's fidgeting drove her to speak. "Okay, I have a recommendation, but it's going to cost the school some money."

Lloyd grimaced. "Let's hear it."

"We make arrangements to home-teach young Mr. Idell until either the excitement dies down or DCFS makes some kind of move." Skye persisted before Lloyd could interrupt her. "By providing a home teacher we kill two birds with one stone, so to speak. We satisfy the Idells that we're protecting Travis from the children who are beating him up, and we appease the other parents by removing him, temporarily, from his alleged victims."

After a moment of thought, Lloyd got up. "This could work. How long do you think we'll have to pay for a home teacher?"

"That depends on a lot of things. Such as what DCFS decides to do and on what time schedule. I don't think I know the Idells. When did they move to Scumble River? Are they fairly affluent?"

"They relocated here about five or six years ago. I'd say they're comfortable. Both parents work in Chicago. With the ninety-minute commute each way they're hardly ever home. I think they do something with the stock exchange, and Travis is their only child."

"One of two things could happen. They may eventually become convinced that Travis did the things he's accused of and get him some professional help. Or they might remain in denial, decide the whole town is against them, and put Travis in a private school." Skye underlined something she had written.

"So, how long do you think this will take?" Lloyd bounced from one foot to the other.

It was Skye's turn to sigh. "This is only a guess, but I'd say a semester would be the longest these circumstances could last without something happening to change the situation."

Abruptly Lloyd ushered her out the door. "Fine. I'll check with the superintendent and get back to you if we need another option."

Finding herself staring at the closed door, she noticed it was oak with a small black nameplate on it: LLOYD STARK, PRINCIPAL.

She thought, *Principal what? Boor?*

Skye wasn't able to leave school until after five, having once again missed lunch. If this continued she'd have to find some sort of food she could eat during the five minutes it took to walk from one appointment to the next. The PPS meeting had lasted past three, and before she could get out of the room, the Idells had arrived. She'd spent two hours trying to work through the issues surrounding Travis's behavior but made little progress.

During a brief break in the conference, she had stolen a few minutes and telephoned her mother to ask if Vince planned on closing the shop for the day. May told Skye that Vince had said he'd be at work the next morning, whether he still had customers or not.

Pulling into Great Expectations about five-fifteen, Skye found the parking lot empty.

Vince was sitting on a stool behind the counter drinking a Coke and reading the *Chicago Tribune* when Skye came through the door.

He got up and came around to hug her. "Sis, I didn't kill her."

"I know." Skye fought the lump gathering in the back of her throat. "Let's sit down."

They settled once again in the plastic-covered chairs by the shampoo sinks and Skye asked gently, "Did most people show up for their appointments?"

"Yes. I was surprised, but there was just the normal number of no-shows."

Skye crossed her legs. "Good. Maybe that means the town's behind you. I suppose they all wanted to ask you questions, though."

"Oh, yeah, but that's pretty normal in this business. I told everyone I wasn't allowed to discuss it."

"That was a good idea."

"I was thinking of changing our double date to Friday. Both Mike and Abby said that was okay. Can you make it then?" Trailing his fingers along the basin, Vince avoided looking Skye in the eye.

"Sure, but maybe we should wait until this is all over."

"No. I want to go out. It will help take my mind off things." Vince continued to appear fascinated with the sink's enamel finish.

"When's your next customer scheduled?"

"Not until six, and that's the last appointment of the day," Vince said, relief evident in his voice.

"Then we have time to talk. What did you think of Loretta?"

"She was amazing, but then so were you and Mom. How did you know what to do?"

"I'm not sure, but ever since all this happened I've been relying on my memories of old TV shows to tell me how to act. I know I watched a lot of television as a kid, but it must have made a greater impact than I ever realized. Every time I get into a jam lately I've done what I've seen them do on TV. I think this latest one was *Perry Mason*." Skye had had little time for television since she'd left Scumble River, so her points of reference were somewhat dated.

"You should've seen Mom," Vince said. "Wally and a couple of his men showed up at my apartment around ten. The news was just coming on. They told me they had a search warrant and were bringing me in for questioning. It took them about forty-five minutes to tear my place apart, then they put me in the back of the squad car and took me to the station. Mom must have gotten to work just a little while before they brought me in, because she wasn't even sitting down yet. She started crying right away, but that didn't slow her down at all. She was on the phone to you before they even got me all the way upstairs."

"Did they have time to ask you anything before Mom stopped you?" Skye posed the question she had been worried about since last night.

"No. Wally was still getting coffee when Mom pushed her way into the room and told me not to say anything."

"If Mom was with you from the time I talked to her until Loretta appeared, how did Dad get there?"

"Mom used the phone in the interrogation room. Wally was so stunned by her actions I think she could have taken me home before he would have thought to object." Vince grabbed a magazine from the stand and started pleating its pages.

"Why did they want to question you? What do you have to do with Mrs. Gumtree?"

"It's a long story." Vince looked embarrassed.

Skye looked at her watch. "Then you'd better get going."

"Well, for starters, they found my styling shears in her neck."

"How can they be sure they were yours?" Skye grabbed the magazine from his hands.

"They had the shop's name engraved on them. But everybody in town gets their hair cut here. Anyone could have taken them without my noticing."

"Wonderful." Skye thought for a moment. "There must be something else."

"In real life Mrs. Gumtree was Honey Adair. Her agent finally returned from his weekend trip and identified her late yesterday afternoon."

When Skye looked puzzled, he explained, "I dated Honey in high school, the end of my senior year. Don't you remember?"

"Now I do. She was really tiny—I was so jealous. The couple of times I was near her I felt like the Incredible

Hulk. The name didn't ring a bell because Mom and Dad only referred to her as 'That Awful Girl.' Why didn't they like her?"

Vince shrugged. "Honey was pretty wild. She was involved with the druggies at school, and everyone said she slept around."

"Did she? With you, I mean?"

"Oh, yeah." Vince squirmed. "That's a big part of the problem."

"They suspect you because of an affair that took place sixteen years ago? Have you seen her since high school?" Skye was getting confused.

"She left town the day we graduated. I don't think she's ever been back."

"Wait a minute. She lived with Uncle Charlie, didn't she? I remember—she was his real niece."

"Right. His youngest sister was her mother. Her parents were killed in a car crash the summer before her senior year, and she moved here from Chicago to live with him." Vince began to fold the towels in the laundry basket next to the dryer.

"It was during that time that he told me to stop coming over to visit. I was really hurt," Skye said in astonishment.

"He probably wanted to protect you from Honey's bad influence."

"Even so, with Mom and Dad being so close to Charlie, I'm surprised they didn't at least try to pretend they liked Honey."

"Honey made it difficult for people to ignore her bad qualities. Charlie had a real rough time that year. I think he was mortified by her behavior. All I could see was how pretty she was," Vince said, looking off into the distance.

"Typical male. Thinking with your crotch instead of your brain."

Vince punched Skye in the arm. She yelped and grabbed for his ponytail. She missed, lost her balance, bumped into a chair, and went sprawling on the floor. Brother and sister both broke into gales of laughter.

They eventually stopped giggling and Skye got back into the chair. "I still don't understand why a high school romance makes you the prime suspect. Anyone who came into the salon could have stolen the scissors."

"I haven't told you the worst part." Vince squatted in front of her. "The morning of our high school graduation Honey asked me to take her for a ride. When I picked her up, she told me she was pregnant and I was the father. All she wanted from me was enough money for an abortion and to get away from Scumble River. Honey hated this town. She said it was full of hicks."

"What did you do?"

Vince glared. "What could I do? I went home, cleaned out my savings, and gave her the five hundred dollars. She promised not to tell Mom and Dad or Charlie, and I thought that would be the end of it."

"It wasn't, though, was it?" Skye guessed.

"No. In December of that year I got a phone call from her. Luckily, none of you were home. She said she'd decided to have the baby after all and she wanted me to pay child support."

"Oh, my God!" Stunned, Skye sagged in her chair.

"That certainly was my reaction too." Vince smiled grimly. "I've been sending her money every month since that phone call."

"Was it a boy or a girl?"

"A boy. Wade. She only let me see the baby once. Probably to convince me to pay up. But twice a year I'd get pictures and copies of his report cards. I never knew where she was. The money went to a post office box in Chicago, and she met me at Louis Joliet Mall."

"Did you know she was Mrs. Gumtree?" Skye reached into her tote and found her notebook.

"I've never seen the TV show, and I didn't look closely

at the posters until this morning. Even then I'm not sure I would have recognized her. The makeup was remarkable."

"This must have had something to do with you needing money?"

"Yeah, she called a week ago and said she wanted to send Wade to private school, and I needed to send her twenty-five hundred dollars by September fifth." He went back to folding towels.

"Have you sent it?"

"No. Since I've been going out with Abby I've started to think about a lot of things. I told Honey I wasn't sending any more money until after she agreed to regular visits. She threatened to talk to Mom and Dad, which is what she did every time I balked at giving her more money. But I stood firm this time."

"You paid all these years just because she threatened to tell Mom and Dad?" Skye asked incredulously.

"That was part of it. They've never been very proud of me, and I thought this would make them think even less of me. Mostly, though, it just seemed like the right thing to do. If I had fathered a child, I should support it. Honey's explanation of why I shouldn't see him seemed logical. Why confuse the kid with a parent who wasn't going to be around?"

"What made you change your mind?"

He shrugged. "I'm not sure. Maybe because he was turning sixteen. I don't know. All I wanted was to see him. I told her I wouldn't even mention I was his father."

"She refused?" Skye was sure she already knew the answer.

"After calling me everything but a gentleman, she hung up. There was a message on my answering machine the next day saying she would talk to me Sunday."

"Sunday was the day she was killed. I wonder if she planned to talk to you in person," Skye speculated. "How much of this do the police know?"

"Only about the styling shears and that we dated in high school. They didn't mention a child at all, but I told Loretta the whole story."

"Good. Who else knows?"

"No one." Vince looked uncomfortable.

"Tell me the kinds of questions the police asked."

"Where was I when the murder was committed? When did I last see Honey? Things like that."

"Nothing about money or the child. Interesting." Skye jotted down a note on her pad. "Where were you when she was killed?"

"Home, alone, getting ready to pick up Abby for the parade."

"Did anyone come to the door or call you on the telephone?"

"No. I picked up Abby about twelve-thirty. Since we were going to watch the parade from the roof of the salon, and it wasn't supposed to start until one, we didn't need to get here early in order to get a good spot." The sound of the front door opening distracted Vince momentarily.

"From the questions the coroner was asking me," Skye said, "they seem to think she was killed shortly before I found her, which would be around eleven-thirty. Plenty of time for you to stab her, go home, shower, and pick up Abby looking fresh and clean."

"Whoa, I thought you said you believed me."

Skye snapped her notebook closed and tucked it back into her tote before standing. "I do, but it's obvious that the police don't."

CHAPTER 10

Money Makes the World Go 'Round

When Skye arrived at the high school on Wednesday morning, she was determined to force the principal, Homer Knapik, to give her some direction. Also, she had several questions regarding scheduling and procedures about which she needed to pin him down. Without his input there was literally nothing she could do for the high school. She didn't know what day or time the PPS meetings were held, or even how often.

Homer was not in his office, but his secretary, Opal Hill, reported that he could probably be found in the library. The school's first IBM computer had arrived late yesterday afternoon, and Mr. Knapik was still in the process of installing and testing it.

Skye walked down the east hall of the high school, astonished at how little it had changed during the time she'd been gone. The beat-up yellow lockers and shabby lime carpet were just as she remembered. Even the faint odor of sweat, hormones, and chalk dust was the same.

The library was located in the center of the building, accessible by either the east or the west halls. Homer was hunched over a stand that held computer components and several open manuals. Skye pulled up a chair from an adjacent table and sat down.

He did not look up until she spoke. "Homer, I need to talk to you, and I need to see the confidential files so I can get started with re-evals and find out who is supposed to be receiving counseling."

It was very hard for Skye not to address him as "Mr. Knapik"; after all, he had been the principal at Scumble River High School for twenty-five years, which included the time she was a student there.

Frowning, he looked up. "Oh, Skye. I told you I didn't want to disturb anything while Neva Llewellyn was away having her baby."

"I understand your hesitation, Homer, but I can't do my job without those folders. And I have as much right to have access to those files as the guidance counselor does."

Homer reluctantly dug in his pocket and retrieved a large set of keys, attached to a key fob that resembled a jailer's ring. He selected two keys and handed the set to Skye. "Here, the big one is for the door and the little one is for the filing cabinets. Don't take the files out of the guidance office, and put them back like you found them."

"Sure. She'll never know I was there," Skye said brightly.

He shook his head mournfully. "She'll know and she'll chew my butt for it." Turning back to the table, he selected a manual and paged through it, wrinkling his forehead in concentration.

Skye persisted, trying to recapture his attention. "When are your PPS meetings scheduled, and are there any other meetings you want me to attend?"

"We only have faculty meetings. The secretary can give you the dates for those, but you don't have to come." Homer didn't take his eyes from the page he was reading.

"You mean you don't meet regularly with the psychologist, social worker, nurse . . ."

"We don't need that here. Anyone gives us any trouble, we kick 'em out. They can't keep up in class, we flunk 'em."

"How about the kids who come to you with an Individual Education Plan in place? We're legally obligated to provide whatever assistance that IEP prescribes," Skye pointed out.

Losing his patience, Homer slammed the book shut. "I told you, Neva takes care of all that."

Skye got up, clutching the keys, afraid he would change his mind and demand them back. Still, she felt obligated to try once more. "So, you never have PPS meetings or staffings or anything like that?"

"Look, if it's really important to you, talk to Neva when she gets back. You two can set things up, but I am not going to any more meetings." Homer turned his back and reached again for the manual.

Having won a small battle in what she was just beginning to suspect might turn into a full-fledged war, Skye hurried toward the guidance office.

It was cool and pleasant—since it was in one of the newer additions to the high school, it was air-conditioned. Although the room was dark, Skye didn't turn on the overhead light; instead she switched on the desk lamp. She noticed one file cabinet after another lining the walls, the drawers labeled with various years. It looked as if all the records since Scumble River High was first opened were stored in this room.

Skye unlocked the drawer identified with the most recent year and inspected its contents. She gathered up a pile of the most promising-looking files, hoping they were confidential special education records that contained Individual Education Plans, and not just cumulative folders containing report cards and group achievement tests.

She sat down behind the desk. The chair was wonderfully comfortable, deep and enveloping, the soft black leather aged and shaped to perfection. She sighed with pleasure at the unexpected physical comfort and started to work.

First she wrote down the name of the student on her

legal pad. In the next column she listed the date on which he or she needed to receive a three-year reevaluation. Finally, after reading the IEP, which usually consisted of fifteen or more pages, Skye determined whether that child was supposed to be receiving counseling. Later she would have to go back and read the most recent psychological evaluation report on each student who was enrolled in the special education program.

Several hours went by, and Skye was about to stop for lunch when she heard a tentative tapping on the frosted-glass window of the door.

Opening it, she found the secretary standing there, twitching. "Were you looking for me, Opal?"

Opal nodded. "Oh, my goodness, yes. Mr. Knapik is out of the building and the police are here."

A sudden wave of nausea left Skye unable to think clearly. *It must be about Vince.*

"Are you all right? You're pale as milk." Opal looked at her curiously.

Skye took a deep breath. "I'm fine. I must have gotten up too fast or my blood sugar's low. It's getting close to lunchtime."

"Could you talk to the police first? With Mrs. Llewellyn gone and Mr. Knapik out of the building, I'm not sure what I should do. Should I call the superintendent?" Opal asked with a touch of panic.

Shaking her head, Skye almost pushed Opal out of the room. "Why don't you ask the police to come in here where we can have some privacy? Give me a minute to put these folders back."

In the few moments it took Skye to tidy up the files and lock them away, she realized how foolish she was to think the police would come to tell her they'd rearrested Vince. The chief had been ready to put Skye in jail Monday night when he found out she was the one responsible for May's behavior and Loretta Steiner's presence. After that incident,

Skye would be the last person on Earth the police would notify.

Opal ushered Deputy McCabe and a Scumble River officer whom Skye didn't know into the office. Opal left, closing the door behind her. Both men stood in front of the desk and looked down at Skye.

"I'm Skye Denison, the district psychologist."

"I'm Deputy McCabe. You remember me from the murder last Sunday?" When she nodded he continued, "This is Officer Roy Quirk. What can you tell us about a girl named Phoebe Unger?"

"Nothing. I'm brand-new here, and I've never heard of her." She indicated chairs. "Please sit. What kind of information are you looking for?"

They sat, the leather of the utility belts around their waists creaking.

Quirk settled back and crossed his legs. "We'd like to know who she hangs out with, who her boyfriend is, what the school's impression of her is."

Skye nodded. "I'm sure we can get that information for you. It's not confidential. But Mr. Knapik, the principal, will want to know why you're so interested in Phoebe."

"That's official police business. There's no need for you to know, little lady." McCabe rubbed a smudge from the toe of his perfectly polished shoe.

Leaning forward, Skye made eye contact with each man in turn. "I certainly understand your need to keep things quiet in an ongoing investigation. And that it isn't always an easy task in a town this size. But you must understand that we need to know what you think she's done. If her actions make her a danger to our other students, we must be informed."

"We've had an anonymous informant tell us that her boyfriend, who does not go to school here, may be involved in a series of arson-style fires." Quirk straightened the crease of his pants.

McCabe glared at him.

"I see. So, at this time she does not appear to be a danger to herself or others. Correct?" Skye looked from one man to the other.

Both men nodded.

"Fine. Then I'll talk to Mr. Knapik when he gets back. With his permission, I'll speak to her teachers and try to get the information you need."

Quirk handed her his card. "Call me as soon as possible."

When school ended that day, Skye drove straight to the Scumble River Police Department. She was going to be a good citizen and deliver the information about Phoebe Unger to Officer Quirk in person. If, while she was there, she happened to chat with Chief Boyd about Honey Adair's murder, who would she be hurting?

Walking up to the counter, she raised her voice. "Hi, Thea. How are you? I haven't seen you in ages."

Thea Jones, one of Scumble River's longtime dispatchers, opened the gate and motioned Skye through, then gave her a hug. "Skye, honey, how you doin'? I'm sure sorry for the trouble your family's havin'."

Skye hugged her back. "Me, too. I hope Chief Boyd finds the real killer soon. It's just silly to think of Vince as a murderer."

"Ain't that right?" Thea sat back down. "Sometimes these men around here don't think too good. None of us dispatchers think he done it."

Leaning over, Skye kissed her on the cheek. "Thanks. I have some information on another case for Officer Quirk. Is he available?"

"Yep. He's in with the chief. I'll let 'em know you're here."

Following a short conversation on the intercom, Thea

turned to Skye. "Go right into the chief's office, honey. They both want to hear what you got to say."

Smiling to herself, Skye thought, *How convenient. I won't even have to ask to see Chief Boyd.*

He was standing on the threshold. When Skye approached, he motioned her inside and closed the door. Office Quirk was in one chair, and Skye took the other visitor's seat.

A faint smell of stale cigarette smoke lingered in the air. Skye looked around but didn't see any ashtrays, so she suspected the odor was from before Chief Boyd's time. His office was small and windowless, its gray walls lined with file cabinets and bookshelves. Linoleum that might have been blue when it was first put down but now looked silvery covered the floor. Shrouding the top of the chief's desk were papers of every shape and color. His chair was cracked green vinyl.

Chief Boyd sat on the edge of his desk, pushing a stack of manila files out of his way. "So, Skye, what can you tell us about Phoebe Unger?"

"Well, she certainly talks tough. No one knows if she carries out her threats, but if anyone crosses her or she thinks anyone has crossed her, she wants revenge."

Roy Quirk asked, "Can you be more specific?"

"I talked to a couple of girls she used to be friendly with last year. They seemed genuinely afraid of her—and it takes a lot to scare a teenager."

"Did they say why?" Chief Boyd looked up from the file he had been sifting through.

"This boyfriend you're investigating tried to break up with her last year. Phoebe was furious and vowed to get him back. She found out who his new girlfriend was, waited until they were out on a date, and trashed the girl's car."

"Why didn't she report it to the police?" demanded Roy.

"Was there any proof Phoebe did it?" asked the chief.

"It wasn't reported to the police because the girl was terrified. She refused to have anything more to do with Phoebe's ex-boyfriend. As to proof, yes, I'd say they had proof."

"You sound pretty sure. What kind of evidence did they have?" The Chief made a note in the file.

"Phoebe didn't give the boyfriend back his school jacket when he broke up with her. When they found the car, there was a dummy behind the wheel, wearing what was left of the jacket. It was stabbed through the chest with a butcher knife."

Both men looked at each other. Roy got up, excused himself, and left the office.

"Why do I think you guys are really after Phoebe and not the boyfriend?" Skye asked, trying to get comfortable on the hard chair.

"You don't want to know."

"You're right, I don't want to, but if the other kids are in danger I need to."

Chief Boyd moved from behind his desk to the chair next to Skye. He took her hand. "Do you trust me, Skye?"

She was having trouble keeping her breathing even. His tone had changed from official to intimate. "Yes, I . . . I guess so." Part of her wanted to jerk her fingers away, but another part of her remembered that summer when she was fifteen.

He seemed to sense her agitation. Letting her hand go, he moved away. "We'll make sure Phoebe doesn't hurt anyone else."

She would have liked to know what was going on with Phoebe Unger, but decided to let that matter drop and see what she could find out about Vince.

"Chief?"

"Do you think you could call me Wally? You make me feel a hundred years old calling me Chief Boyd all the time.

I'm only eight years older than you, and those eight years seem a lot shorter now that you're not fifteen anymore."

This was definitely not what Skye expected. She didn't know how to react. In her confusion she wasn't sure if he was flirting or just being friendly. The feelings she'd once had for him were resurfacing, but he was married, and she wasn't about to forget that.

"No, I'm far from fifteen. It seems like lots of things have changed since I've been gone. How's the murder investigation going?"

"I really can't talk about that."

"Oh, I know you can't go into detail, but it must have been quite a surprise when Mrs. Gumtree's agent identified her as Honey Adair." When the chief didn't answer, Skye went on, "Or did you already have an inkling as to her real identity?"

"What makes you say that?"

"Mom says there was a lot of secret activity going on here night before last." Skye watched him carefully. "And I find it hard to believe that no one recognized her. After all, she lived here for almost a year."

Wally said, "That was over sixteen years ago. And you have to remember she didn't want to be recognized, so she stayed away from people. She only appeared outside of her trailer for storytelling on Saturday. The only ones who saw her close up were children."

"Still, the whole thing is very convenient for someone. You don't seriously suspect Vince, do you?" Skye's eyes never left his face.

"They were his scissors."

"Half the town gets their hair cut at his salon. Anyone could have stolen them."

"True, but how many people dated Honey Adair in high school?" Chief Boyd went around his desk and sat down. The barriers were back in place.

"Half the town, or so I've heard."

"But Vince was the last one before she disappeared. Why did she leave so mysteriously?"

"What did Charlie Patukas say about her leaving?" Skye put both hands on the edge of the desk and leaned forward.

"This whole thing has been quite a surprise for him. He hadn't heard from or seen Honey since she left town. I thought the guy was going to have a stroke when I told him who Mrs. Gumtree really was. And then to find out she had left him all her money—the poor old man is still in shock."

Skye worded her next question carefully, not wanting to arouse his suspicions. "Did Honey leave anything else to him?"

Chief Boyd looked puzzled. "Like what?"

"You know, property, things like that." Skye glanced at the top papers on his pile, but found nothing interesting.

"She owned a condo in Chicago, but besides that and her personal possessions, her estate is mainly cash and, of course, her life insurance policy."

"How much do you figure the total inheritance will come to?" Skye picked up a pencil from the desktop and twirled it between her palms.

He flipped open a file. "Because she was a TV star, she had an unusually large life insurance policy. It's worth a million dollars by itself. Add the condo and the cash and I'd say we're talking in the neighborhood of one point five million dollars."

"That's a pretty nice neighborhood for Charlie to move into," Skye said thoughtfully. "Of course, a move into such a nice neighborhood usually comes with a pretty high price tag."

In this case the price had been a young woman's life.

CHAPTER 11

Somewhere in the Night

That afternoon when Skye got home from the police station, her mother's car was in the driveway and she was washing the front windows of the house. With the temperature continuing to hover in the nineties, May's face was an alarming shade of red, and sweat was dripping from the tip of her nose.

Skye turned her key in the locked door and entered the centrally air-conditioned cottage. She held the door open and looked questioningly at her mother. May gave the window one more swipe, picked up her bottle of Windex, and went inside.

Skye headed for her bedroom. "So, Mom, is the president of the United States coming to visit, or did you just have an uncontrollable urge to give yourself heatstroke?"

May didn't respond to Skye's sarcasm. Instead she stood in the doorway to Skye's bedroom and watched her change into blue chambray shorts and a plain white T-shirt. Slipping on a pair of white sandals, Skye walked past her mother into the great room and sat down in a camp chair.

"You really need to get some more furniture. Where would your dad sit if he was here?" May looked at the other camp chair with distaste.

Skye was not about to be distracted. "So, you came to furnish my house as well as to clean it. Fine. Don't forget to scrub the grout around the tub, and I'd like a Queen Anne–style desk set."

Rubbing the wooden arm of the chair with her rag, May paused before sitting. "Vince needs your help."

"Oh." Skye recognized a trap when she heard one. "Has he said he wants it, or is this all your idea? I got him a good lawyer, and I know he's not back in jail. I was just at the police station."

May looked up sharply. "What were you doing there?"

"Officer Quirk needed some information on one of the high school students, so I stopped after work to give it to him. Why shouldn't I be there?"

"You were always sweet on Wally, but he's out to put your brother in jail."

"He didn't seem to be on a vendetta when I spoke to him a few minutes ago. I'm sure they're looking into other suspects too, like people she knew in Chicago."

"Aha, you just talked to him. I thought you said you went to talk to Roy Quirk." May stood up and attacked the inside windows.

Skye handed her mother the bottle of Windex. "I did go to talk to Officer Quirk, but he was with the chief, and so I talked to them both."

"When I was dispatching last night I looked through the Honey Adair file, and Vince is their only suspect. They aren't looking at anyone else."

"How did you get a chance to see that file? Don't they keep stuff like that locked up?"

May smiled. "I've changed a lot since I've been working at the P.D. The locks on the file cabinets are a piece of cake."

"Then what do you need me for?" Skye asked, unnerved to discover her mother had a dark, criminal side.

"You need to find out who really killed her. People talk to you. At least they should after what we paid to send you to college."

Skye narrowed her eyes as she studied her mother.

"Have you been watching *Murder, She Wrote* again? In real
life the police solve crimes, amateurs don't."

"The police think they've already solved the case.
They're too busy gathering evidence against Vince to look
at anyone else. We can't afford a private detective, even if
I knew where to find one. As a psychologist, you know
how to make people talk and you can tell if they're lying.
Plus, I can help by getting police information. I know how
to use the computer at work to find out lots of stuff." May
moved over to the wall mirror and began wiping vigor-
ously.

Skye considered what her mother had said. *I'm amazed
the way people assume that because I have a degree in
psychology, I also have magical powers. Would I be back
in Scumble River if I were that good?* She closed her eyes
and sighed. *On the other hand, Mom has a point. If the
police aren't looking for anyone else and Vince remains
their prime suspect, something has to be done. Why do I
have this sinking feeling that I'm about to get into trouble
again?*

"Okay, Mom, I'll see what I can do. I'm not sure where
to start, though."

"You'll have to find out about Honey. Try to discover
where she's been all these years and why someone would
want her dead." May's eyes searched the room for something else to clean.

"Any idea where I should begin that little task?"

Apparently sarcasm was wasted on May. "At the beginning. Go talk to Charlie. He knows more than he's saying."

The only light on at the Up A Lazy River Motor Court
was in Charlie's cabin. Even the parking lot lay in darkness.
Skye glanced at her watch. It was a little past eight, not too
late for a visit. Waiting on the step after ringing the doorbell, she remembered how, when she was growing up,

doors weren't locked in Scumble River and friends just walked in unannounced.

What was taking Charlie so long? The cabin was tiny, having only a bedroom, kitchenette, living room, and bath. She was beginning to get a bad feeling when a car turned into the parking lot, its lights momentarily blinding her.

With a sensation of relief, she saw Charlie get out of the car and heard him say, "Thanks for the ride, Eldon. See you tomorrow."

When Charlie spotted Skye standing on the step, he hurried toward her. "Skye, honey, what are you doing waiting out here like a door-to-door salesman? Don't you remember where I keep the key? You should've let yourself in."

"That's okay. I just got here. When I saw the light, I thought you were home."

Charlie frowned. "I don't remember leaving a light on, but of course my memory's not what it used to be, and after these past few days . . ."

"Uncle Charlie, I'm so sorry. I had no idea about Honey."

Shrugging, Charlie unlocked the door and stood aside to let Skye enter first. She let out a gasp and stopped dead in her tracks. Charlie pushed in behind her and halted too. The cabin had been ransacked. All the cushions had been sliced open and stuffing was spilling out; the chairs were upended, their bottoms also slashed. Pictures were torn off the walls, their glass smashed and the photographs shredded into confetti. The carpet had been ripped up at the corners and dragged to the middle of the room.

Silently they moved to the kitchen. There the cupboard doors stood agape, dishes and glasses shattered on the floor, and food smeared on the counter. A window over the sink was open, and jelly footprints indicated that this was the way the person had entered and exited the cabin.

They found the bedroom and bath in similar shape. Charlie appeared to be in shock, all of his seventy years evident in his face. He sank down on the bed and buried his head in his hands.

Even as Skye dialed the police, she knew she shouldn't have touched the telephone. But no fingerprints had been found in Mrs. Gumtree's trailer, according to her mother's report, and she certainly wasn't leaving Charlie there alone while she located another phone.

Chief Boyd and Officer Quirk arrived with sirens blaring and lights flashing. Skye and Charlie were hustled out of the cabin. They climbed into Skye's car. Charlie sat with his head leaning against the back of the seat. Skye battled her conscience. One part of her wanted to leave Charlie alone, while another part of her said this was the perfect time to get information.

The practical side won. "Mom's really worried about Vince being arrested for Honey's murder."

Without opening his eyes, Charlie said, "So am I. Honey always did manage to stir things up. I guess now she's doing it from the grave."

"I know this isn't the time, but would you mind telling me about Honey? I only remember her a little."

Rubbing his eyes with his knuckles, Charlie straightened. "It isn't all that strange that you hardly remember her. To begin with, Honey was completely selfish and had no interest in other females. At fourteen you probably didn't even exist to her. Also, your parents and I agreed that she wasn't someone we'd have wanted you to have as a role model. You may have run into her only once or twice."

"But if Vince dated her, wouldn't I have seen her more often?"

"Vince kept his relationship with Honey pretty quiet. Your parents and I didn't find out about it until the end."

Turning toward Charlie, Skye sat with one knee tucked under her, and her arm along the back of the seat. "How did she end up in Scumble River?"

"Honey's mother was my younger sister. There were only the two of us left from my family, so when she and her husband were killed in an auto accident there was nowhere else for Honey to go. Her father had no family at all."

"Is it true she was uncontrollable? Was that a reaction to her parents' deaths?"

Charlie shook his head. "No, as a matter of fact, her parents were looking into a military-type boarding school for Honey the day they were killed."

"Do you remember the details of their accident?"

"Their brakes failed, and they were hit by a tractor-trailer truck."

Skye whistled. "How awful. I'm sure that losing her parents in such a dreadful way contributed to her problems here."

"Maybe, but Honey wouldn't talk to the therapist I took her to, and her behavior when she lived with me sounded just like her mother had described it."

"People have said she was . . . ah, sexually active. Do you know the names of her partners?" Skye couldn't meet his eyes.

Charlie's face turned red. "No. Back then things like that were kept more quiet." Charlie hesitated. "Honey did spend a lot of time with Mike Young. I suspected she was getting drugs from him."

"Interesting. Can you think of anyone else she spent time with?"

"No, when she first got here she behaved pretty good for the first couple of months. She got on the softball team and spent a lot of time at practices and games, which kept her out of trouble. Then, about Thanksgiving, she hooked up with Mike, and after that she seemed to run through a bunch of boys, one after the other. She started with Vince around Valentine's Day, and her behavior improved again."

"Did Honey tell you she was leaving?" Noticing the

sweat on Charlie's brow, Skye leaned across him and opened the window.

"No. I came home after the graduation ceremony, and all her things were gone. She took my car and all the petty cash, about two hundred dollars."

"Did you call the police?"

He looked away. "No. I was glad she was gone. It seemed a cheap price to pay, two hundred bucks and an old clunker, to get my peaceful life back."

Skye patted him on the arm. "You just tell me to mind my own business if I'm getting too personal here or there's something you don't want to answer." She waited, but when Charlie didn't say anything she went on. "Where did Honey go to school before she moved here?"

"Bogart? No, Bogan High School on the south side of Chicago."

"What do you know about her more recent life?"

Charlie kneaded the fingers of one hand with the other. "Only what her agent told me when she called. Honey owned a condo on the Gold Coast in the Raven Building. She spent most of her time either taping her TV show or out on the road promoting it. The agent said Honey didn't seem to have any friends and work was her life."

"That's pretty sad. Will her agent be coming down for the funeral?"

"Yeah. I'm supposed to call her once the arrangements are made. She said Honey's producer and publicist will be coming too."

Having covered everything but the inheritance, Skye found her resolve faltering. She decided to take the plunge before Chief Boyd or Officer Quirk came to talk to them and ruined the moment. Charlie might not be so forthcoming tomorrow when the shock wore off.

"Chief Boyd mentioned that you were Honey's beneficiary. Were you surprised?"

Charlie gripped Skye's knee so hard that it frightened her. "You have to believe me, I hadn't seen or talked to Honey since the day she left here. I can't imagine why she left me her money. My gut feeling says that that money is going to bring me nothing but pain and heartache."

CHAPTER 12

A Taste of Honey

Chief Boyd finally allowed Skye to go home, just before midnight. He questioned her and Charlie separately, making each wait while he talked to the other. When the county sheriff's technicians were finished, he also insisted that Charlie go through the cabin and make a list of everything that had been taken. Charlie wasn't missing a single thing.

The phone started ringing the next morning at five-thirty. Skye was having a nightmare about police cars, so the shrilling of the phone merged into the sirens of her dreams, and it took her some time to understand what was going on.

"Hello?" she mumbled, still not fully awake.

Her mother said anxiously, "Where were you last night? I tried to reach you until almost midnight."

At the sound of May's voice Skye sat up and swung her feet to the floor. "When I got to Charlie's, his cabin had been vandalized. The police kept me until nearly twelve o'clock."

"Oh, my God! Are you all right? Is Charlie okay?" May's voice cracked.

"We're fine. No one was home when it happened. Nothing was missing, but Charlie's pretty upset."

"I'll bake him a pie this morning and go visiting this afternoon."

"That sounds good. He probably needs help cleaning up, too. I'll stop after work and do that," Skye said.

"You just concentrate on your new job and clearing Vince. I'll clean up at Charlie's. It won't take long, his place is so small."

"Okay, Mom, but don't overdo." Skye waited for a reply. "Do you hear me?"

"Yes, I hear you. Just remember I'm not an old lady yet." With that pronouncement May returned to her original purpose in calling. "So, did you find out anything from Charlie?"

"You called me at five-thirty in the morning to ask me that?"

"I wanted to catch you before you left for school. Tonight I'm working the three-to-eleven shift, so if you need any information, let me know."

Skye itched to remind May, once again, that she didn't have to be at school until seven-thirty, but realizing that her mom only heard what she wanted to hear, she said instead, "Let me think about it. I'll call you back in half an hour."

After showering and making herself a cup of tea, Skye sat and thought about what she'd learned from Charlie last night. *Mm, Honey was in trouble before she got to Scumble River, which makes it safe to assume that she didn't change when she moved away. It's also interesting that Honey hung around with Mike Young during his druggie period. And why doesn't anyone seem to know a thing about a child?*

Skye decided she wanted May to use the police computers to find out about Mr. and Mrs. Adair's accident and Mike Young's arrest record. Meanwhile, she was going to talk to some of the people who would have been in high school during Honey's senior year.

A low-pressure system had rolled in during the night, and the predawn skies were overcast and threatening rain. It was only eighty degrees, but the humidity remained near

100 percent. Skye's sinuses were throbbing, and she knew there would be a thunderstorm before the end of the day.

Her schedule called for Thursday mornings at the elementary school, because of the PPS meeting at seven-thirty. Thanks to May's early wake-up call, Skye arrived in plenty of time. She had been told by Caroline Green, the principal, that the meetings were held in the special education classroom.

Standing awkwardly by the door, Skye was unsure of where to sit or what to do. She surveyed the room. Twelve desks were arranged in three pods of four each. The chairs were of molded orange plastic, designed for the height and build of six- and seven-year-old children. The sole adult chair was behind the teacher's desk.

Only a few minutes passed before Abby arrived, followed closely by two other women.

"Skye, have you met everyone?" Abby started to take the chairs off the top of the student desks.

"No, I haven't."

Abby pointed to the woman at the teacher's desk, who was dressed in a full denim skirt and a white oxford-cloth blouse. "This is Yvonne Smith, the special education teacher." Turning to the other woman, who was now seated, Abby continued, "And this is Belle Whitney, the speech therapist."

Smiling, Skye sat down next to Belle. "I'm Skye Denison, the new psychologist."

Yvonne was what most people pictured when they thought of an elementary school teacher—round and soft, with a halo of gray-brown curls and a smiling face.

She carried the teacher chair over to where Skye was sitting, then settled in and patted Skye on the arm. "Nice to meet you. I hope we'll see a lot of you down here. I could sure use some new ideas. The kids seem to get tougher every year."

Belle nodded. "Yes, and each year there are more kids who need help."

The speech therapist looked like a whipped-cream factory that had exploded. She wore her pale-blond hair in elaborate curls and waves. Her white dress was made of a gauzy material, with rows of ruffles around the neck, sleeves, and hem. Even her eyeglasses had loops and curlicues on the frames.

Skye looked at her watch. It was quarter to eight. "Does the principal usually attend these meetings?"

"If she remembers," Abby answered. "I didn't put a note in her box this time, so she probably won't show. We might as well get started." Abby flipped open her notebook.

"Okay, I'll go first." Yvonne poised her pencil over the list she had put on the table. "Since this is only our ninth day of school, I don't have any kids to discuss, but the kindergarten teachers have asked for help with a fall screening."

"What kind of help? Help administering the test?" Skye leaned over to look at Yvonne's paper.

Yvonne nodded. "That, too, but first they need a test to administer."

"They don't like the instrument they have now? Do you know if they're looking for something that measures readiness skills or processing abilities?" Skye rummaged in her tote, looking for a test catalog.

Yvonne laughed, not unkindly. "We've never had kindergarten screening before. There is no test to like or dislike. They probably don't even know what they want to assess. My advice would be to start with something that tells them if the kids are ready for kindergarten. Looking at memory or the ability to distinguish one sound from another is more information than they would know what to do with at this point."

"Oh." Skye was overwhelmed by the idea of single-handedly setting up a screening for 150 five-year-olds. "I guess I'd better talk to the kindergarten teachers myself."

She flipped through her appointment book. "How about next Tuesday before school?"

After making a note, Yvonne patted Skye's arm again. "Don't worry, I'll let them know that's when you're free and they'll be there."

"I'd like to attend too, if that's okay?" Belle looked up from her own appointment book. "Since I have to screen all kindergartners for speech and language delays anyway, maybe we can pick a test that will do double duty."

"That would be great." Skye's pencil hovered. "Is Tuesday morning all right with you?"

"It's fine. I'll bring some test catalogs." Belle made a note in the margin of her book.

Abby said, "I'll be doing the vision and hearing screenings on Monday."

"Do you screen the whole school?" asked Skye.

"Almost. I test all the kids in special education, all the kindergartners, all the new kids who have moved in, and all of the third and fifth grades."

"Is there anything else? It's almost nine o'clock, so the kids will be here any minute." Yvonne stood.

Skye handed each of the women a list of twenty-six names. "These are the children who are past due for reevaluation. We all have a part in the case study, so I wanted to know what timetable you all would like to follow in getting these assessments up to code."

"Well, I don't have any part in a case study," Yvonne said, picking up her chair.

Skye tried to decide the best way of phrasing her request. "I know you haven't been consulted in the past, but that really was a waste of knowledge. Who knows these kids better than you? We need your input, and I was thinking that maybe you could do the section titled 'Current Educational Functioning.'"

"But I wouldn't have any idea how to write that type of report." Yvonne let the chair drop.

"I'll give you a model to go by." It was Skye's turn to pat Yvonne's arm.

After a moment Yvonne nodded. "Okay, I've always said you guys didn't listen enough to what the teacher had to say about the student you were evaluating. I guess it's time to put my money where my mouth is. This will give me a chance to be heard."

Skye was surprised at how easy that had been. She turned to Abby. "Lloyd mentioned that you do the health history, since we don't have a social worker, and I do the adaptive part. Is this how it works in all the schools?"

"That's how we've done it in the past. But I was think-ing—I have to talk to the parents anyway, so if you gave me the social history form you want to use, I could ask them the questions on it and you could use that for your re-port. It would save both you and the parents some time."

"I'd owe you big time. I was dreading that aspect of the job. Why don't they hire a social worker?" Skye looked at all three women.

"We've tried," Abby answered. "We put ads in the pro-fessional social work journals and the Chicago newspapers. Last year we even sent a representative to the school social worker convention. Not one person signed up to be inter-viewed."

"But why?" Skye asked. "The salary is a little low, but not that far out of alignment."

Abby and Belle looked at each other. Abby nudged Belle with her elbow. "I think we've been blackballed."

Everyone laughed.

"Seriously, the social workers we've had since I've been here wanted everything to be their own way, and that's just not going to happen in Scumble River. When you add the fact that they were all outsiders, and no one in town would tell them anything . . ." Abby looked to the others for con-firmation.

Belle nodded. "I've lived here for ten years, and people

are only now beginning to trust me. And I don't ask them personal questions."

"It is an advantage, having lived here all of my life." Abby stood. "Half the time I don't even have to ask questions, I already know all the dirt."

Skye tapped the list she was holding. "Back to my original question. When, and at what rate, are we going to tackle this list?"

No one answered.

"How about three a month? Since the three of us are all split among three schools, I figure we're all here about a day and a half a week."

Everyone nodded.

Before anyone could say anything else, a stream of students started filling the room.

A little redheaded boy with a crew cut marched up to Skye. He looked familiar, but she couldn't place him. "You're sitting in my chair."

She got up and squatted down in front of him. "I apologize. My name is Ms. Denison, and sometimes I have to come to your room before school. Would it be okay if I use your chair when you're not here?"

The boy smiled, revealing that his front teeth were missing. "Sure, but you gotta get off it when I say so."

Skye stuck out her hand. "Deal."

Yvonne noticed the boy for the first time. She walked around her desk and stood near him. "Junior, it's time to sit down. Maybe Ms. Denison will visit you again sometime."

Junior. Where have I heard that name before? Skye tapped her chin, lost in thought.

Belle and Abby had gathered their folders and appointment books and were heading out the door when Skye caught up with them. "Abby, were you in Vince's class during high school?"

"No, I was a year behind."

"Did you know Honey Adair?"

"That little ponytailed porcelain doll? How could I forget her?"

Putting her arm through Abby's, Skye steered her toward the health room. "Can we talk?"

With a wave, Belle set out in the opposite direction.

Skye and Abby settled themselves in the health room after shutting the door. This room looked just like the one at the junior high, and Skye was betting that the one at the high school would also be the same. Abby sat at the desk while Skye made do with the cot.

"So, why do you want to know about Honey?" Abby asked, leaning back and crossing her legs.

"You know the police had Vince in for questioning?"

She nodded. "Yeah, but they let him go that same night."

"Only because the attorney I found for him wouldn't let him say anything. They didn't have enough evidence to arrest him, but he's still their number-one suspect. According to Mom, he's their *only* suspect."

"So, what are you doing?" Abby frowned.

"My mom thinks, and I have to agree, that unless we find out who really killed Honey, the police are going to keep trying to nail Vince.

"In order to find out who killed her, I need to know as much about her as possible. Right now I'm trying to get a picture of what she was like. What do you remember about her?" Skye squirmed, trying to get comfortable on the lumpy vinyl cot, and vowed to race Abby for the chair next time.

"She was the only person I've ever met that Gandhi would have slapped."

"Why was that?"

"Honey was just plain mean. She was so tiny, you weren't prepared for her to turn on you. She went out of her way to say hurtful things to people. That one had a talent for picking out the weakest kids around and tearing them to shreds. When you add the fact that she was never interested in a boy unless he was dating someone else . . ." The expression on Abby's face was one of disgust.

"Boy, she was a real witch."

"With a capital B," added Abby.

Skye grabbed a pencil from the desk. "Who were some of her loves du jour?"

"Most guys were just one-night stands, and their girlfriends eventually took them back."

"So you're saying if sex were fast food there would have been golden arches over her head."

Abby didn't smile. "Before she latched on to Mike Young, he was pretty serious about Darleen Ames. They never did get back together."

"Darleen Ames. Is she Darleen Boyd now?"

"Yep."

"Who else's life did she mess around with?" Skye lifted her tote onto her lap.

"Well, we were on the softball team together that summer she moved here, and she seemed very close to the coach."

Skye leaned forward. "Who was the coach? Is he still in town?"

"Sure, you see him every day. It was Lloyd Stark." Abby hastened to add, "Just remember that was only an impression I had, not a fact."

"Understood. But it certainly is food for thought." She hated to broach the next question. "Who was Vince going out with when she hooked him?"

Abby looked away. "He wasn't seeing anyone seriously, but he and I had dated a couple of times."

"That must have made you feel pretty angry."

"I wanted to kill her."

CHAPTER 13

All Shook Up

After speaking to Abby, Skye had tried to concentrate on setting up a counseling schedule and observing in different classrooms. At eleven-thirty she gave up and called May, suggesting that they meet for lunch. Now she sat in a booth at McDonald's, waiting for her mother and gazing out the window at the parking lot. If she craned her neck she could see the spot that Mrs. Gumtree's trailer had occupied. She was surprised that the area showed no trace of either the parade or the murder.

May slid onto the bench opposite Skye. "I'm glad you called me. Meeting for lunch was a good idea. This way we can discuss the case without your father knowing what we're up to."

"Why don't you want Dad to know?"

"Because he doesn't know how to keep a secret."

"That's true." Skye stood up. "I'll get our food, and we can talk while we eat. I only have half an hour. What do you want, Mom?"

"Gee, I don't know. I guess a grilled chicken sandwich and a Diet Coke. I'll eat some of your fries." May reached into her wallet and thrust a ten-dollar bill at Skye. "My treat."

"I can buy my own lunch."

They glared at each other for an instant before Skye acquiesced and reluctantly accepted the money. She shot May one more look before leaving to place their order.

Skye was gone less than five minutes. She handed May her change before putting the brown plastic tray on the table and settling back on her side of the booth. While May put away the money, Skye unwrapped her Big Mac and took a bite.

May removed a foil pack of moistened towelettes from her purse and tore it open. She shook out the paper square and thoroughly wiped the tabletop. After flattening the wrinkled paper from her sandwich into a makeshift place mat, she took a handful of Skye's fries and put a straw in her cup. She smoothed a napkin on her lap.

Skye watched this ritual with interest, having seen it only a million or so times before today. "Are we comfy yet?"

May looked up, but did not respond to Skye's sarcasm. "That's a pretty outfit. Don't forget to put your napkin in your lap."

Having forgotten momentarily what she'd put on that morning, Skye looked down at what she was wearing—a deep blue wrap-style dress with a cascade collar. "Thanks."

"Why don't your shoes match?"

Since the pumps she was wearing were made for walking, Skye walked away from that booby trap. "If we're through with our housekeeping chores and fashion bloopers, perhaps we can discuss what I've uncovered so far this morning."

"Shoot."

Leaning forward, Skye lowered her voice, even though there was no one anywhere near them. "Okay, you remember the things you're supposed to research for me tonight?"

May nodded impatiently. "Yes, I wrote it all down. I'm not senile. What else have you found out?"

"After my meeting this morning I chatted with Abby Fleming, the school nurse. You know she's dating Vince now, but did you remember she went out with him a few times in high school?"

May smiled indulgently. "I couldn't keep track of all the girls Vince dated. He was so popular."

Skye wondered if her mother was reminding her that she had not been very sought after in high school. Talking with her mother always required being on the alert for ambushes.

She ignored that unwelcome thought. "Anyway, Vince dated her right before he got involved with Honey Adair. And Abby was really ticked off at Honey for stealing Vince."

"This all happened so long ago. She can't still be upset about it."

"Think of it this way. She's dating Vince again, everything is going really well, and suddenly she finds out that Honey is coming back to town. I'd say all the old resentment would resurface."

"How would she know that Honey was Mrs. Gumtree?" May took a few more fries from Skye's pile.

"I haven't worked out that part yet." Skye shrugged. "But she could have recognized her from her picture on those posters that were all over town."

May shook her head. "Abby is such a sweet girl. She couldn't do something like that."

"Right." Skye opened another ketchup packet. "And there were no drugs in Scumble River when I was in high school. At least that's what you always told me when I complained about the pushers in class."

"Did you find out anything else?"

"Oh, my, yes. Did you know that Chief Boyd's wife, Darleen, dated Mike Young in high school, while he was so involved in drugs? Honey broke up that relationship, too."

"No, I didn't know any of that. Well, that might explain his wanting to pin this murder on Vince without much investigating. He probably doesn't want anything about his wife's past to come out." May shook some salt on her sandwich.

"I would imagine not, but I just can't picture Chief Boyd with Darleen. She's the special ed teacher at the junior high, and there's something about her that bothers me."

"Like what?"

"Let me think. To begin with, she's emaciated, not just fashionably thin but skeletal. Also, her eyes bulge out. I keep trying to remember what medical condition causes that. But mostly it's her extremely submissive behavior around the principal that disturbs me." Taking a sip of her Diet Coke, she tried to put the pieces together.

May finished her meal and started to clean up the debris, putting everything back on the tray. "Everyone doesn't have to be as bossy as you are."

"Thanks a lot, Mom."

May got up and dumped the trash in the garbage. "You've found out a lot already."

"That's not all." Skye followed May to the door. "Abby said that Honey was very friendly with her softball coach back then. And you'll never guess who that was." She paused for effect. "It was Lloyd Stark, the junior high principal."

"Do you really think someone like him would get involved with a student?"

"Remember, this was sixteen years ago. He may have changed considerably since then. Nevertheless, I'm going to talk to him too."

They walked toward their cars, parked side by side. May opened her door, then cautioned, "Be careful. If one of these people did kill Honey, they may already think you saw something, and by asking questions you could be stirring up a hornet's nest."

Skye hugged her mother and kissed her on the cheek. "When you asked me to help Vince, what did you think would happen?"

"I guess I didn't think, but I don't want to put one of my kids in danger to save the other."

"Sure, Mom, I'll watch it."

*   *   *

Skye was scheduled to spend the rest of the day at Scumble River Junior High. As soon as she arrived, she asked to speak to Lloyd but was told by Ursula, the school secretary, that he was unavailable.

Next, she went to the special ed classroom. There she found Darleen, along with eleven students, who were studying for a math quiz.

Skye whispered to Darleen from the doorway, "Mind if I watch?"

Darleen shook her head, but she kept glancing uneasily at Skye as she taught.

Making her way to the back of the room, Skye sat in a yellow plastic folding chair. From reading their files she knew the kids had a mixed bag of disabilities, with the majority having either learning or behavior problems. They all had study sheets, and most had written in their solutions. Darleen was going over those answers.

Skye was visiting the classrooms in an attempt to match faces to the names on file folders, allow the teachers and students to become accustomed to her, and get a feel for the different teaching styles.

The bell rang at two-fifteen and the students piled out of the room. Gym was last period, and they had a lot of bottled-up energy to expend.

Turning to Skye, Darleen gestured to the sheaf of papers she was holding. "This is my planning period, so there won't be any more students today."

Skye nodded. She recognized a dismissal when she heard one, but she persisted. "Are you going to the teachers' lounge?"

Darleen gave Skye a deer-in-the-headlights look. "Yes, I thought I'd get a soda while I grade these papers."

Skye ignored Darleen's attempt to make it perfectly clear that she didn't want company. "Great. Mind if I join you? Maybe we can get to know each other."

Sighing, Darleen trudged down the hall.

The teachers' lounge was decorated in Early Grandma's Attic. Nothing matched, and everything was at least fifty years old. A refrigerator had been placed in the back corner, next to a counter with a sink full of used coffee cups. The microwave, located on an old library cart, was stained both inside and out. Several tables had been shoved together, plastic folding chairs arranged haphazardly around them. A couch covered in nubby orange fabric occupied the opposite wall, and next to it a child-size desk held a telephone.

Darleen opened the fridge and took a half-empty can of soda from the shelf. She sat down at the table and started grading papers.

Skye looked around for the pop machine but did not see it. "Where's the soda machine?"

Darleen shrugged listlessly. "It must still be out for repair."

Making a mental note to bring in a few cans of Diet Coke to put in the fridge, Skye joined her. While Skye waited for Darleen to look up, she studied her. If anything, the teacher looked worse now than she did the first day of school. Her skin was pasty, and she had dark circles under her eyes. She wore an overall romper over a Spandex crop top.

Skye thought, *Why would a teacher who deals with disturbed adolescent boys dress like that? Talk about asking for trouble.*

The silence lengthened and Skye's impatience grew. "So, are you from Scumble River?"

Darleen nodded but did not look up.

This conversation was more of a chore than getting a sixteen-year-old to talk. "You must have gone to high school here then, right?"

Again a nod but no eye contact.

"That murder Sunday was awful. Did you know Honey Adair?"

Finally Darleen looked at Skye and started to nibble on a fingernail. The rest of her nails showed evidence that this was a long-standing habit. Her fingers also had yellow stains, suggesting she was a chronic smoker. "No, not really. Well, sort of. I mean we were in the same class, but I never hung around with her or anything. I don't think she had any girlfriends."

Skye took the opening that statement provided. "Yes, but I hear she had a lot of boyfriends."

Darleen looked down at the papers in front of her and shrugged.

"In fact, I just heard today that before she started dating my brother, Honey and Mike Young were closer than two ones in an eleven." Skye stared at Darleen, daring her to deny the truth.

"I don't remember." Darleen's face had turned an unhealthy shade of red.

Feeling as if she was pulling the wings off a butterfly, Skye leaned closer and said, "Oh, I'm surprised to hear that. I thought you and Mike were dating before Honey stole him away."

Darleen stood up so suddenly that the chair she was sitting on went flying back and toppled onto the floor. She was trembling when she turned to Skye, and tears were running down her cheeks. "You're like all the rest of them, asking questions, prying into the past. Leave me alone. Why can't everybody just leave me alone?"

Darleen ran out of the lounge. Skye sat there, stunned. *I wonder who all the rest of them are? Who else has been prying into her past?*

At five o'clock, on her way out of the building, Skye stopped at the front office to try once again to talk to Lloyd. Ursula had been telling her all afternoon that he wasn't seeing anyone. This time she found Ursula gone and the room vacant.

She called out as she walked back toward the principal's office, "Lloyd, are you busy?"

There was no answer, but she could see that the light in his office was still on. Standing at the partially closed door, she knocked. "Lloyd, it's Skye Denison. Could I talk to you a minute?"

Silence, except for the humming of a computer monitor. This was beginning to feel like déjà vu. First Mrs. Gumtree's trailer, then Charlie's cabin, and now this. Skye forced herself to push the door all the way open and stick her head inside.

The office was trashed. All the desk drawers had been taken out and their contents strewn on the floor. Certificates and plaques that usually hung on the wall were thrown into a pile. It was clear that someone was searching for something and didn't care who or what got in the way.

CHAPTER 14

As Time Goes By

Once again Skye found herself in the backseat of Chief Boyd's squad car. Scumble River had recently purchased all new police vehicles, which meant buying two of them. Chevy Caprice Classics had been the mayor's selection after an arduous brainstorming session. This was not exactly a risky choice, since most police officers in the country drove similar sedans, and Chevrolet manufactured a special line of this model especially for law enforcement departments.

Scumble River's Caprices were robin's-egg blue with a map of the river painted in black on both front doors. Chief Boyd's squad smelled faintly of his aftershave, and something else Skye couldn't identify.

The interior was exceptionally neat. No candy wrappers, empty soda cans, or other debris littered the floor. The dashboard was dust free and the windshield sparkled. Skye wondered if her mother routinely washed the windows before each of her shifts.

She felt unsettled. After the initial shock of discovering Mrs. Gumtree's body had worn off, Skye had found the situation fascinating, in a morbid way. Of course, she was upset when Vince was arrested, but she felt resourceful as she took charge and saved him. Talking to people was interesting, and she was astounded at how easily they told her their secrets. But she was getting tired of finding rooms vandalized everywhere she went.

Chief Boyd interrupted her thoughts by opening the door. "Okay, Skye, we're finished. You can come back inside. I have a few questions to ask." He smiled. "You know the drill by now."

Slowly, Skye followed him into the school. He led her to the health room and closed the door. After they were seated, he took out his notebook and clicked his pen. "Tell me what happened. Start with why you were here after everyone else went home."

She shrugged. "What can I say? I'm either dedicated or foolish, take your pick. The school system hasn't had a psychologist in almost a year. They still don't have a social worker. There's a ton of paperwork that the state and federal agencies require be done . . . in triplicate. I'm trying to catch up so I can do my real job of working with kids."

"It sounds like my job. More paperwork than police work."

"In a small town you have to do both—be an administrator and go out in the field." Skye tried to gain brownie points by demonstrating her empathy.

Chief Boyd nodded and leaned toward her. "Okay, when did Ursula and Lloyd leave?"

"They usually leave between four and four-thirty. I checked with Ursula at about three-fifteen to see if Lloyd could see me. She said he was unavailable but didn't give any details. Then I got involved with what I was doing and forgot to go back until I decided to call it a day at five."

"Did you see anyone when you walked from your office to Lloyd's?"

"No. It was sort of spooky. Like someone gave a signal and the place just cleared out. Or like they'd all been beamed aboard the *Enterprise*."

The chief made a note. "I'll have to check and see if this is typical behavior. I don't suppose you've been around long enough to tell?"

Skye shook her head. "Was there anyone in the building when you searched it?"

"We found a custodian in the boiler room, but that was it. Tell me what you did when you found Lloyd's office trashed."

"I backed out the door, used the phone on Ursula's desk, and called you."

"What did you do until we got here?"

"Well, I knew there was no one in Lloyd's room or up here in the front office, so I sat in Ursula's chair where I could see the entrance. The only thing I touched was the telephone and Lloyd's door. Do you think this has anything to do with the murder?"

He shrugged. "I can't see how, but you never know."

Sitting silently, Skye debated whether to mention his wife's peculiar behavior and what she had found out about Lloyd. She finally decided to tell him what she knew about Lloyd but not mention Darleen. "Ah, Chief, I did happen to hear about a connection between Lloyd and Honey."

He raised an eyebrow. "How did you 'happen to hear' about this connection?"

"I was chatting with Abby Fleming, the district nurse, and she mentioned that Lloyd coached a softball team that she and Honey were on the summer before their senior year in high school."

"That's not exactly a close association. He coached various sports for several years. There are a lot of people in town who were on those teams."

Skye hesitated, not wanting to start an unsubstantiated rumor. "Abby did allude to a closer relationship than student and coach."

"What do you mean by 'allude to'?"

"She said they seemed very close. More so than he and other students."

"This was just an opinion, right? Abby didn't actually witness any impropriety?"

"No, I think it was only an impression."

He took her hand. "I know you don't want to think that Vince could have killed her, but you have to consider the facts. They all point to him."

Skye snatched her hand from his grasp. "All the facts do not point to him. You have to consider that you haven't looked at anyone but him. Which makes me wonder why. There are a lot of people in this town who hated Honey Adair and had good reasons to want to see her dead."

She paused, knowing that if she continued she'd be sorry. Stealing a peek at the chief, she saw a look of condescension on his face and lost control.

Her words tumbled out with no pauses for breath. "Lloyd Stark may have been intimate with her when she was underage. Abby Fleming certainly hated her for breaking up the relationship Abby and Vince had in high school. Charlie Patukas inherits a lot of money with her dead. Mike Young had an intense relationship with Honey until she went after Vince. And last, but definitely not least, your wife had reason to hate her for stealing Mike away."

Without giving him a chance to reply, Skye stood up and stalked out of the room. She got into her car and drove home, refusing to think about what she had just done. It wasn't until she was in her bedroom changing clothes that she allowed herself to consider the consequences of her impulsiveness.

She sat on the bed and pounded her knee with her fist. *I hate it when I put my mouth in gear without first engaging my brain. What have I accomplished by provoking Chief Boyd? Nothing. Up until now he has treated me like the old friend I was. He hasn't done anything to deserve that abuse.*

Then an idea crossed her mind, and she stopped hitting her leg. This whole thing could force the chief to look at other suspects. *Maybe this isn't such a bad thing. Maybe he won't be angry that I threw his wife's high school fling in his face. Yeah, and maybe pigs will fly, too.*

A glance at her clock radio told her it was five after seven. That Big Mac had been a long time ago. She went into her kitchen, and over to the refrigerator. The shelves were empty. It was time to go to the grocery store.

Clouds had continued to roll in, and it was beginning to get dark when Skye pulled into the parking lot of the supermarket. She winced as a flash of lightning illuminated the asphalt. Hunger, stress, and heat had given her a raging headache.

As she cruised the lot looking for an open slot, her emotions ranged from self-pity to outrage, settling somewhere near resignation. In her exhausted state she felt as if she had been looking for a parking place for hours. She recovered somewhat when she saw someone getting into a car parked only three spaces from the door.

Pulling up almost behind the occupied vehicle, Skye put her turn signal on, indicating her intention to claim the spot. True to the tenor of her day, the people in the car took an eternity to get settled and start to move out. Finally their brake lights came on and they began to inch backward.

They were barely out of the parking place when a white Lexus zipped into the space, narrowly missing Skye's right front bumper. She pounded on her horn, which produced only a feeble whimper, but the auburn-haired driver exited his car and entered the store without glancing back.

Still fuming, Skye finally made her way into the store after being forced to park what seemed like a mile and a half from the door. By that time the rain had started and she was soaked.

Scraping her wet hair back into a ponytail, she headed for the soda aisle. It looked almost as barren as her refrigerator.

She was reaching for the last six-pack of Diet Coke on the shelf when a long, tanned arm reached above her and grabbed it.

Whirling around, Skye came face-to-chest with the man who had stolen her parking spot. As her eyes reached his face, she realized she knew him. It was the coroner, Simon Reid.

Resentment she had only partially contained all day broke loose. "Give that back to me right now!"

"I can't give it back to you. You never had it to begin with."

Skye seethed; her voice rose. "First, you snatch my parking place when it was evident to any moron that I was waiting for that car to leave so I could pull in. Then, you rip the last cans of Diet Coke from my hands. What's next? Are you on your way to steal the Social Security checks from little old ladies?"

The man leaned on his grocery cart, completely at ease and comfortable with himself. "Boy, you sure have a temper. I like a woman who—"

Interrupting him in midsentence, she fought the urge to scream. "I have a temper? You ill-bred, mannerless boor. How dare you? You give that soda back to me or you're going to be sorry."

"What are you going to do? Kick me in the shins?" he asked over his shoulder as he walked around the end of the aisle. In his grocery cart, the six-pack of Diet Coke sat in solitary splendor.

Skye started to run after him but stopped before reaching the next aisle. Sagging against the shelves, she thought, *He's right. What can I do? I'm powerless.*

Simon reminded her of her ex-fiancé—selfish and egotistical. It had been only a few months, and the pain he had caused her hadn't diminished. Not only had he robbed her of her dream to join New Orleans society, he had also taken her self-confidence.

Her head drooped and her shoulders bowed as she returned to the soda aisle and settled for a six-pack of Diet Pepsi. Just like her ex-fiancé, Simon was long gone and she had to live with the consequences. She hated men who made her lose her temper and her Diet Coke.

She finished her shopping and was headed toward the checkout when a voice stopped her. "Hey, Skye, what are you doing here so late?"

She turned to find her cousin Ginger Leofanti Allen hurrying toward her. Ginger was dressed in a garishly striped muumuu that hung on her tiny frame and had rollers the size of juice cans on her head. Her feet were stuffed into canvas shoes that had holes in the toes, and her face was devoid of makeup.

"I got home late from school and found the cupboards bare." Skye attempted to edge around her cousin.

Ginger gave Skye a hug. "I heard the news about Charlie's niece. That poor man. How's he doing?"

Leaning back against the cart, Skye made herself comfortable. She knew there was no graceful way to hurry this conversation along. "He's doing okay."

"He's such a sweet guy. He comes in the bank two or three times a week, and he always stands in line for my window." Ginger absently rewound a wisp of hair that had escaped from its curler.

"So, what are you doing here so late?" Skye asked. Most people in Scumble River did their grocery shopping right after work and were tucked in watching TV by eight o'clock.

Ginger looked down at her attire. "I was just getting ready to sit down and relax when Bert spilled an entire gallon of milk on the floor."

"Bert's your four-year-old, right?"

"Yes, and he's not supposed to touch the gallon cartons of milk. Anyway, that meant I wouldn't have any for the kids' cereal tomorrow."

"Your other two are in school, but who takes care of Bert while you work?" Skye switched the strap of her purse from one shoulder to the other.

"Either my mom or Flip's."

"What a great arrangement. I understand good child care is hard to find." Skye judged that her social obligation was almost fulfilled. She turned and took hold of the cart's handle. "How are the kids and Flip?"

"The kids are growing like weeds. I had to buy them all new clothes for school. And Flip's doing real fine. This time of year he's got more construction jobs than he can deal with. How're your folks?"

Skye started to edge her cart down the first aisle. "Fine."

"How's poor Vince taking this thing about Honey?" Ginger followed closely behind Skye.

It always amused Skye the way people shied away from certain words like *murder* and *death*. "He's hanging in there, hoping they find the killer."

"At first we were all real worried about a murderer stalking the citizens of Scumble River, but now we figure it was someone Honey knew from Chicago."

"That's probably true," Skye said noncommittally. "Well, I'd better let you get going. We both have an early day tomorrow. Tell everyone hello."

Ginger was not easily dismissed. She kept pace as Skye quickened her steps. "You know, we were all real sad for you when your fiancé jilted you."

Skye bit her lip. She did not want to talk about him to anyone, let alone a cousin she didn't really like. "Thanks, but I'm fine. I've put that behind me."

"Good. Then it's true. You are dating Mike Young."

"No. I mean, it's just one double date with Vince and Abby."

"Do I hear wedding bells?"

"If you do, it's time to recharge the old Miracle Ear," answered Skye, making her escape.

When she reached the front of the store, three of the eight lanes were open. The two nearest her had several people in line, all of whom had their carts piled high.

Skye hurried toward the farthest row, where two people with only a few items were waiting. An instant before she stepped into line someone cut in front of her. She looked up into Simon's lively gaze.

"My, you are having bad luck today," he said. "Tell you what—I'll take pity on you and let you go in front of me. After all, women are naturally slower than men."

Her head throbbed. "I wouldn't dream of taking your place or anything else of yours."

"Do you often cut off your nose to spite your face?"

"Turn around and leave me alone, or I'll call the manager."

"And say what? Some horrible man offered to let you go in front of him in line?" With that, he leaned back against his cart and stared at her until it was his turn at the register.

CHAPTER 15

That'll Be the Day

Timing is everything in a junior high. Too early and you have to wait around for the next bell. Too late and you have to face a hostile teacher as you interrupt his class. It's the tyranny of the forty-minute hour.

Keeping this in mind, Skye arrived at Scumble River Junior High on Friday with only a few minutes to spare before sixth period began. She hurried to the office and wrote a pass for Zach Van Stee, asking Ursula to give it to him when the bell rang. Zach was the lucky boy who had won the reevaluation lottery, his good fortune due to his parents' being the first to sign and return the consent form.

Still trying to beat the clock, Skye nabbed an additional chair and cleared a corner of her desk. A quick review of Zach's file indicated he was classified as learning disabled, but had not been assessed since second grade. Because of this, she decided to administer the full test battery, which included measures of intelligence, achievement, and processing skills.

The sound of anxious breathing caused Skye to look up from the various test protocols she was filling out. A student stood in her doorway with his mouth open and a distinctive orange slip of paper in his hand.

She smiled at him reassuringly. "Are you Zach Van Stee?"

Nodding, he clutched the pass tighter.

Skye got up and motioned to the other chair. "Hi, I'm Ms. Denison. Please sit here. You can put your backpack on the floor. You're in sixth grade, right?"

Taking the seat she pointed at, Zach nodded again. He was short and stocky. This, along with his tightly curled hair, made Skye think of a Chia Pet. She jotted this down in her private notes to help remind herself of the boy when she went to write her report.

"Do you know why you're here?"

He shook his head.

"Did either of your parents talk to you about this?" she asked.

Again he shook his head.

"Okay. You know how you get help from Mrs. Boyd and her assistants?"

When he nodded for the third time, Skye was ready to recheck his file to see if he was mute.

"Well, because you get that special help, every three years we need to give you some tests to see how you're progressing. We want to see if you still need that assistance. Do you remember in second grade taking some tests without your classmates?"

Zach picked up a pencil and spoke to it. "Mrs. Boyd is nice. I don't think I could do junior high without help."

"It must be scary coming over from fifth grade." Skye gave him an opening to share his feelings. "The junior high is pretty big."

When Zach returned to his vow of silence, she went on. "Okay, the tests I'm going to give you are nothing like the tests you take in school. There's no grade. I want you to do the best you can, but it's all right to say, 'I don't know.' These tests are given to kids who are as old as sixteen, so I don't expect you to know all the answers."

He still looked uncomfortable.

She reached into her drawer and pulled out a bag of Tootsie Roll Pops. "How about one of these before we get started?"

Selecting a chocolate-flavored pop, he unwrapped it and began to suck contentedly.

The canvas case holding the Wechsler Intelligence Scale for Children—Third Edition, was placed next to her chair. Skye took a spiral-bound booklet from the case and opened it to a few pages from the front. "What's missing from this picture?"

Touching the button on her stopwatch, she started timing how long it took him to answer. If he took over the allowed limit, he would not get credit even if his answer was correct.

Once that subtest was completed, they went on to the second, in which Skye asked Zach questions designed to measure his general knowledge. In all, there were ten required subtests and three optional ones. They measured abilities ranging from attention to detail to short-term visual memory. Half the subtests were given and responded to verbally. The remaining required no language skills on the part of the student.

Since the WISC-III took ninety minutes to administer, only thirty minutes of the school day remained when they had finished. Knowing that the achievement test would take at least an hour, Skye decided to give the Bender Visual-Motor Gestalt Test instead so she wouldn't have to stop partway through the other instrument.

She got out the manila envelope that contained the index cards and laid it on the desk in front of her. "Zach, for this measure I want you to make your drawing look as much like the one on the card as you can." She tried to avoid using the word *test* as much as possible, since many children become anxious hearing it.

Skye put a sheet of white paper in front of Zach. The longest side was placed parallel to the table edge. Next she gave him a sharpened pencil with a good eraser. Finally she set the first of the nine index cards in front of him.

She watched carefully as he began, making notes about how he approached the task and how long it took him to execute each picture.

After he finished drawing the last geometric shape, Skye said, "Take a good look at what you've drawn." She paused. "Have you looked it over?"

"Yes."

Taking away that paper, she replaced it with another blank sheet. "This time I want to see how many shapes you can remember. They don't have to be drawn as well as the first time, but try to remember as many as you can."

Zach drew six figures, then squirmed in his seat and chewed on his pencil before giving up. "Why did you have me do that?"

"On the first part, when you were copying the figures, I was trying to see how well your eye and your hand work together. This last portion was to measure how well you remember what you see. When I asked you to repeat the numbers after me and then say other sequences backward, it was to assess how well you remember what you hear."

"That number thing was hard, especially going backward."

"Yeah, remembering what you hear is difficult for you. That's why when teachers *tell* you something instead of *showing* it to you, it's hard for you to learn."

"Why do they teach that way, then?"

"Because some kids remember things they hear better than what they see. It's impossible to please everyone. That's why Mrs. Boyd and her assistants are there to help you."

The ringing of the dismissal bell took them both by surprise.

Zach got up and grabbed his backpack. "Do I come back here tomorrow?"

"Yes, we need to look at your reading, math, and spelling, and then I have to ask you a few questions. I'll leave a pass for you telling when you're supposed to come."

" 'Bye, Ms. Denison."

" 'Bye, Zach."

Skye packed up her equipment and put the cases near the door. She kept everything in her car trunk, since most of the instruments had to be shared among the schools. After locking the file cabinet, she put her purse over her shoulder and hoisted the test kits off the floor.

In the parking lot she set the cases on the ground near her car while she fished her keys out of her purse and unlocked the trunk to put the cases inside. Suddenly a hand reached around her and banged down the trunk lid.

Lloyd was standing right behind her. His eyes bulged and his face was rigid. He grabbed her by the upper arm and yanked. "Come to my office immediately."

Caught off guard, Skye stumbled as she went along with him. His fingers were cutting off the circulation in her arm. He shoved her into his office and slammed the door.

Skye tried to stay calm. "What is it, Lloyd?"

" 'What is it, Lloyd?' " he mimicked. "I want to know whatever gave you the idea that you had the authority to call the police?"

"You're talking about yesterday when your office was ransacked?"

"Of course I'm talking about that. Are you in the habit of calling the police?"

She deciding not to answer that question on the grounds it could incriminate her. Instead, she asked a question of her own. "Why would I not call the police after discovering that your office was vandalized?"

"Are you questioning my orders?" Lloyd grabbed her again.

She was ready this time and used a self-defense technique she'd been taught in the Peace Corps—shoving her thumb into his wrist and applying pressure until his hand bent backward. Lloyd yelped and released her, stumbling back into his desk.

"Don't touch me again, or when I call the police this time it will be to report an assault." Skye backed away, putting a chair between them.

Lloyd stopped. She could almost see his mind working. He visibly forced himself to calm down. "In the future I would prefer to make those kinds of decisions. We often handle minor problems in-house." He smiled insincerely and sat down behind his desk. "You do understand."

Uninvited, Skye also sat. "Yes, I understand that. What I don't understand is what makes you think you have the right to shout and manhandle me."

Pushing up the sleeve of her blouse, she displayed the angry red mark where his fingers had grabbed her.

He looked uneasy.

"I sure hope Uncle Charlie doesn't notice if this turns into a bruise."

"I apologize." He spoke through gritted teeth. "We'll want to keep this episode between ourselves. You know how easily rumors get started."

Skye smiled slightly. "Yes. Rumors certainly do start easily and die hard. In fact, there was something I heard about you yesterday that I wanted you to clarify."

"Fine. I have no secrets," Lloyd replied jovially, apparently attempting to make up for his earlier behavior.

"You've probably heard that my brother, Vince, was taken in for questioning regarding Honey Adair's murder?" Skye looked at Lloyd, who nodded. "I'm very concerned about this, and so I've been trying to find out more about Honey when she lived here."

"What has this got to do with me?" Lloyd fidgeted in his chair.

"Someone told me you were her softball coach the summer before her senior year."

"Really? I don't recall." Lloyd continued in a patronizing tone. "After all, I coached numerous sports for many years. I can't be expected to remember every student on every team."

"From what I was told, you should remember Honey. I understand the two of you had a closer relationship than you would have had with most of your students."

Lloyd's face reddened with angry color, and he lunged to his feet. "Who told you that? It's a lie! If I hear you repeating that piece of crap, I'll not only sue you for slander, I'll make sure you're dismissed. And don't think Charlie Patukas can protect your job. I've been talking to people at your old school. I know that you were fired, and I know why."

Skye was so upset by her confrontation with Lloyd that she was halfway home before she remembered that she had to get her paycheck in the bank before her account was overdrawn.

She pulled up behind a bright-green "duallie" truck with four rear tires instead of two, giving it the appearance of a toad. A purple bumper sticker read, MY KID CAN BEAT UP YOUR HONOR STUDENT. Skye had liked the original bumper stickers boasting of having a child who was an honor student, but trust Scumble River to come up with a grotesque variation.

Her banking took longer than she planned. Gillian, one of her least favorite relatives, was on duty at the teller's window, dressed in a hot-pink zip-front suit. The jacket was open to the waist, revealing a black stretch-lace camisole with a low neckline. Skye blinked and looked again. She didn't remember Gillian's being so well endowed. Skye would have bet money that Gillian was wearing either silicone or a Wonderbra.

"Well, if it isn't my long-lost cousin Skye. Ginger said she saw you last night at the grocery store. When are you going to come visit?" Gillian asked.

Gillian was Ginger's twin sister. Both worked as tellers at Scumble River First National Bank. This often confused the customers, as well as the management. The twins were proof that evolution can go in reverse. Instead of getting smarter and learning from their experiences, both women tended to repeat the same mistakes over and over, with increasingly dire results.

"As soon as I get settled, I thought I'd have you and my other cousins over for lunch." Skye dodged Gillian's question while nudging the deposit slip toward her.

"We were sure surprised to hear you were coming home. This is such a *small* town, and we all have such *small* minds. Everyone thought you'd be living in New York or California by now."

Pasting a smile on her face, Skye shoved the check closer to Gillian. "Life is full of surprises. Maybe next year I'll be in Alaska. You can never tell."

"After all the times you said you'd never come back, it must be hard to face people." Gillian slowly started to tap the keys of the adding machine. "Especially after having gained so much weight."

Skye managed to keep a pleasant look on her face by thinking, *Yes, it is. Thank you for announcing it to the world. If brains were lard, you wouldn't have enough to grease a skillet.* She looked pointedly at the line growing behind her. "It's been great talking to you. We'll have to have lunch sometime. But I really need to get going now."

"Sure. We've really missed you at the family gatherings. It's a shame we never got to meet that fiancé of yours before he broke up with you." Gillian completed the transaction, giving Skye the deposit receipt and counting the cash into her hand.

Skye made her escape and hurried next door to the dry cleaners. For once it was a relief to pay the ransom for her clothing. At least none of her relatives worked there.

CHAPTER 16

It's Impossible

Skye was stretched out across her bed with an ice-cube–filled washcloth covering her eyes. Her only movement was a fingertip idly tracing the stitching on the quilt. It had deep rose-colored diamonds and ivory rings on a cranberry background, and had been on every bed she'd owned since her Grandma Leofanti gave it to her when she turned sixteen.

After the scene at the junior high and the run-in with her cousin at the bank, Skye was emotionally exhausted. Upon reaching home, almost before closing the door, she'd shed her clothes and kicked off her shoes. She'd grabbed a handful of ice from the freezer and a cloth from the bathroom, then flung herself across the bed and tried to forget her encounters with Lloyd and Gillian.

The harder she tried to think of something else, the more the confrontations bothered her. *As a psychologist I'm supposed to know how to deal with people. Instead, I'm alienating them left and right. First Darleen, then Wally, and now Lloyd. Who will be next? Gee, I haven't spoken to the superintendent of schools yet. Or how about the mayor? Maybe the pope will grant me an audience.*

A loud ring from the telephone interrupted her self-castigation. She reached for the handset without removing the washcloth from her eyes. "Hello?"

"Good, you're finally home. Where have you been? It's almost five-thirty."

"Vince, I've had a bad day," Skye said in a don't-mess-with-me tone.

"I'm just calling to make sure you remember our double date tonight."

"Oh, my God!"

"You did forget," Vince said accusingly.

Skye responded petulantly, "Gee, I'm sorry I forgot something so important, but I have been a little busy trying to clear your name."

There was silence on the line, and Skye wondered briefly if he had hung up.

"Yeah, well, ah, thanks. That's good, because Wally was by the shop again today," Vince mumbled.

"You didn't say anything, did you?"

"No. He said he just wanted to make an appointment for a haircut."

"Well, you don't really believe that, do you?" Skye sat up.

"Of course I don't. I'm not as stupid as everyone in the family thinks."

"This is a stressful time, Vince. No one thinks you're stupid. We need to stick together." She swung her feet to the floor.

"Okay. Let's forget this stuff and have a good time tonight. What are you wearing?"

"Where are we going exactly?"

"We'll pick you up at six, which would put us in Joliet around seven. If we eat at the Red Lobster near Louis Joliet Mall, we could catch the nine o'clock movie at the cinema." Vince's voice became more animated.

"That sounds good. I guess I'll wear my black-and-white gingham shorts suit. Will that be all right? Or should I call Abby?" she teased.

Vince responded seriously, "No, that sounds fine. Do you have white flats?"

"Sure, they're ballet-style flats with bows."

"Great. What are you going to do with your hair?"

"Oh, I thought I'd wear it. Unless you think I should shave it off. What's going on here? I thought this was a casual date." She rubbed her throbbing temples.

"It is. I just want you to look nice. Mike hasn't seen you in a long time."

"Is this about my weight?" Skye threw the damp cloth in the direction of the bathroom door.

"No, no, that's not it at all. Mike's a little conservative, and sometimes you dress a little wild," Vince hurried to explain.

"Are you kidding? I dress about as flashy as Marie Osmond. How conservative is this guy?"

Vince ignored her question. "Everything will be fine. We'll see you at six."

Skye had a bad feeling about this date, but reassured herself by thinking, *After all, it's just one date. It's only a few hours out of my life. Vince and Abby will be with us the whole time. And I do want to ask Mike some questions about Honey.*

She rolled off the bed and retrieved the wet cloth from the floor, using it to mop up the puddles from the melted ice cubes. After disposing of it in the bathroom hamper, she slipped into her robe, which had been hanging on a hook on the back of the door.

Skye took a moment to admire it. Running her hands over the powder-blue damask cotton, she snuggled in the French terry lining. It had cost more than she made in a day, but she couldn't resist it when she'd spotted it at Marshall Field's.

She had developed a clothes addiction when she returned from her stint in the Peace Corps. After wearing nothing but denim shorts, jeans, and T-shirts for four years, she had gone on a shopping spree that rivaled Imelda Marcos's. She still liked nothing better than to shop until she dropped.

Skye took one look at her rumpled hair and pale skin in the bathroom mirror and switched on her electric curlers. While she was waiting for them to heat up, she washed her face and applied a generous dollop of moisturizer.

Allowing the lotion to soak in, she set her hair before applying her makeup. Skye employed a lot of cosmetics to appear as if she used none. First came the base. Next she used a concealer to cover the circles under her eyes. After a light dusting of translucent powder and some blush she was ready to work on her eyes.

Skye's eyes had always been her best feature. Their effervescent color and large size drew admiring glances and comments wherever she went. The cream and taupe eye shadows, dark green eyeliner, and mascara were merely embellishments.

It was five minutes to six by the time she finished dressing. She was fastening her watch when the doorbell rang. Slipping on an onyx ring shaped like a cat's face, she walked to the front door.

Abby, Vince, and Mike were all standing on her porch. Mike was dressed in a conservatively cut navy suit. His light blue shirt matched his eyes, and his hair was cut as short as possible without edging into a crew cut. Belatedly, Skye realized that she should have had something ready to serve them.

Stepping to one side, she gestured them into the foyer. "Please come in. I'm sorry the place isn't more furnished, but I'm still getting settled."

Vince saved her. "We really don't have time to stay. You know Abby, and this is my friend Mike Young."

Mike held out his hand. "Hi. I'm sure you don't remember me, but I certainly remember you. I always thought Vince's little sister was going to be a beauty when she grew up."

Having no answer to that statement, Skye smiled uncomfortably and wondered if he was disappointed with the reality.

Mike and Vince did most of the talking on the drive up. They thoroughly discussed the Cubs' latest season before moving on to the best way to work out at the gym. Abby was able to contribute an occasional comment on both subjects, but it sounded to Skye as if they were speaking Swahili.

Red Lobster was mobbed when they arrived. The lobby was full, and people were standing outside on the front walk, making it difficult to negotiate passage through the throng. Vince offered to fight his way to the front to find out how long a wait there would be.

The loudspeaker squawked, "Martin, party of four."

A group rose from one of the two benches outside the door. Skye was not able to see how it was accomplished, but miraculously she found herself seated between Mike and Abby.

Mike leaned back, stretching out his long legs, seemingly unaware of the dirty looks from the people standing in front of him. "Ah, this is better. You comfortable, girls?"

At the word *girls* Skye shot Abby a look. A slight shrug of Abby's shoulders stopped Skye from pursuing the matter.

"We're fine, Mike. Thanks for snagging the bench. I've been on my feet all day." Abby slipped off a sandal and rubbed her instep.

"Oh, anything special happen at school or just the usual disasters?" Skye turned slightly to look at Abby.

Before Abby could answer, Vince pushed his way back out the door and plopped himself down on the bench next to her. "It's a madhouse in there. The hostess said it would be about forty-five minutes. You guys want to stay or try somewhere else?"

"It's Friday night. Everywhere will be crowded. Let's just stay here." Skye looked at the others for agreement.

Mike reached across the women and lightly punched Vince in the arm. "I told you we should have gone someplace where they take reservations."

Vince muttered under his breath, "You did not."

Skye was surprised to hear Vince answer back. He usually avoided confrontation. The silence became uncomfortable as the men silently stared at each other.

It occurred to Skye that this might be the time to ask about Honey and Mike's past relationship. She didn't want the conversation to end like the one with Lloyd had earlier, so she chose her words carefully. "Mike, you and Vince go way back, huh?"

"Yep, we were in kindergarten together." Mike sat back and extended his arm across the back of the bench.

Vince added, "Yeah, he was the one who borrowed the class hamster, and I was the one who got into trouble for it."

Wow, two confrontations in a row. This isn't like the Vince I know. Maybe he changed while I was gone. Skye looked at her brother thoughtfully

"Vince, why bring up ancient history?" Mike replied. "Remember Matthew, chapter six, verse twelve: 'Forgive us our debts, as we forgive our debtors.'"

Skye frowned. "I thought that was from the Lord's Prayer."

"You Catholics do not know your Bible."

Not wanting to get sidetracked from her original line of questioning, Skye asked, "Were you two friends throughout school?"

"Yeah, I guess. More so in high school, when we were both on the basketball team," Vince answered.

"That must have been tough. If it was anything like when I was in school, all the popular girls went out with the basketball team. I remember my junior year two of our stars fought the whole season over one girl. They never talked except on the court."

Mike laughed. "We never seemed to have the same taste in girls. Vince always liked the ice queens and I preferred the sex kittens."

"I recall one girl you both liked," Abby said softly.

Skye could have kissed her. This was exactly where she wanted the conversation to go. Disregarding the dirty looks that both Vince and Mike shot at Abby, Skye asked, "Would that have been Honey Adair? I understand almost every male in Scumble River was attracted to her."

"She and I were through by the time Vince started dating her," Mike said. "In fact, I think it was my idea that he ask her out."

Once again Vince muttered to himself, "It was not."

"It seems that no one went with her for very long," Skye said. "I was told she was always after greener pastures. Why did you break up with her, Mike?" Skye looked him in the eye.

He got up from the bench, stepped over to the door, and peered inside. "I wonder if we're getting close to a table? Maybe I should check."

Smiling, she patted the vacant spot next to her. "Oh, that's not necessary. The time goes fast when you're having a nice conversation."

Reluctantly, Mike sat back down.

"Mike, you were going to tell us about your breakup with Honey," Skye reminded him after a few moments of silence.

"Why are you so interested in a past romance? Not jealous, are you?" Mike put his arm around Skye's shoulder.

"No, you moron," Abby suddenly broke in. "She's trying to figure out who killed Honey Adair, and you're one of her suspects."

"Talking to a man in that manner is why you're still single, Abby." Mike smiled cruelly.

Abby's face mirrored her fury, but before she could speak Vince whispered something in her ear. He turned to Mike and Skye. "We'll be right back."

After they left, Mike drew Skye closer. "You really ought to leave the investigating to the police. An innocent young lady like yourself could get hurt asking questions of the wrong people."

"So, you're not going to answer my question?" She shrugged out of his embrace and scooted to the far side of the bench.

"Is there any reason I shouldn't tell you?" When she didn't respond, he slouched down farther and examined his fingernails. "She wanted to get married and I didn't. Even tried to tell me she was pregnant—but she couldn't prove it when I confronted her."

"Why did you sic her on Vince?"

Mike shrugged, unconcerned. "He always dated such nice girls, I thought it was time he had a taste of the wild side. Now that I've found Jesus, I can see I was wrong. 'There is no peace, saith the Lord, unto the wicked.' Isaiah, chapter forty-eight, verse twenty-two."

"Did you find God while you were in prison?" Skye asked pointedly.

"Yes, I did. I'm not ashamed of my past. I learned a trade and was born again."

"Which church do you belong to, Mike?" Skye looked in the direction Abby and Vince had disappeared.

"The Church of Forgiveness. I founded it myself. You'll have to come to one of our services."

"Where is it? I don't remember seeing a new church building."

"It's on Springfield, between Basin and Kinsman." Mike slid closer to Skye.

She thought a moment. "Oh, yeah, I know where it is." She had passed by it one day and wondered about its origins. After all, it's not often that you see a church in a double-wide trailer. "When are services?"

"Tuesdays at seven and Sunday at eight. Why don't you come this Tuesday?"

"I certainly will . . . if I'm free." *Right after I dye my hair black and get a tattoo.*

"You should come. It would help you after your awful experience." Mike took her hand.

Skye wasn't sure which awful experience he was referring to but guessed. "You mean when I found Honey's body?"

"Yes, that must have been awful for you. I'll bet you dropped everything and ran out screaming."

"Well, actually, I was pretty calm when it was happening. I didn't have my breakdown until afterward."

"Did you see anything?" Mike didn't seem upset when Skye withdrew her hand from his grasp.

"No. I was inside the trailer for less than a minute. I didn't have time to look around."

"Sometimes we see things without them registering right away."

"I guess so, but like I said, I was there for such a short time and I didn't touch anything but Honey."

Mike put his arm back around her shoulders and squeezed hard. "Let's hope the murderer believes that."

CHAPTER 17

Lonely Street

Saturday morning, thanks to the school district's lack of a social worker, Skye found herself driving in and around the outskirts of Scumble River. While attempting to get the special education files in order, she had discovered several with no telephone numbers and only sketchy addresses. All but one family had proved to be accessible through neighbors or relations.

Earl Doozier, Jr., needed a reevaluation. In order for this testing to take place, Skye needed a signed Consent for Assessment form. Parents couldn't be asked for a signature if they were unreachable, and since the Dooziers had no telephone number and an iffy address, obtaining permission would require the dreaded *home visit*.

As she drove up and down streets, searching for the correct address, Skye thought of an assembly she had attended her senior year in high school. The speaker talked about the history of the town. Most of the other students were bored, but Skye had been enthralled. It was the only time she had found anything interesting about Scumble River, and what the man had said remained clear in her memory even now.

She could still hear his voice weaving the story of the community's establishment. "The town of Scumble River was originally built in the eighteen-thirties in the fork between the two branches of the Scumble River. Since then it has spread along both banks. Some might say overflowed.

"Railroad tracks encircle the village. They creep up from

the south and curve west before continuing north. As you all may have noticed, it's often possible while driving through Scumble River to be stopped twice by the same train.

"Consisting of the six blocks that run along Basin Street, the center of town is like the yolk of an egg. To the west of this area, houses were built in the nineteen-thirties by Italian immigrants who were imported by the Sherman Coal Company.

"When the mines played out in the late sixties, most of the initial settlers were ready to retire. Their offspring, having served in World War II and the Korean conflict, had gained other skills and worked in the factories springing up in nearby towns. Thus the closing of the mines had little effect on the local economy.

"Children of those coal miners built their fifties-style ranch houses both north and south of Scumble River's core, surrounding it like the egg white.

"On the extreme west there is still farmland, owned chiefly by the descendants of the first farmers, who arrived from Sweden at approximately the same time that Italians were pouring into the area. Most acreage is still being worked by the original families. But with fewer and fewer children and less interest in agriculture, this too is beginning to change.

"Two groups of people live in an uneasy alliance along the river. A few years ago, people from the city discovered Scumble River and decided to build summer cottages or retirement homes along its south bank. While this 'outside' interest served to line the pockets of some citizens, it invaded the privacy of others. Here is the shell of the egg, and it's starting to crack.

"The original group of people who have always lived along the river are known as Red Raggers to the locals. No one seems sure how this term came into being, but it is definitely disparaging."

It had been more than twelve years since Skye heard that speech, but she remembered every word. She was thinking about the way the talk had ended as she slowly steered her Impala down Cattail Path, deep in Red Ragger territory.

The man had said, "These are not folks who appreciate uninvited guests."

Skye squinted at the faded names on rusty mailboxes. When she saw a redheaded boy who looked vaguely familiar, she stopped the car and leaned out the window. "Hi. Do you know where the Dooziers live?"

"Yep." The boy continued bouncing his ball.

"Great. Where?"

"Said I knew, didn't say I'd tell you."

She thought quickly. "It's really important that I find them. I could offer a reward."

He stopped playing and moved closer to her car. "What kinda reward?"

Her eyes swept the front seat. A foil-wrapped packet glittered in the sunlight. She had found it in her cereal that morning and stuck it in the car to bring to school to use as a prize. Skye held it up for his inspection. "How about a set of Bulls basketball cards?"

"Depends who's on them," he hedged.

Skye shrugged. "It's an unopened package, so it's kind of like the lottery. You take your chances. How about it?"

The boy hesitated, then grabbed the cards from her hand, and pointed to the house in back of him. "Dooziers live there. Don't tell Daddy I told ya."

It suddenly came to Skye. Junior Doozier. The boy who was throwing rocks at Vince's sign, the same child she had negotiated with for a chair in the elementary school's special ed room.

Scumble River is way too small. What if his mother recognizes me from the beauty shop? She'll never sign anything for me after the confrontation we had. Here I go again, getting myself into trouble by opening my big mouth.

Skye pulled her car into the dirt driveway and scanned the lot. Weeds lined the cracked sidewalk and choked what little grass showed between the junked cars and old appliances littering the yard. The house had been white at one time, but now was an ashen shade from long years of neglect. It looked about as stable as a house of cards. A dog's barking echoed in the motionless air, and flies buzzed over the evidence of his recent visit to the front lawn.

She stuffed a clipboard with the consent form attached and a pen in her canvas tote bag before opening the car door. She had taken only a few steps when a heavily tattooed man sauntered out of the house's side door. He was very thin, except for a small pot belly that hung over his boxer shorts, which were the only garment he wore.

At least it's not Mrs. Doozier, Skye comforted herself. "Hi, I'm from the junior high. My name's Skye Denison."

"Funny name, Skye."

"It was my grandmother's maiden name," Skye explained, and then felt foolish for doing so.

"What ya want?"

Skye worded the next question carefully, well aware of the reputation of the people in this area—often fathers, brothers, and uncles were all the same people. "Are you Earl Doozier's father?"

"Maybe. What's he done?"

"He hasn't done anything that I'm aware of, but it is time for his reevaluation."

"His what?"

"Every three years we need to take a look at kids that receive special help and see if they still need it," Skye explained.

"Oh, you wanna see if he's still dumb. Don't waste your time. He is."

"I don't think he's dumb at all. In order to be classified as Learning Disabled you have to have at least average intelligence." Skye felt she had to try to explain, even knowing it was futile. "The school just wants to see how he's doing and if he still needs help. We just want to make sure he's getting all the services he's entitled to have."

"Okay. So, whadda ya want from me?" The man was busy investigating a substance he had extracted from his ear.

"We need your written consent."

"I don't like signin' things. Last time I signed somethin' I ended up owin' money for magazines I couldn't make head nor tails of." He finally gave up his analysis of the earwax and wiped it on his already filthy shorts.

Skye took the form from her purse and handed it to Mr. Doozier. "I promise this won't cost you a thing. Just sign here and check these two boxes."

He took the form and the pen she offered and scrawled his name. "Is 'at all? I got chores to do."

"One more thing. Is there a telephone number you can be reached at?"

"Don't got no phone."

"What's your mailing address, then?" Skye asked, desperately envisioning future trips to obtain consents.

He shrugged. "Jus' put Cattail Path. It'll get 'ere."

It was almost noon when Skye pulled up to the police station. Before setting out for the Dooziers', she had phoned her mother to ask what shift she was working that day. When Skye found out May was working seven-to-three, she decided to stop by as close to lunch as possible. By arriving then, she hoped the policeman on duty would be safely tucked away at McDonald's or the local restaurant, and the P.D. would be clear of walk-in patrons.

Pushing the door open, she was greeted with a refreshing blast of cool air. The temperature had been lingering in the high eighties with humidity to match.

Wearing black walking shorts and a black-and-white-striped shirt, Skye had felt underdressed for a home visit.

She had considered wearing something more businesslike, but the heat and the knowledge of the area's standards had quickly changed her mind.

When she'd glanced into the open garage on the way in, she'd seen that both cruisers were gone. The chief always drove one, and the officer of the day had the other. The waiting area was also empty.

Skye pushed the buzzer, and after a few minutes May came hurrying out of the back room. "I was in the bathroom."

When the latch was released, Skye came around the counter. "What happens if the phone rings or you have radio traffic while you're away?"

"They call back. Or if it's more than a few minutes, County picks up."

Sitting in the visitor's chair, Skye took a yellow legal pad from her tote and looked around furtively. "Are we alone?"

May nodded and settled behind the dispatcher's desk. "Yes. Roy just went to lunch and Wally had some personal business."

"Good. Did you get the information I wanted?"

May withdrew a copy of *Better Homes and Gardens* from her purse and put it on the counter. "Yes, the reports are between the pages of this magazine. There's not much to them. The Adairs' accident was nothing more than that, and you already know Mike was convicted of selling drugs."

"Yeah, I figured as much, but I like to be thorough. I'll take a look myself when I get some time." Skye reached for the publication.

"Not so fast." May whisked the periodical out of Skye's grasp. "Tell me what you've found out so far."

"You don't have to treat me like a child. You could just ask." Skye's tone was petulant.

May folded her arms across her chest and stared at Skye.

Skye gave in. "Fine. I wanted to get it all down on paper anyway."

"That's a good idea, dear. I'll take notes while you talk."

"No, I'd rather write it out myself." Clinging to the legal pad, Skye grabbed a pen.

"Whatever you say." May got up and went into the next room. "I'm getting a Diet Pepsi. Do you want one?"

She followed her mother and looked at the machine. "Yeah, I guess so. I prefer Diet Coke."

"Yes, dear, but we only have Pepsi products." May smiled with false patience.

They settled back into their chairs, and Skye picked up the pen again. "Okay, first there's Abby. She has no alibi and is very jealous of Vince's attentions.

"Next, we have Darleen and Chief Boyd. I haven't been able to find out where she was at the time of the murder, but he certainly had opportunity. I'm also not sure what the motive is for her, but she overreacted when I brought up Honey's name, and it certainly seems funny that he's not investigating anyone but Vince."

Leaning forward, May seemed as if she were going to say something, but Skye held up her hand. "Let me finish."

May sat back.

"Okay, Lloyd definitely has something to hide. He was really ticked off that I called the police after his office was ransacked, and he threatened to have me fired when I asked about his past relationship with Honey.

"It would have been awkward for me to ask him directly about his whereabouts, so I called his wife and pretended to be Barb, from the paper. As Barb, I told her the *Star* was planning on running a picture taken while the parade was being set up, and I was trying to identify the people in the photo. I said I thought one of them was Lloyd but couldn't tell for sure. She told me Lloyd wasn't feeling well that day and stayed home while she and the kids went to the parade."

May got up to throw away her empty soda can. "Is there anyone in town you don't suspect?"

"Vince. I know he's innocent, and I'm going to prove it," Skye answered seriously. Her voice softened as she continued, "I do wonder about Charlie. After all, he does inherit a lot of money, and Vince said that Charlie has been short of cash lately. Maybe you could find out where he was before I found the body."

May put her hands on her hips. "Come on. That's going too far. Charlie would never do anything to hurt Vince or you."

"True, but he couldn't have known Vince would be implicated."

"How about the fact that the shears had the name of the shop on them? That definitely makes it look like whoever did it was trying to point to Vince."

Skye paused. "Well, that could be the case, but it could also be that whoever plunged those scissors into Honey did it on the spur of the moment and didn't know they were engraved. The question is how they were removed from Vince's shop—and if the police lab found any fingerprints on them."

"No prints. They were wiped clean." May began straightening papers and putting files away. "So, is there anyone else on your list?"

"Mike Young. He was roaming around taking pictures for the paper that day, so he has no alibi. Maybe she knew something about his past—when they were in high school together."

"How was your date with him last night?" May looked at Skye with hope in her eyes.

"Okay. He is nice-looking, but he's pretty chauvinistic and he quotes the Bible all the time. Abby sure didn't seem to like him."

"Are you going to see him again?"

"I don't think so. He asked me to attend the Tuesday

night service at his church, but I'm going to pass. In fact, I think I'll stop at his studio on my way home. I can thank him for taking me out and at the same time tell him I'm busy Tuesday. Also, I seem to have misplaced my sunglasses. Maybe he remembers where I left them." Skye stood up and started walking toward the door.

May asked plaintively, "Am I ever going to hear wedding bells?"

"Only if you start to have auditory hallucinations," Skye shot back.

At that moment the chime over the front door jingled. Skye and May looked at each other and burst out laughing.

Chief Boyd rounded the counter and stopped dead. "What's going on with you two?"

Glancing guiltily at Skye, May couldn't meet his eyes. "Nothing. We were just, ah . . . ah."

Skye interrupted, "I just stopped in to say hi. I've got to be going now."

She was nearly through the gate when May rushed over. "You forgot this." She was waving the magazine with the reports still hidden inside.

"Oh, right. Thanks, Mom. I'll get it back to you as soon as possible." Skye showed the cover to Chief Boyd. "I'm trying to get some decorating ideas for the new place. You know, rugs, drapes, flowers . . . that sort of thing. 'Bye, Mom. I'll call you later at home. 'Bye, Chief."

CHAPTER 18

Make Believe

Skye sat in her car for a few minutes, trying to slow her heartbeat and catch her breath. Clearly she was not cut out for a life of crime.

Driving carefully to Mike's studio, she was half afraid Chief Boyd would tail her. After parking, she combed her hair, powdered her nose, and put on lipstick before approaching the door. Just because she didn't want to go out with the guy didn't mean that she didn't want him to want to go out with her.

There was no one in the waiting room, so she tapped on the closed connecting door.

Mike's voice yelled, "I'm in the darkroom. Have a seat. I'll be out in a couple of minutes."

She yelled back. "It's only me, Skye Denison. Don't rush."

For a moment Skye wondered if she smelled smoke but decided she was just overwrought. As she sat on the sofa and leaned toward the table of magazines, she noticed an ashtray with the Red Lobster logo. She turned to the end tables and spotted two other ashtrays, also with restaurant names on them.

Gee, I wonder which Bible verse says it's okay to steal?

It was only two o'clock, and Skye had already tried watching TV and reading. Nothing seemed to hold her interest. Finally she gave in and decided to go visit Charlie. She still had a lot of unanswered questions.

When she pulled into the motor court's parking lot, the first thing she saw was a white Lexus with gold trim, the same one she had encountered at the grocery store. She considered turning around and going home, but curiosity won out and she climbed the steps.

Charlie had cleaned up after Wednesday's vandalism. The carpeting had been tacked back down, the furniture righted, and the books replaced on their shelves. The only evidence of that night's destruction was the squares of lighter-colored paint on the walls where pictures had hung.

Simon and Charlie were sitting on the sofa, paging through what at first looked like a book of wallpaper samples. When Charlie saw Skye at the screen door, he motioned her inside. Not knowing what to expect, she reluctantly pushed the door open and headed for a chair.

"Come sit over here, sweetheart. I need you to help me pick things out for Honey's funeral."

Reluctantly, Skye went to the couch and sat in the only space available, next to Simon. "What's going on, Uncle Charlie?"

"When Simon called this afternoon to let me know they were finished with the autopsy and were going to release Honey's body tomorrow, I asked if his funeral parlor could handle the arrangements. He said yes and offered to bring me these books tonight so I wouldn't have to find a ride over to him. Wasn't that obliging?"

"Very," said Skye, thinking to herself, *So, Mr. Simon Reid, you've heard about Charlie's inheritance.* She looked at Simon and said aloud, "How kind of you, but Charlie knows my parents or I would be glad to drive him anywhere he wants to go."

Simon sat back, looking totally at ease. "Oh, it's nothing. I often go to people's houses to make the arrangements. It's so hard for older people to get around. That's why I got these books made up. It makes the whole process somewhat easier."

"I've got the cemetery plot already," Charlie said. "I bought it when her folks died. There's plenty of room for Honey, and me too when it's my time." He pointed to a picture of a casket on the open page in Simon's lap. "I thought this white one would be nice, with pink satin lining. Do you think it's okay?"

Skye noticed that it was one of the most expensive on the page. "Did Simon suggest that one?"

Simon shot her a look before answering smoothly, "I try not to influence people's selections. It's such a personal matter."

She wondered if he was intimating that she had no business helping Charlie choose. "It's kind of expensive. I'm sure Mr. Reid could show you something a little simpler."

Before Simon could speak Charlie said, "I didn't like the cheap ones he showed me first. After all, she was a TV star. We don't want the Chicago people who come to her funeral to think we're hicks."

Skye noticed that Charlie's eyes were tearing up. "That one would be perfect."

Simon put the catalog he was holding on the coffee table and took another from the briefcase at his feet. Skye noticed that the attaché was made of expensive Italian leather.

He opened the new volume. "Now for the headstone."

Skye and Charlie looked closely as he turned the pages. Coming to the last page, Simon gazed at them expectantly.

"Skye, which did you like?" Charlie asked.

"Well, Simon is right. It's a very personal decision," hedged Skye.

Charlie looked at her helplessly. "I've always thought of you like a daughter. Who else could I ask?"

"I thought the white granite one with the gold letters looked nice." Skye swallowed a lump in her throat. She sometimes forgot how alone Charlie really was.

He nodded. "Me too. We could put a gold star on it, and it would be like her dressing room door."

"What would you like on the stone besides the star?" Simon asked.

"Her name and the dates of her birth and death." Charlie turned to Skye. "It seems like there should be a saying or something."

Skye thought a moment and then smiled softly. "How about: *And throughout all Eternity I forgive you, you forgive me.*"

Simon looked at her, a surprised expression on his face. "That's beautiful. I guess I need to hire you as my epitaph consultant."

"It's Blake. I have a minor in English," Skye answered, disconcerted by Simon's approval.

"That's perfect. Honey caused a lot of heartache while she was on this Earth, but that don't give anyone the right to kill her. Now they can all forgive each other." Charlie reached across Simon and patted Skye's hand.

Simon put his pile of books in his briefcase and pulled out an appointment book. "When would you like to schedule the service?"

"I'm not having any wake, and I want the funeral on this coming Monday. It's Labor Day, so most people won't have to take a day off work. Honey didn't have many friends here in Scumble River, so it'll mostly be people paying their respects to me. I don't want to inconvenience them any more than I have to. Her agent said he didn't think many people from Chicago would come."

"Will we be going to a church?" asked Simon.

"No." Charlie shook his head. "She never believed in any of that when she lived with me, and her agent said she hadn't changed. Could you say a few words?"

"Sure, and anyone else who might want to will be welcome." Simon added, "You know it takes a while for the headstone. It won't be ready on Monday."

Charlie nodded and got up, sticking out his hand. "Thank you for your time. I appreciate your kindness."

Simon shook Charlie's hand and picked up his attaché. "Skye, would you walk out to the car with me?"

"What?" Skye looked at Charlie, puzzled. He nodded slightly. "Okay, just for a minute."

After holding the door open for Skye, Simon led the way toward the Lexus. He unlocked the doors and put his things in the backseat. For once he seemed at a loss for words. "Ah, Skye, I was wondering—ah, I mean, if you're not busy, would you like to go out tomorrow? We could go to brunch."

"You've got to be kidding." The words flew out of Skye's mouth before she could stop them.

He raised an eyebrow. "I beg your pardon?"

"As well you should. What makes you think I would want to go out with you after the way you acted in the store Thursday night?"

"I really didn't do anything wrong at the supermarket." Before Skye could reply, he hurried on. "But I am sorry if my conduct caused you any distress. Truce?"

Skye was not by any means completely satisfied by this equivocation. She might forgive his caddish demeanor, but it wouldn't be forgotten.

She opened her mouth to dismiss him, but before she could speak his golden eyes bored into hers and she forgot what she was going to say.

Taking her hand, Simon held it between both of his. "I'd really like to get to know you better. I promise to be on my best behavior. Please come to brunch with me tomorrow."

"Yes, I'd like that." Skye was tempted to look around to see who had said that. She certainly had not intended to go out with him. She found him obnoxious, didn't she?

"You're probably wondering why Sunday brunch." Simon's thumb made lazy circles on her palm.

His touch made her feel light-headed, and she fought to keep her voice even. "A little."

"I generally have funerals Friday and Saturday, but since

no one gets buried on Sunday I can always count on that day off."

"That makes sense."

Simon let go of her hand. "Great. Is ten all right?"

"Fine. I'll see you then." She felt strangely bereft when he got into his car and drove off.

As Skye walked back into Charlie's, her mind cleared and she firmly pushed away the memory of Simon's touch. By the time she reached the door, she had almost convinced herself that what she had felt wasn't real.

She found Charlie standing by the bookshelves, holding a slim black volume in his hands. The cover was graced by a giant red scorpion.

"What do you have there, Uncle Charlie?" Skye looked over his shoulder.

"It's Honey's yearbook. I found it stuck inside another book when I was straightening out the mess from Wednesday. Look at all the people who signed it."

Skye took the book from his hands and idly leafed through it. Suddenly she stopped. There, on the page showing the pictures of the faculty, right below Lloyd Stark's photograph, was an inscription. It said: *I hate and I love. Perhaps you ask why I do so. I do not know, but I feel it, and I am in torment.* There was no signature, but Skye intended to get a sample of Lloyd's handwriting first thing tomorrow morning.

Skye thought to herself, *If you really want to know about someone, read their yearbook.*

CHAPTER 19

It's My Party

Before nine-thirty Sunday morning, Skye had already tried on seven outfits and completely redone her hair twice. It would have been easier to choose what to wear if she'd known where they were going. If it was someplace local, casual attire would be fine, but if they were going into Chicago, she needed to dress for a city crowd. Glancing at the clock, Skye noted it was now one minute to ten. Time to fish or cut bait, as her dad would say.

She finally settled on what she hoped was a sensible compromise, another shorts suit, this one in mint green. Its vestlike top had French knot buttons, a weskit hem, and side slits. The shorts were full-cut with inverted pleats that gave them the illusion of a skirt.

While giving herself one last spritz of Chanel, she heard the doorbell ring. She walked swiftly through her bedroom and paused in the center of the great room.

Saturday night, after Mass, she'd spent lugging the rest of her belongings from her parents' garage to her cottage and finishing the unpacking. The room now contained a futon-type sofa that faced the sliding glass doors leading to the deck. Two camp chairs faced the couch, with an old wooden trunk that doubled as a coffee table in front of it. The shelves situated between the doors were full of books, pictures, and souvenirs.

It wasn't exactly the Ritz Carlton, but it was a vast improvement from her graduate school dorm room or the wooden shack of her Peace Corps days. She had put a tray containing a carafe of coffee, mugs, spoons, napkins, and a sugar and creamer on the trunk. Tiny Danish pastries were arranged on a separate plate.

When Skye opened the door, she caught her breath. Simon was wearing a straw fedora with a green band, a beige short-sleeved oxford-cloth shirt with a button-down collar, and pleated Dockers in an olive check. The penny loafers on his feet looked newly polished.

Beneath the brim of his hat, Skye saw, his short auburn hair had a fresh barber line. His features hinted at elegance and refinement. In his hand he held a dozen yellow roses.

Finding it hard to speak, Skye managed only, "Hi. Please come in."

Simon walked into the foyer, removed his hat, and handed her the bouquet. "I thought these might make up for the Diet Coke."

"Wow, my favorite. What do I get for the parking space and the place in line?" Her best defense when faced with intense emotion had always been humor.

He smiled. "Won't it be interesting to find out?"

This was a man who could definitely become a problem. Unlike the boys Skye had dated in college or the other students at grad school, Simon had poise and polish. A dangerous combination. The same treacherous savoir-faire her ex-fiancé had possessed in abundance. Why was she attracted to this kind of man? A lump formed in her throat. They only brought her pain.

Skye forced herself to speak. "I'll get a vase. You can put your hat on the hall table. Please make yourself comfortable." Skye gestured him into the great room.

When she came back with the flowers in their hastily improvised vase, a plastic pitcher, Simon was sitting on the sofa leafing through a magazine.

Coming closer, she noticed it was the copy of *Better*

Homes and Gardens in which her mother had concealed the police report—the report she had not yet removed.

Trying to distract him before he came to those pages, Skye hurriedly placed the roses on a shelf and sat down beside him. "Would you like a cup of coffee before we leave?"

As he put the magazine down, a sheet of computer paper slid to the floor. Skye and Simon reached for it simultaneously. He won.

He glanced down while handing it to Skye and stopped abruptly. "How did you get this?"

"That's none of your business."

"This looks like an official police report. As an officer of the court, it certainly is my business." Simon's expression was implacable.

Skye struggled to answer him without whining, which she knew was not an attractive trait. "Look, I'm trying to figure out who killed Honey Adair."

"Isn't that the police department's job?"

"Maybe, but they're doing an extremely poor job of it. Chief Boyd is convinced my brother is the culprit, and he refuses to look for any other evidence."

Simon put the paper down and absentmindedly poured himself a cup of coffee. "I know it's hard to think of your sibling being involved in a murder, but facts are facts."

"That's just it. He's not looking at all the facts." Skye took the opportunity to surreptitiously push the offending page under a pile of other magazines.

"What do you mean? And hiding it is not going to stop me from wanting to know how you got it." Simon sipped his coffee and reached for a Danish.

Skye held on to her temper, though with difficulty. She hated losing control of a situation. "I've found six other people who had motive and opportunity to kill Honey."

"Who?" Simon asked, setting his cup in its saucer with a clink.

After Skye listed her suspects and explained why and how each of them could be the murderer, Simon sat without speaking.

Nervously nibbling on a pastry, she waited.

"I see your point," he conceded grudgingly, "but I think what you're doing could be very risky. And you still haven't told me how you got hold of that document."

Getting up, she plucked a rose from the pitcher and twirled it between her fingers. "I'll tell you, but you have to promise not to reveal my source."

"Okay, I promise."

"Actually, you could figure it out pretty easily just by asking around," Skye said, excusing her lack of discretion. "My mother is a police dispatcher." Skye watched him carefully as she revealed this information.

Simon smiled as if in relief. "That explains it. I thought maybe you had a relationship with one of the cops, or even Wally."

"Chief Boyd is a married man." Skye put the blossom back in the vase.

"True, but women seem to find him attractive, and he appears to be quite fond of you." Simon stood up and straightened the crease in his trousers. "Are you ready to go? Our reservation is for one o'clock."

He followed her into the hall, where she picked up her purse. "If Wally's so devoted to me, why is he after my brother?"

Brunch was wonderful. They drove to Chicago and ate at Cité, a revolving restaurant on top of Lake Point Tower. It offered views of both the skyline and Lake Michigan. Their conversation was animated, with no awkward pauses or uncomfortable silences. The subject of murder was not raised again.

They talked of travel—where they'd been and where they'd like to go. Both confessed to being addicted to books and chocolate. Best of all, Simon revealed himself to be a bridge player.

Sitting back, Skye watched a seagull swoop and dive over the water. "Do you play in a club?" she asked.

"No, unfortunately I haven't been able to locate one in the area. Friends in the city occasionally call me to fill in when one of their group members can't make it, but it's a long drive." Simon took a last swallow of coffee and pushed the cup away. "How about you?"

"Nope. I played all the time in grad school, but I don't know anyone in Scumble River who plays."

"Too bad. Maybe we can find another couple and teach them."

So we're a couple. Skye wasn't sure how she felt about that. Out loud she said, "That would be fun."

The waiter brought over the check in its leather folder and put it on the table. Simon took out his wallet and selected a credit card.

She tried to stop herself, but she couldn't resist an attempt to peek at how much the meal had cost him. But he was too smooth for her to catch a glimpse.

While they were waiting for the server to return, Simon asked, "Do you feel like a walk by the lake?"

"What a good idea. It'll be good to feel a fresh breeze after these last couple of weeks of air-conditioning." Skye stood up. "I'll use the rest room and meet you up in front."

They strolled hand in hand down the sidewalk bordering the lake. When the breeze blew a strand of hair into Skye's eyes, Simon tucked it behind her ear. The memory of his touch lingered on her cheek.

The moment was broken when another jogger—the third one—knocked into Simon. Both the pathway and the beach were teeming with people enjoying both the Labor Day weekend and the break in the heat.

Simon pulled Skye to one side. "Maybe this wasn't such a great idea."

Having had a stroller wheeled over her foot only moments before, Skye had to agree with him. "It is a little crowded. I do have another idea of what to do."

"Sure, whatever you'd like."

Skye grinned wickedly. "Anything?"

Simon faltered. "I . . . I guess so. What did you have in mind?"

Skye had easily convinced the doorman that she was helping out Honey's uncle. Convincing Simon was a little more difficult.

"Are you sure Charlie asked you to do this?" Simon looked nervously over his shoulder. "Did he clear it with the police?"

Skye, busy trying to figure out how to get the door open without letting Simon see she didn't have a key, didn't reply.

"What are you doing?"

"The key must have slipped out of my pocket when I was in your car. Could you run down and check?" Skye asked.

Once he was gone, she took her trusty Swiss Army knife from her purse and opened it to the thinnest blade. She inserted it into the space between the door and the jamb and prayed that Honey hadn't invested in a good dead bolt. This only worked with cheap thumb-button locks.

As Simon reappeared at the end of the hall, the door opened and she walked inside.

When he didn't follow immediately she went back, grabbed him by the arm, and pulled him inside, shutting the door behind them.

"So, you found the key after all."

When she didn't answer, he put his hand on her shoulder. "This is a really bad idea. We could both get into a lot of trouble. Let's leave before the doorman changes his mind and calls the police."

"No, Charlie asked me to look around for him. You can wait in the car, but I'm going to search Honey's condo." By this time she almost believed that what she said was true.

They were in a tiny foyer. To the left was a small kitchen, straight ahead was a living room, and a short hallway went to the right.

"Why do you have to search it? I'm sure the police already have."

At the kitchen doorway, Skye was greeted with a scene similar to the one she had found at Charlie's. She stepped aside so Simon could see. "Someone sure has, but I don't think it was the cops."

"Well, that takes care of that. Let's go."

"I'm still going to have a look."

He gestured at the mess in the kitchen. "Anything worth finding is gone."

"Maybe they didn't know what they were looking for and passed it by."

"And you do? Know what you're looking for, I mean."

Skye nodded. "I'll know it when I see it. Look at it this way, now that we don't have to be careful it will be much quicker."

"If there were any other way for you to get home I'd leave you here." Simon's jaw was set, and the muscle in his cheek was rigid.

She laid her hand on his chest and smiled up at him through her lashes. "I appreciate your not abandoning me." Feeling him relax his stance, she continued, "If we both look we'll be out of here that much quicker."

He was examining the last of the shelves in the living room while Skye investigated the bathroom. There had been nothing of interest in the bedroom, the home office, or the kitchen.

It looked as if everything had been ripped apart and left in the middle of the floor. This did not stop Skye from crawling into the cupboard under the sink. Wedged into a corner was a package of Stayfree Maxi Pads. At first glance it appeared to be unopened, but Skye's heart beat faster when she noticed the irregular seam in the plastic.

"Come quick, Simon, I think I've found something," she called excitedly.

His running footsteps faltered when he saw the container she held aloft in one hand. His fair-skinned face turned red. They stared at each other for a moment before Skye giggled and Simon dissolved into laughter.

When she was able to stop, she said, "Okay, so this wasn't what you expected on a first date, but look, this package has been opened and sealed shut again."

He took the container from her and examined it closely. While he was doing that, she got to her feet and dug out her pocketknife. "Give it back and I'll open it."

"Maybe we should take it to the police while it's still sealed," Simon suggested.

"And how would we explain having it?"

"I thought you had Charlie's permission to be here."

Ignoring him, she worked the edge of the blade between the two pieces of melted-together plastic. It opened with ease, further indicating that it had been tampered with before. She reached in and felt among the wrapped pads. Her fingers touched one that was more rigid than the others, and she pulled it out. Peering inside, where the packet wasn't completely fastened, she stuck in two fingers and withdrew a small address book.

On the front was a picture of a puppy and a kitten frolicking in the grass. Skye looked at Simon and then opened it up. Only a few pages had been written on, and they weren't covered with addresses. Instead, there were columns of initials and numerals.

* * *

Skye refused to talk about their find on the way home. She felt that anyone driving in the city needed to concentrate on the road and not be distracted, especially anyone driving a beautiful and expensive car like Simon's Lexus.

By the time they reached I-55 and she could relax her vigil, she was caught up in her own thoughts and didn't want to explain them until she was sure. Digging out a small pad of paper and a pen from her purse, Skye began making notes.

She twisted the pen point back into the casing just as they pulled into her driveway. "I've figured it out."

"You know who the murderer is?" Simon turned toward her with an incredulous look on his face.

"No, but I know what the killer has been searching for and why."

"And the answer is . . ." Simon made a "go on" motion with his hand.

"Let's go inside. It'll be easier if I show you."

Simon got out of the car, coming around to Skye's side to help her out, and had them both at the front door in record time. Skye had her keys ready and they were inside and at the kitchen table before the screen door finished swinging shut.

"Would you like something to drink?" Skye indicated the refrigerator.

He smiled stiffly. "No, but I would like to see the object for which I risked getting arrested."

She started to spread out the papers she had been writing on in the car but stopped. "Gee, I'd sort of like a soda before I explain. My throat's awfully dry. Oh, darn, I forgot. I don't have any Diet Coke."

"Skye," he said softly, "show me. Now."

"Fine, be that way." When she finished straightening the sheets, Skye handed him a copy of the address book.

Before they had left the condo, she'd used Honey's well-equipped home office to duplicate the book. Then, after having carefully wiped her fingerprints off its surface, she had put the original in an envelope addressed to Chief Boyd and dropped it into a mailbox in Chicago.

"See if you can figure it out," she said.

Simon got up and turned his chair around. Resting his chin on the high back, he looked from the copies in his hand to what Skye had written. After a while he asked, "Is this a record of payments?"

She nodded.

"It looks to me like Honey was blackmailing four people. Four identical sets of letters and numbers appear repeatedly. The letters must refer to who and the numbers to how much. Do the columns refer to monthly payments?"

"Probably. It looks like she started blackmailing the first person about sixteen years ago. Maybe just before she left town. She added another cash cow six months after that. The next was six years later, and the fourth started to pay only about two years ago."

"I'm surprised anyone would or could pay as long as those first victims." Simon tapped the pages in front of him.

Leaning forward, Skye pointed to her notes. "If I figured this right, she demanded very small amounts, only fifty dollars a month to start with, and the increases were small, too. So, as the person grew older and made more money she upped the ante, but only a little at a time. She made sure they never felt the pinch."

"Are you figuring that the numbers in the address book should be multiplied by ten to get the actual cash value? How did you come up with that?" Simon got up again and turned his chair back around.

Skye cocked an eyebrow at him. "Bored?"

"No, I've just always had a lot of nervous energy. Go on."

"I'll explain my reasoning if you promise not to tell anyone what I tell you."

"Hey, I've already sworn not to tell on your mom." Simon took Skye's hand and squeezed it reassuringly.

Taking a deep breath, she squeezed back before gently removing her hand. "Okay, we have four sets of two letters, obviously initials of some sort. But *OH, NB, EW,* and *WY* fit no one's name who is involved."

"How do you know? Couldn't it be people from her city life that you aren't aware of?"

"Possibly," Skye conceded, twisting a strand of hair around her finger. "But the truth is, my brother was one of her victims, and since I know that and the amount of the last demand . . ."

"You worked backward."

"Yep. He was supposed to pay her twenty-five hundred dollars the week after the parade. So, I looked for the latest entry after each initial. Two, *NB* and *OH,* had a hundred and fifty written next to them, and *WY* had a fifty after it. But *EW* had two hundred and fifty in its column. And the one before that was one hundred.

"*EW* had to be Vince because he was supposed to pay twenty-five hundred and he was asking to borrow fifteen hundred, which is the difference between the prior month's payment and the current month's."

Simon got up and strolled over to the refrigerator. He took out a can of Diet Pepsi and waved it at Skye, who nodded. "Why did the payments go up so much the last month? And who are the others?"

Skye retrieved two glasses from the cupboard. She filled them with ice and, taking the can from Simon's hand, split the contents between the tumblers. After a healthy swallow she took a clean sheet of paper from the pad and wrote the alphabet. On top of those letters she wrote it backward.

She put her pen tip on the bottom *E*. "If Vince Denison equals *EW,* then the letter on top of this *V* should be an *E* and the *D*'s letter should be *W,* which they are. Who else on my list of suspects has a *V* or a *D* in their name?"

"Darleen Boyd," Simon said after thinking briefly.

"Right, and in this code *B* equals *Y,* so *WY* is Darleen. Using the same logic, *OH* is Lloyd Stark and *NB* is Mike Young," Skye finished with a flourish.

Simon ran his long fingers up and down his glass of soda. "There's only one thing," he said hesitatingly. "This makes Vince look even more guilty. He was paying more than anyone else, and he was supposed to see her the day of the parade."

"I don't care. We are operating on the premise he is innocent. If you can't agree with that, you should leave now."

For a few minutes Simon silently made interconnecting water rings on the table's white tile top. He sighed. "I can live with that for now, but if we find insurmountable evidence against him, I'll have to turn it over to the police."

"You won't do it without telling me first?"

"Okay. It would be better if we did it together."

"We'll see."

Simon finished his drink and put the glass in the sink. Not looking at her, he asked, "What was Vince being blackmailed about?"

"Honey claimed to have had his baby fifteen years ago. She called it child support."

"Did Vince ever see this baby or have visits?"

Skye started gathering up the papers. "Only once, right after it was born. But he's seen pictures. Why?"

"Because according to the autopsy report, Honey Adair never had a child."

"Just as I thought. She aborted the baby and still put Vince through the wringer."

"No. Honey never had an abortion either. She was sterile. The medical examiner hypothesizes that she had a sexually transmitted disease that caused an infection in her fallopian tubes."

"That's interesting. She claimed to be pregnant to try to get Mike Young to marry her, but he found out she was lying. So, next time, when she told Vince she was pregnant, she demanded money instead of marriage and then conveniently disappeared." Skye pounded the table with her fist so hard her glass trembled.

"The real question is, what was she blackmailing everyone else about?"

"Lloyd is easy. It has to be about his affair with her when she was his underage student."

Simon nodded. "How about Darleen and Mike?"

"I have no idea about Darleen. Her only connection was dating Mike before he hooked up with Honey." Skye tapped her finger against her lip. "Mike, on the other hand, was heavily involved in drugs at that time."

"Didn't he serve prison time for that already?"

"Yes, but maybe he did something awful while under the influence, and she was holding that act, not the drugs themselves, over his head. From the dates, it looks like she didn't start blackmailing him until after he got out of prison and was trying to turn his life around."

"That makes sense," Simon agreed. "And having experienced prison once, Mike might not have been willing to take any chances of returning."

CHAPTER 20

Monday, Monday

After a restless night, Skye rose early on Monday. She dressed in a black linen A-line dress, black hose and shoes, then put her hair into a French twist, spraying it until she was sure no curl would escape at an inopportune moment. Adding the string of pearls her parents had given her when she graduated from college, she was ready for Honey's funeral.

On the way to the funeral home, Skye noticed that the Labor Day sky was drab and cloudy. A pall draped Scumble River like a mantle of shame and made it seem that the town had been singled out as degenerate and corrupt. It was a perfect day to bury someone who had been murdered.

May wanted them to walk in together as a family, and she had instructed Skye to meet them at eight-thirty outside of Reid's. Skye arrived a few minutes early, only to find her parents' white Oldsmobile already parked in the nearly full lot.

She got into the backseat of her parents' car. "Where's Vince? He usually beats all of us."

Twisting in her seat, May looked back at Skye. "I don't know. Right before we left, I tried calling him, but no one answered. We thought he must be on his way already."

"Could he have spent the night somewhere else?" Skye was proud of herself for wording her question so delicately.

May didn't answer, but Jed caught Skye's eye in the rearview mirror and winked.

Her head rested against the back of the seat, and she let her mind wander. The car's dark-red-velvet interior reminded Skye of an old sofa that had been in her grandmother Leofanti's parlor. She must have been hovering between wakefulness and sleep, because the sound of a car door slamming made her heart skip a beat. Her father was standing outside the car.

"Dad's decided we'd better go on in without Vince," May said. "You call Abby's when we get inside." May joined Jed on the pavement.

Skye struggled out of the backseat. The velour gripping her dress made a graceful exit impossible. "Why do I have to be the one to call?"

"Because if I called, it would embarrass Abby." May gave Skye a withering look.

The three Denisons walked up to the frosted-glass doors. Reid's Funeral Home had been in business since the nineteen-thirties. It was a large one-story building with a red-brick exterior, white pillars, and a circular drive. One almost expected the governor to reside there.

Inside, a blast of cold air carried an overwhelmingly floral odor, yet held a hint of a less pleasant scent. Double doors opened to a small flight of carpeted stairs with a metal railing going up the center. One wall was completely mirrored, allowing mourners to arrange both their clothing and their expressions into appropriate lines.

After mounting the stairs, Skye and her parents parted. Jed and May went to the right, stopping to sign the guest book before making their way to the front, where Charlie stood facing the mourners, his back to Honey's closed coffin. Sprays of flowers, potted plants, and wreaths flanked the casket.

Skye turned to the left and walked along the narrow aisle formed by folding chairs set in rows that faced the front of the room. Tucked behind the seats was a short hallway with rest rooms on one side and an office on the other.

The door to the office was open, and inside, Simon was talking to a small man in a shiny navy blue suit.

Simon motioned Skye in as soon as he saw her. "Skye, I'd like you to meet my assistant, Xavier Ryan. Xavier, this is Skye Denison."

Xavier dipped his head slightly. "Nice to meet you, Miss." His pale blue lashless eyes were magnified behind old-fashioned horn-rimmed glasses, making them seem reptilian.

Although the last thing she wanted to do was touch this man, Skye pasted a smile on her face and held out her hand. "How do you do?"

His grip was surprisingly warm and gentle. After a brief squeeze, he turned to Simon. "I'll go see if we need more chairs, Mr. Reid."

Xavier left, and Simon moved closer to Skye. Taking her chin in his hand, he looked into her eyes. "I had a really good time yesterday. I'd like to see you again, soon. Are you free Wednesday night?"

She was pleased. *Gee, a second date. Even after I forced him into a life of crime. He must really be interested.*

Aloud she said, "Yes. I'm usually home from school by five. Is six okay for you?"

Simon carried her hand to his lips and lightly kissed her fingertips. "How about five-thirty?"

Although she was having that breathing problem again, she managed to nod.

"I'd better go and check on Charlie. It's about time to start."

"Could you hold off beginning for a few minutes? I need to try and call Vince. He was supposed to have met us here at eight-thirty."

"Sure. Use the phone on the desk. Let me tell Charlie what's happening." Simon looked over his shoulder as he left the room.

Knowing how few rings her mother allowed before

hanging up, Skye tried Vince's number first. His answering machine picked up after four rings. Next, she tried the shop, and got the same results.

Reluctantly, she dialed Abby's number, having first looked it up in the book conveniently located beneath the telephone. Abby answered immediately, as if she were waiting by the phone.

"Abby, this is Skye Denison. Is Vince there?" Skye sat in the upholstered chair behind the desk.

"No. He was supposed to call me this morning before he left for the funeral, but he never did." The worry in Abby's voice was clearly audible.

"He hasn't showed up at Reid's, either. No one answers at his house or at the shop."

"This isn't like him."

Skye started to doodle on a pink message pad. "Do you have any idea how to locate him? My parents will go ballistic if I tell them I can't find him."

"He's not at the gym, and I can't think of anywhere else he could be."

She added a star to her drawing. "I hate to impose, but could you drive by his apartment and see if his car is there?"

"I'd be glad to. Where can I reach you?"

"Where I'm going to end up as a paying guest, if this whole thing doesn't get settled soon: Reid's Funeral Home."

The service was brief. Simon looked handsome and dignified in a black double-breasted suit. Skye admired his tie, with its hexagonal design of black and gold. He talked about mercy and forgiveness, and ended his remarks with the announcement that a luncheon was being served at Charlie's cabin after the interment at the cemetery. All in attendance were invited.

Xavier tapped Skye on the shoulder as she was waiting

with her parents to file by the casket. "You have a telephone call, Miss."

She turned to her mother. "It must be Abby."

May and Jed looked at her pleadingly. Neither had taken the news of Vince's disappearance well.

Skye walked back to Simon's office to take the call.

Loretta Steiner's voice boomed from the handset. "God, you're hard to track down."

"What's wrong? How did you find me?" Skye's stomach was doing flip-flops.

"After trying your house and your parents', I called Abby. Doesn't anyone in your family believe in answering machines?"

"I'm planning to get one the next time I get to Kankakee or Joliet." Her answer was mechanical. "Why were you so intent on reaching me?"

"Vince is in jail. They arrested him this morning about seven-thirty. He called me as soon as they let him make a phone call. I just got to the station." Loretta's tone was impatient. "What is it with these cops? The chief's not here, and the guy on duty refused to believe I was Vince's attorney. I know you said they'd never had a black woman lawyer in Stumble Waters, but, hell, you guys do get cable, don't you?"

"I'll be right down."

"No, I convinced him. As soon as I mentioned a civil rights lawsuit he seemed to catch my drift." Loretta sighed. "You might want to make watching *Law and Order* a mandatory course in your high school, though."

"Sorry. Why do you think I was so anxious to get out of this town?" Skye felt her face flush with embarrassment. "But what about Vince? Can you spring him?"

"No, not right away."

Standing up from the chair she had sunk into at the news of Vince's arrest, Skye stretched the phone cord to its limit. "I'll get my parents and be there in a few minutes."

"Don't. They're serious this time. They won't let you or your parents see him. They've found new evidence, and they're turning him over to the county for processing. I'll follow him over to the county seat."

"We can drive to Laurel."

"No. I'll be meeting with the county's prosecutor to find out what evidence they have. You sit tight and I'll be in touch," Loretta cautioned.

Skye gave Loretta Charlie's number and told her to call there if no one answered at her house or her parents'. She then went to tell her parents the bad news.

Jed and May were standing outside. The hearse had already left for the cemetery, followed by Charlie in the funeral home's limousine. Other cars were falling into line as Skye approached her parents.

"Let's walk to the car." Skye guided her parents to their Olds.

"Was that Abby? Did she find Vince?" May anxiously seized Skye's hand.

"Why don't we get in so we can talk in private?" Skye opened her mother's door.

After they were all seated, Skye leaned her arms across the back of the front seat. "That was Loretta Steiner. Vince has been arrested."

Gasping, May clutched her chest. Jed sat staring out the windshield, the only evidence of his emotions the white of his knuckles where he was clenching the steering wheel.

May grabbed Jed's arm. "Hurry. We've got to get to the station."

Before Jed could react, Skye put a hand on both their shoulders. "Loretta said for us not to go there."

"Why not?" May twitched her shoulder anxiously.

"She said they were taking him to Laurel and we wouldn't be allowed to see him there, either."

"We have to be there for him. We can at least talk to Loretta." May turned to Jed.

"I think we should go to the cemetery and then to the luncheon. There's nothing we can do for Vince right now, and Charlie hasn't got anyone else." Skye also looked to her father.

Jed started the car and backed out, getting in line behind the last vehicle in the procession. "Right now we can do something for Charlie. We can't for Vince," Jed said in a case-closed tone.

May asked questions all the way to the cemetery, but because she had no answers Skye concentrated on the scenery crawling past her window. She allowed her mind to wander, trying to block out her mother's voice.

As the column of cars turned left on Basin and headed south of town, Skye glanced at the orange and white exterior of the Strike and Spare Bowling Alley. Its blackened windows and peeling paint gave it a jack-o'-lantern appearance.

Skye sighed and closed her eyes. When she opened them, the car was inching past McDonald's plaza. People were walking out, carrying cups of coffee and brown paper sacks. Turning her head, she gazed at the cornfield on the other side. A billboard announced it was the future home of the newest Castleview housing development.

She watched the yellow-green stalks heavy with ripe ears of corn rustle in the breeze. Soon the farmers would be out on the combine harvesting them, but right now the blackbirds were enjoying a morning snack.

Brick and wrought-iron gates loomed on the east side of the road, spelling out the words "Scumble River Cemetery." Winding their way down the narrow dirt lane, the cars turned first right, then left, then left again before stopping within sight of a dark-green canvas awning.

The coffin and the flowers from the funeral home were set up in the front of the shelter. Charlie and Simon stood together. By the time the Denisons trudged up from the rear of the procession, the space under the tent was full. As they stood to one side, Charlie motioned for them to come next to him.

Before Simon started the interment ceremony, Charlie whispered into Skye's ear, "What happened to you guys? I wanted you to ride with me."

"Vince was arrested," Skye whispered back. "His lawyer called just as we were leaving."

Simon must have heard what she said because he gave her a quizzical look before beginning. After he said a short prayer and gave a few inspirational words, the crowd filed by Charlie and the casket once again.

Standing up front, Skye noticed that all her suspects had come for the funeral. Darleen, looking like a corpse herself, was dressed in a slinky black dress that hugged her skeletal frame and accentuated her chalk-white complexion.

Looking every inch a principal, Lloyd was impeccably outfitted in an expensive blue suit with coordinating shirt and tie. Not to be outdone, Mike wore a charcoal-gray pin-striped suit that made him look as if he had stepped off the pages of a Marshall Field's ad.

If she were judging them on the crime of bad taste, Darleen would have to be the killer. Maybe she was using drugs. The clothes she wore had to have some pharmaceutical explanation.

Skye's attention wandered to a group standing on the edge of the crowd. She had been introduced to them by Charlie at the funeral home. The short, square-shaped woman was Honey's agent, Blanche Herman. She kept glancing at her watch and sighing.

Next to Blanche stood Roxanne Dunn, Honey's publicist. She was busy scribbling in a pocket-size notebook.

The last of the Chicago Three, as Skye had dubbed them, was the producer of *Gumdrop Lane,* Adrian Warner. As Skye watched him, he examined his manicured nails and adjusted the collar of his lilac silk shirt. She quickly scanned the crowd to see if anyone else noticed. All eyes were facing forward. Skye hoped the Chicago people would come to the luncheon; Adrian would certainly liven things up. May had taken another peek at Honey's file and reported to Skye this morning. It was too bad that all three had alibis for the time of Honey's death. Each of them looked as if killing would be all in a day's work.

CHAPTER 21

Luck Be a Lady

Charlie's friends and neighbors had done him proud. His kitchen table and all available counter space were covered with dishes of food. Walters' Supermarket had sent over a sliced roast beef, and the grocery store had contributed a spiral-cut ham. There were pies and cakes of every flavor. Jell-O molds jockeyed for position with green-bean-and-french-fried-onion casseroles.

Skye circulated through the assembly. People were balancing plates and cups while standing in little knots gossiping. She refilled coffee, dispensed napkins, and eavesdropped on her suspects' conversations.

Mike and Lloyd stood with their heads together for their entire stay. Skye caught the words "Chokeberry Days" once and the phrase "this should take the wind out of his sails" another time, but for the most part they stopped talking whenever she appeared. Skye knew the two men were against continuing the festival, but she thought it was incredibly tacky of them to discuss it while under Charlie's roof, considering that he was so clearly in favor of the event.

On his way out, Mike took her hand and inclined his head. "I wish you'd reconsider and come to the services at my church tomorrow."

"If I get out of my meeting early, I'll do that," Skye promised insincerely, removing her hand from his grasp and holding the screen door open. "Thanks for coming. I'm sure Charlie appreciates it."

Lloyd was next to leave. He shook hands with Charlie and made his way over to Skye. "Can I speak to you a moment in private?"

She glanced at the people still filling Charlie's small house. "How about the office? It's through the connecting door at the end of the hall."

He followed her silently. When they reached the office, he said, "Someone called my wife Saturday morning, pretending to be from the paper. Do you know anything about that?"

"How would I know about something like that? What do you mean, 'pretending to be from the paper'?"

Lloyd backed Skye into the counter and poked her with his finger, breathing angrily into her face. "Someone called pretending to be Barb, but Barb's in St. Louis visiting her sister this weekend. Her husband is our custodian. He mentioned they were leaving right after school Friday."

Skye tried to move away from Lloyd, but he put a hand on either side of her. She thought fast. "That's pretty odd. Could your wife have misunderstood? Maybe what they said was that they were calling for Barb."

"Wrong!" he roared, french-fried-onion fumes smacking her in the face. "You can't fool me that easily. I called the *Star*. There are no pictures from Chokeberry Days that they're trying to identify."

"That's strange, but I don't know why you think I'm involved." Skye shoved Lloyd away.

"Because it occurred to me that whoever made that call was trying to check to see if I had an alibi for the time of Honey's death."

Skye had been edging toward the door as he spoke. She fumbled behind her for the knob. "How clever. Maybe it was the police." She pushed the door open.

"I didn't kill Honey Adair. If you keep trying to prove I did, all you're going to do is bring up the past and ruin my marriage." Lloyd's voice was low and beseeching.

Now that she was steps away from other people, Skye felt safer. "I'll do whatever I have to do to save Vince."

"If I catch you talking to my wife or spreading any more lies about me, I'll see that you're fired. Remember, I know what happened at your last job. I will not be a scapegoat for your brother." Lloyd thrust his finger at Skye again.

Just then Charlie emerged from the bedroom next to the connecting door. "You'll what?" he thundered. "Believe me, Stark, Scumble River will see the backside of you long before my goddaughter is ever fired."

Lloyd stalked past Skye and Charlie without replying. He shouldered people out of his way and slammed the front door behind him.

"Well, Uncle Charlie, I think I'm in trouble now."

Charlie put his arm around her shoulders. "Don't worry, honey. Lloyd's reign of terror is just about over."

"What do you mean?"

"Come to the board meeting tomorrow night and you'll see."

"You've got something on him. Could it help Vince?"

"It won't help Vince, but it will get Mr. Lloyd Stark out of our hair."

Before Skye could ask more questions she heard a voice calling her name. She turned and saw Honey's agent beckoning to her. After excusing herself to Charlie, Skye joined the Chicago Three.

"Skye, I couldn't help but notice that you and Charlie seem very close," Blanche stated as soon as Skye walked over.

"Yes?" Skye waited to see what was on the agent's agenda.

"We have an exciting project to honor Honey, but Charlie is reluctant to give us the go-ahead, and we thought maybe you could explain it to him." Blanche moved closer to Skye. "See, the thing is, the terms of Honey's will give Charlie the rights to her life story."

"I really don't think I should get involved." Skye tried to move away, but both the producer and the publicist blocked all possible avenues of escape.

"Just listen." Adrian adjusted the cuff of his lilac shirt. "It's a fabulous idea."

Roxanne whipped open her notebook. "We think the Honey/Mrs. Gumtree story would be a marvelous made-for-TV movie. It has everything: sex, violence, deception. The murder scene with that hairdresser plunging his scissors into Honey's throat would be boffo."

Skye shook them off like raindrops. " 'That hairdresser' is my brother, and he did not kill Honey. Any suggestion in a book, movie, or cartoon that he did and you'll be speaking with our attorney."

No one blinked. Finally Blanche said, "Does this mean you won't help us get Charlie to sign a release?"

The last of the crowd was slowly taking their leave. Charlie and May stood by the door, easing them out. After the ceremony at the cemetery, Jed had dropped Skye off at the funeral home to get her car, then gone to the farm to work on some machinery. She was to drive May home after they finished cleaning up at Charlie's.

Skye grabbed a tray from the kitchen and started fetching dirty plates, silverware, and cups. The places where people crammed them were amazing. Someone had even deposited their debris in a file drawer in the desk.

Skye put her tray on the floor and knelt down. Warily she picked out the dirty plate. Several papers clung to it. She put them aside, meaning to wipe them with a damp cloth. The knife and fork were easily retrieved, but the cup had spilled its liquid dregs into the bottom of the drawer.

Taking out the wet papers, Skye added them to the soiled pile. She picked up the pages in her left hand and then used her right hand and the edge of her left to lift the tray.

Once in the kitchen, she ran hot water and squeezed dish soap into the sink, placing the dirty dishes, cups, and utensils in the water to soak. After clearing the table of containers and serving dishes, she spread the moist papers from the desk on the tabletop and started to blot them with paper towels.

As she was doing this, the letterhead caught her eye. It depicted a stylized drawing of a woman's face with an elaborate crown and read: "Baroness Riverboat Casino." Alarmed, she looked closer. Most of the papers bore the same insignia, although a few were from other riverboat casinos in the area. All were letters demanding payment of credit extended for gambling. Some were over a year old.

Skye debated returning for a look at the files remaining in the drawer, but before she could decide, Charlie and May walked in.

Charlie's eyes were immediately drawn to the papers on the table. "What are you doing with those?" he roared.

"Someone opened the drawer of your desk and stuffed their dirty plate and cup inside. Coffee and food were spilled on some of the papers so I took them out to wipe them off." Skye felt her face turn red and looked away. "I'm sorry, Uncle Charlie."

Coming around Charlie, May put her arm around Skye and quickly skimmed the papers. "Charlie Patukas, what's the meaning of this, yelling at Skye like she was the one who did something wrong."

Charlie pulled out a kitchen chair and sat down heavily in it. He buried his face in his hands.

Skye knelt beside him and hugged him. "Tell us about it. You'll feel better."

He sighed. "It started a few years ago. I always did like a good poker game, but stakes around here are usually pretty low and I never lost more than I could afford. Then I started going to the boats. They had senior citizens' day and free breakfast for the early-bird cruises and this and that until I was so far in debt I didn't know what to do."

"That's why you couldn't lend Vince the money," Skye murmured.

May gave her a funny look. "So, what did you do, Charlie?"

"I sold everything I could—my car, my investments, everything but the motor court, and they wanted that too." Charlie looked down and rolled the edge of the nearest letter. "Finally, I asked Honey for a loan."

"I thought you didn't know where she was." Skye pulled up a chair and sat down next to him.

"She wrote me a few years ago and gave me a post office box address, in case of an emergency. I figured this was as close to an emergency as I was likely to get."

"Did she give you the money?"

"No, she said she didn't have it." Charlie wouldn't look up.

"So then what did you do?" May walked to the sink and started to wash the dishes.

"Before I could decide what to do, she was murdered and I inherited that money. The casino is glad to wait until the will is probated."

"I'll bet they are. What have you done about this gambling problem of yours?" Skye looked at him sternly, forcing him to meet her eyes.

He put his right hand over his heart. "You don't have to worry. I started going to Gamblers Anonymous in Joliet three months ago and haven't placed a bet since."

Skye gathered up the letters and stooped to kiss him on the cheek. "Good for you."

They remained quiet for a moment.

"I didn't kill Honey." Charlie looked from May to Skye.

"We don't think you did." May turned away from the sink.

"Good, because I have an alibi. Fayanne Emerick was

with me from nine o'clock until Skye found me at eleven. I wish you'd ask her."

Skye squeezed his hand. "We believe you."

The phone rang, startling them all. Charlie answered, then handed the receiver to Skye. "It's Loretta Steiner."

May rushed to the phone, trying to hear what Loretta was saying.

After a few "okays" and "ahas" Skye hung up. She turned to May and Charlie. "They're charging Vince with first-degree murder. They just got verification of a letter they found in Honey's condo last week. It's in Vince's handwriting, and he threatens to get rid of her if she doesn't leave him alone."

CHAPTER 22

Jailhouse Rock

First thing the next morning Skye phoned Fayanne and confirmed that the liquor store owner and Charlie had been together during the time he claimed.

Fayanne's exact words were, "Nope, the man never left my sight. I stuck to him like the printing on a T-shirt."

Skye sat in the high school guidance office chewing on the end of her pencil. Her appointment book lay open on the desk, a sprinkle of eraser crumbs scattered like dandruff across its pages. *Shit, there is no way I can avoid the junior high. I've got to finish testing Zach today or everything else gets screwed up.* She dreaded coming face-to-face with Lloyd after yesterday's confrontation.

The warning bell rang, startling her out of her reverie, and she quickly got ready for her first student. In rapid succession Skye saw a girl with a habit of hiding in the rest room during her afternoon classes, a young man caught wearing gang colors, and three teens who had long-standing problems.

Skye hypothesized that the girl might be bulimic and was hiding in there to make herself vomit or use laxatives after eating lunch, the boy was a wannabe gang member, and the remaining trio probably knew more about therapy than she did. Nevertheless, she put them down for weekly appointments.

Instead of eating lunch, Skye telephoned Loretta Steiner. The lawyer dispensed with the normal chitchat. "He can have one visitor from two to four and another in the evening from six to eight."

"You mean both of my parents can't see him? Can one go in for the first hour and another for the second?"

"Probably. Small-town jail. Upstanding local family. Yeah, they'll probably cut you some slack." Loretta paused. "Of course, you could always get some hard-ass guard. No way of telling."

Next Skye called her mother.

May's voice was shrill. "Fine. Then your dad and I are going over right now. I'll trade my shift with another dispatcher. You can go right after school."

"I'll probably stop at my place so I can change and grab something to eat. I can't get in until six and it's only a forty-five-minute drive."

May snorted and the phone went dead.

Skye wondered why she had even tried to explain. If she was going to survive living in Scumble River, practically on her mother's doorstep, she was going to have to be more selective about what information she shared with her parents.

Walking over to the junior high, Skye didn't notice the freshly cut grass or the singing birds. Instead, she planned the best route through the school if she wanted to avoid Lloyd.

When she entered the main hall, she saw that the coast was clear and sprinted to her room. A true sense of accomplishment filled her as she settled behind her desk. Only then did she realize that if she wanted to see Zach for testing she would have to send for him from the main office. The school felt that a telephone for her office was one luxury too many.

Skye steeled herself for an attack by Lloyd and went to the office. Ursula was dividing index cards into five different piles. Skye waited for a break in the action.

Ursula glanced up. "Mr. Stark wants to see you."

"Now?" Skye felt her heart accelerate.

"Yep, said to send you in as soon as you got here."

Skye moved toward the rear of the office and tapped on the partly open door before pushing it open farther. "You wanted to see me?"

Lloyd did not look up from his desk. "Right. Come in and close the door."

She complied, the blood pounding in her ears.

After an interminable wait Lloyd finally put down his pen and looked up. "The superintendent has asked me to let you know that the incident with the boy hosting the sex parties has been resolved per your recommendations and he thanks you for your good work." Lloyd's mouth was pursed as if he had just bitten into a bug.

"Well, ah, thanks for telling me. I wondered what had happened with that case." Skye waited for further directions, but Lloyd picked up the phone and dialed.

She let herself out of his office and walked over to the secretary to continue her original mission. "Ursula."

"Yes?"

"Ah, could you . . . ah . . . call Zach Van Stee and send him to my office?" Skye stumbled, intimidated by the secretary's sharp gaze.

"What class is he in?" Ursula turned toward the intercom controls, her finger poised over the multicolored levers.

"Ah, I don't know." Skye cringed, expecting the worst.

Ursula jerked her head toward a table by the wall. "Look up his schedule in the box."

She waited impatiently while Skye fingered through the large white cards in the bin indicated. Pulling out Zach's, she looked at it blankly. "I'm sorry, I know this is sixth period, but there are two different classes listed for him."

"Those are the semester classes. Look at the class marked 'one.'" Ursula sighed loudly. "Semester classes are marked one or two to indicate which semester the student is taking them."

"He's in Home Economics." Then more quietly to herself, she added, "I hope."

After thanking Ursula, Skye fled the office. While she waited for Zach, she set up the room for the assessment.

Today she would be administering the Wechsler Individual Achievement Test. Skye routinely gave only six of the eight subtests—the ones measuring reading decoding, reading comprehension, spelling, paper-and-pencil math, story problems, and written language. The other two subtests measured language skills, and she felt those were better left to the speech pathologist.

Zach walked in quietly and dumped his backpack on the floor. "Too bad you called me from Home Ec. We were making cookies."

"Oh, that is a shame. Would a Tootsie Roll Pop ease your suffering?" Skye reached into a drawer.

"It'd help some," Zach allowed. "What're we going to do today?"

Skye handed him the bag of suckers, and he again selected a chocolate one.

She then answered his question. "I'm going to see how good you are at reading, spelling, and math. We're going to start with some story problems. Here's a piece of scratch paper and a pencil. You can use it on all the problems except the ones I tell you not to. Ready?"

Zach nodded.

"Okay, since you're in sixth grade we'll start with number eleven. Remember, it's just like last time. Some questions will be too easy for you and some will be too hard. It's all right not to know some."

He nodded again.

"Look at the picture of the fish. Find the fourth fish from the aquarium."

They finished the last subtest, written expression, half an

hour before the final bell. Skye had one more part of the testing to complete with Zach, the clinical interview.

"That's it for this test, Zach. Now I'd like to ask you some questions about you and how you feel about things. Then we'll be done."

"What kinda questions?" Zach asked warily.

"Stuff like, When's your birthday?"

"That's easy. November twenty-third." Zach grinned.

"Do you know the year?"

Things were going smoothly until Skye asked, "If you had three wishes, what would you wish for?"

"Three more wishes," Zach answered promptly.

"What would be the first three things you would ask for with all your wishes?" Skye attempted to pin him down.

"More wishes."

She gave up, recognizing this as a typical preadolescent response.

With a few more questions and answers Skye finished the interview and handed him a piece of unlined paper. "Here's a sheet of blank paper. Draw a picture of a complete person."

"I'm not very good at drawing. Can it be a stick figure?"

"Make it as complete as you can. Just do the best you're able to."

Zach turned the page several times before settling down to work. He finished the drawing moments before the final bell. Standing, he picked up his backpack. "Will I see you again?"

Skye smiled. "I'll be visiting your class to see how your teacher teaches you, but you won't need to come here again."

"Oh." Zach hovered in the doorway. "This was sorta fun."

"You did a good job for me. I appreciate how hard you worked."

"Is it true that you saw that dead lady?" Zach's hand was on the knob.

"Yes," she answered cautiously.

"Was there blood everywhere?"

She shook her head. "No. Did you know Mrs. Gumtree?"

"Nah, but my uncle dated her in high school." Zach looked down at his feet. "When I told him about taking all these tests with you, he asked if you mentioned seeing anything when you found her."

"Who's your uncle?"

"Mike Young."

Before Skye could respond, a voice from the hall yelled, "Zee, ya comin' or not?"

Zach waved and ran out the door.

Skye put the materials back in their case and began to score the various tests she had given Zach. *First Lloyd and now Mike. Everyone seems really interested in what I saw.*

The town of Laurel was the county seat of Stanley County. It contained the courthouse, the sheriff's office, and the jail. Skye spent the time driving there trying to figure out what to say to Vince.

She pulled into a metered space at a quarter to six. Digging through her wallet and tote bag, she came up with two quarters, a dime, and a nickel in change. This bought her two and a half hours. With visiting hours ending at eight she would have fifteen minutes to get from the jail to her car before it was parked illegally and ticketed or towed.

Skye wasn't sure of the proper attire for a jail visit, but knowing Vince's fastidiousness, she had worn crisply pressed khaki pants, a light-blue oxford-cloth shirt and loafers. Going for a low-key effect, she had pulled her hair back with a tortoiseshell barrette.

She didn't know where the entrance to the jail was located. Looking around, she decided the most likely direction would be through the sheriff's office.

Its interior was similar to that of the police station in Scumble River. Walking in, she saw a bench to the left and a glassed-in counter to the right. Ahead was a closed steel door. There was a button on the counter, which Skye pushed.

A woman around May's age stepped up to the window, leaned forward, and spoke through the grate. "Yes, what can I do for you?"

"I'm here to see my brother, Vince Denison." Skye found herself somewhat embarrassed to admit that she had a brother in jail. "I was told that I could visit him between six and eight."

The woman smiled warmly. "You must be Skye. I'm Betty. May and I know each other from dispatching. She told me all about you. Vince is really anxious to see you. Come on back and I'll take you to the jail."

Betty met Skye on the other side of the door and guided her up a corridor and down some steps. A man in a tan deputy's uniform sat behind a desk, reading a newspaper and eating a sandwich.

Betty marched up and snatched the paper off the desk-top. "Ed, this here is Skye Denison. Her mother is May Denison from the Scumble River P.D. She's here to visit her brother, Vince. You treat her nice, and there'll be cook-ies for you tomorrow."

Ed put his half-eaten sandwich down, wiped his hands on his pants, and stood up. "Now, Betty, you're going to make this girl think I'm not nice to everyone."

She sniffed and started back. "You just remember she's got to come back by my desk, and I'll be asking her if she had a good visit."

"Okay, Miss, you'll have to leave your purse here, and I got to ask if you have any concealed weapons on you."

Shaking her head, Skye handed over her tote bag. "I brought Vince a few magazines. Can I give them to him?"

"Let's see 'em."

"They're in my tote, right on top."

Ed examined the magazines, then turned them over and shook. A shower of subscription cards was the only thing to fall out. He handed the magazines to her. "We haven't got a visiting room, so you'll have to sit in his cell. You can take that folding chair by the desk. You're lucky there's only one other prisoner—it's not too bad."

Ed unlocked the steel door and led her into the jail. Skye followed, carrying the metal chair. The cell closest to the door held a short man with a barrel chest and shaved head. He appeared to have no neck. He lay on his cot with his eyes closed.

The next four cells were empty. Vince was in the last one, seated on the cot with his back supported by the beige cinder-block wall. The only other furnishings were a sink and a toilet without a seat.

While the deputy inserted the key he said, "Vince, stay right where you are." Turning to Skye, he explained, "The prisoners are supposed to be leaning against the far wall whenever we open a door."

Vince stayed seated and Skye walked in. She set up the chair. "Is there anything else, Ed?"

"Nope. I'll leave the door by my desk open. Just yell when you're ready to leave." He slammed the cell door and walked away.

Vince got off the bed and held out his arms. "Thanks, Sis. I sure never wanted you to see me this way."

Skye hugged him and gave him the magazines. "Here, I thought you might need something to read. Is there anything else I can get you?"

"No, Mom and Dad brought some clothes and stuff. They get our meals from the local restaurants." Vince sank back onto the bunk.

She tried to make herself comfortable on the metal chair. "Tell me about the letter."

"I wrote it after Honey started demanding more money. That letter was only meant as a bluff."

Studying a scuff on her loafers, Skye avoided his eyes. "You never were too good at poker. I used to clean you out of your allowance all the time."

"Have you found out anything? Loretta said you gave her the names of some other people who had motive and opportunity."

Looking over her shoulder, Skye lowered her voice. "I had a date with Simon Reid on Sunday."

"So? Is that the big secret?"

"He's the county coroner."

"Yeah, I know, and he owns Reid's Funeral Home. How can you date someone who works with dead bodies?" Vince screwed up his face in distaste.

"Fine. How could you have slept with a woman who hit the floor anytime someone yelled 'hoedown'?" Skye shot back.

He ducked his head. "Hey, let's not fight. This whole situation is just so frustrating."

"That's okay. I'm sorry too. But Simon seems like a really nice guy. He knows how to keep a secret, and he's helping me investigate."

Vince got up and went to the sink. He toyed with the handles on the faucet. "How?"

"Simon was with me when I searched Honey's condo, and he told me the results of the autopsy." Skye stared at the graffiti behind Vince's head. It claimed that Bubba loved Charlene.

"What did you find out? Where's my son?"

"I'm sorry, Vince, you don't have a son." Skye was not happy to be the one to break the news to him. "Honey lied. The autopsy showed she'd never been pregnant. She was sterile."

His shoulders sagged. "I think I always knew there was no child. She must have borrowed a baby that one time she let me see him, and sent pictures of a friend's kid. Her bluff certainly worked better than mine did."

"We did find a record of all her blackmailing activity." Skye hastily added, "Besides you, she was getting money from Lloyd Stark, Darleen Boyd, and Mike Young. I'm pretty sure what she had on Lloyd—he had an affair with her when she was his student—but I haven't got a clue what Darleen and Mike were paying her to keep quiet about. Do you have any ideas?"

Vince thought for a minute, pacing the length of the cell and back. "What Darleen could have done I can't even imagine, but Honey used to hint about something she and Mike were up to."

"We're guessing that whatever she was blackmailing him about took place after she left town. She may even have snuck back into Scumble River from time to time. Her records show that Mike didn't start paying until after he got out of prison, so I don't think it was about drugs. And it probably happened after she left town." Skye paused, then asked, "Can you think of anywhere she might have hidden something in town? Something that would give her the power to blackmail people?"

"Honey loved secrets and hiding and sneaking around. I think it was going behind Charlie's back that turned her on more than I did."

"Where did you two, ah, you know, do it?" Skye asked, curious as to the mechanics of the situation. "I mean, Charlie owned the only motel. Neither of you had any privacy where you lived, and as I remember you drove a Camaro—not exactly roomy enough for sex."

"She had a few places all decked out and ready. But each boyfriend only got to know about one of them. Our place was the boathouse at the recreational club." Vince frowned. "Wait a minute. I remember Honey talking about another of her rendezvous spots. She said 'Union' would be a good name for it."

Skye thought hard. "There's a lot of different ways you could take that. The Union versus the Confederacy, the union of two people in holy matrimony . . ."

"That doesn't help much, does it?" Vince's voice reflected his disappointment.

"It's on the tip of my tongue. It'll come to me if I think of something else."

CHAPTER 23

Time in a Bottle

Vince kept urging Skye to leave before it got too late. He was worried about her lonely drive home. The roads between Laurel and Scumble River were rural and deserted at night. At quarter to eight, she gave in and called to the deputy.

After hugging Vince good-bye, she accompanied Ed out of the jail. As she walked by the guy in the first cell, she asked casually, "What's he in for?"

Ed locked the door and grinned. "That's a funny one, Miss. That fellow walked into the travel agency in town and asked for an airline ticket. Didn't care about the cost. He just wanted the next flight to Miami.

"The agent asked him the date of his return. He said no return, he wanted a one-way ticket. She wanted to know how he'd pay. He took out a roll of bills thick enough to choke a horse. They finished their business, he took the ticket and left. She figured it was sorta unusual, but . . . what the heck, it's a weird business.

"Except he came in the next week and they went through the same routine. This time she called us. We checked things out. Shot his description to the feds, and what do you know? He's wanted for drug smuggling in three states. We're holding him until their agent gets here."

Skye reclaimed her tote from the desk. "Pretty sharp travel agent."

"They get real suspicious. There're a lot of scams people try to play on them."

"Thanks, Ed. I'd better get going before my meter runs out."

"Tell Betty not to forget those cookies," Ed shouted after Skye's retreating back.

Betty looked up from her word search puzzle when Skye stopped at her counter to say good-bye. "Did Ed treat you okay?"

"He was very nice. What does he usually do?"

She walked with Skye to the outside door. "He likes to scare girls. You know, pretend he won't let them out."

"Well, thanks for taking care of him. I'm in no mood for that nonsense." Skye waved and made her way to her car. It was eight-fifteen exactly, and the meter's red flag popped up just as she pulled away.

Pondering the word *union,* Skye drove toward Scumble River. She turned on the radio, but WCCQ out of Crest Hill was full of static, so she tuned in to the Chicago country music station, US99.

According to the radio, it was nine on the dot when Skye turned onto Maryland Street in Scumble River. The news and weather were being broadcast, interrupting the music.

There was a moment of silence, then the announcer's voice said, "Our big story for today is an explosion in a passenger train at Union Station."

Skye was thinking, *Nowhere is safe,* when it hit her: *Union Station. "Union" could mean that old railroad depot on Kinsman Road. It had been vacant for years.*

Without a second thought she went through the intersection at Basin, past Center Street, and turned left on Kinsman. Four blocks down, past the railroad tracks, on the left side, was the old terminal, a small clapboard building with peeling paint and broken windows.

Skye took the flashlight from the glove compartment and slid out of the car. She left her purse inside, locked the door, and pocketed the keys. It was a bright night and the moon was almost full, so she didn't switch on the light. Cautiously, she picked her way across the loose boards and up the rotting wooden steps.

Because the door was off its hinges, she was able to shove it aside. She stepped into the room, turned on the flashlight, and played it over the interior. A dirty mattress with springs poking through the torn cover lay against one wall. Beer cans and wine bottles were scattered everywhere. An old oil lantern, melted candle stubs and empty matchbooks littered the floor.

Short of carbon dating, there was no way to tell how long this debris had been here.

Feeling discouraged, Skye was about to leave when it occurred to her. *Honey liked to hide things. Maybe she hid something here.*

She looked over everything again and thought, *It can't be in something movable. Honey would have been afraid someone would carry it off unknowingly.*

Okay, the walls and floor look solid. What else is permanent?

A counter that ran the length of the rear wall was the only other fixed feature in the room. Skye walked around it. It was open in the back. She pointed her flashlight inside but found nothing.

She had already made her way back around the ledge and was almost out the door when she thought, *I never looked up.*

Retracing her steps, she squatted down and shone the light on the underside of the counter. Nothing. Next, she reached up into the inverted crevice at the joining of the top and the front board.

Duck-walking the length of the shelf, Skye trailed her fingers along the vee. In the furthest corner she felt something. By turning around and sitting inside the opening, she could see a manila envelope attached to the wood with gray duct tape.

As Skye tore it down, she heard a cracking sound, as if one of the outside wooden steps had given way. Before coming from under the counter, she took her shirttail out of her pants and stuck the bulky envelope down the back waistband of her slacks. She blessed both elastic-waist pants and oversized blouses while she tucked her shirt back in.

A police siren sounded in the distance as she crawled backwards. It was the last thing she heard before she felt her head explode and the world disappeared.

I can sleep a few minutes more. My alarm hasn't gone off yet. It smells as if Mom is burning the toast again, Skye thought as she stretched her hand out, encountering rough wood instead of a smooth sheet.

Prying her eyes open, she squinted. Where was she and why did she have such a headache? Struggling to her knees, she saw that the room was full of smoke. Nausea welled up in her throat when she started to rise, so she crawled instead.

Skye was nearly to the entrance when she realized the fire was stronger in that direction and the door was completely blocked by flames. Concentrating, she remembered a window in the center of the back wall, but she didn't know if it was large enough to squeeze through.

She dragged herself back. The smoke was so thick that she began coughing and gasping for air. Without standing up, she took off one loafer and tried to knock out the remaining shards of glass from the broken window. When she was sure the space was clear, she put her shoe back on and grasped the sill.

Skye hauled herself up and rested her midriff on the window frame. Although she had never had much upper-body strength, and couldn't complete even one chin-up, she somehow managed to squirm through the opening. Covering her head with her arms, she thrust herself outside with her feet.

She fell the short distance to the grass and somersaulted to a stop. She felt the small of her back—the envelope was still there. She hoped that the person who had hit her in the head was gone, because she could go no farther.

Skye was thoroughly sick of the back of Chief Boyd's cruiser. She had already examined every inch of the floor, seat, and ceiling, and nothing had changed from her previous occupancy. Now she sat holding a cold pack to the back of her head and watching the Scumble River Volunteer Fire Department at work.

The squad car was parked on the other side of Kinsman. Next to it was Skye's car. A police officer had asked her for the keys and moved it after the fire trucks started to arrive.

Roy Quirk had been on routine patrol when he'd spotted smoke coming from the railroad station. Driving past, he saw Skye's Impala and radioed in the fire. He was walking around the building trying to see what had happened to the car's owner when he'd heard Skye moaning.

When the firefighters arrived, the paramedic examined Skye and said that although she appeared to be okay, she should go to the Laurel hospital to check for a possible concussion. She had refused.

Her head was throbbing and she was considering the possibility of retrieving some Nuprin from her purse when Chief Boyd opened the cruiser's door.

He slid in next to her and shook his head. "Have you always attracted this much trouble or does it only happen when you're in Scumble River?"

Skye bristled but held her temper. "None of this is my fault. Do you think I hit myself in the head and then set the place on fire?"

"No, but I do think you were sticking your nose where it doesn't belong." He turned sideways on the seat and scrutinized her.

She met his gaze without flinching. "If you would admit that even a small possibility exists that someone other than Vince might have killed Honey, I wouldn't be forced into these situations."

"We're not getting anywhere like this. Besides, I have orders to bring you to the police station right away. We'll talk more there." He got out of the back and into the front of the car.

"Wait. Whose orders? How about my car? Am I under arrest?" Her questions became more panicky as Chief Boyd started the engine and pulled onto the road before answering.

He looked at her in the rearview mirror. "Your mother, an officer will bring it to the station, and not quite yet."

"This is kidnapping, and I want my purse," Skye grumbled.

Reaching beside him, he lifted her tote bag up so it was visible. "You can have it back when we get there . . . after I've taken a look inside."

May was waiting for them in the doorway. Seeing Skye's soot-streaked face and torn clothes, she turned on Chief Boyd. "Walter Boyd, why isn't this girl in the hospital?"

He raised his hands in mock surrender. "She refused to go, and you ordered me to bring her here."

"I'm okay, Mom. I just need a shower and a couple of Nuprin and I'll be fine."

Reaching up, May ran her fingers over the back of Skye's head. "Well, there's hardly any lump."

"Can I go home now?" Skye asked tiredly.

Chief Boyd patted her on the shoulder. "Why don't you wash up a little and wait for me in my office? I want to talk to the fire chief and Roy before I let you go. I don't suppose you saw who hit you?"

Skye shook her head, which wasn't a good idea since that made the throbbing intensify. Once inside the ladies' room with the door safely locked, she took the envelope out from its hiding place and examined it. It was about six inches wide by nine inches long and had two bulges in the middle. She didn't have time to open it, so she stuck it back into her waistband.

Along with washing her face and smoothing her hair back into its barrette, Skye brushed off her clothing. A button had been ripped from her shirt and it now gaped open, exposing her midriff. Her elbow peeked from the hole in her sleeve, and there was a large tear across the knee of her pants. She had no cuts, so her clothes must have protected her from the exposed glass and nails.

When she finished, Skye went to the chief's office. It was empty and dark. Flipping on the light, she looked around. His padded chair beckoned, and she sank wearily into its cushioned depths. She noticed that his middle drawer, the one with the lock, wasn't closed all the way.

Deciding to test it, Skye put her finger underneath and tugged. It came open with no resistance. A white business-size envelope lay on top of the pile. Its typed label showed it had been sent to Mrs. Walter Boyd at her home address. The return address was the Carle Clinic, a large medical facility in Urbana.

Skye got up and looked out into the hall. There was no sign of the chief. Going back, she took the envelope out of the drawer, extracted the contents, and skimmed the pages quickly. It was a medical report concerning Darleen. The gist of it was that she was infertile due to a previous infection in her fallopian tubes, most probably caused by an untreated sexually transmitted disease.

Where have I heard that before? she wondered. *Wasn't that what Simon said about Honey?*

Hearing footsteps in the corridor, Skye hastily stuffed the letter back into the envelope and the whole thing back into the drawer. She was sliding it shut as Chief Boyd entered. She leaned against the desk and tried to look nonchalant.

The chief walked around her and sat in his chair. Skye glanced down and saw a white corner sticking out of the closed drawer. Following her eyes, he frowned and opened the drawer, pulling the envelope out.

As his gaze went from Skye to the envelope, his voice became dangerously quiet. "Were you snooping?"

Her face mirrored her contrition. "I'm sorry. It was an awful thing to do. I'm just so worried about Vince."

Chief Boyd sighed and sat back. "Did you read it all?"

She nodded miserably.

"Darleen is obsessed with having a baby," he said, almost to himself. "Oh, sit down, before you fall down," he said when he noticed Skye swaying.

Gratefully, she sank into a chair. "I am sorry, Chief. Does this have anything to do with why she got upset when I brought up Honey Adair?"

He tapped the edge of the report on his cheek. "Yeah. It seems Mike Young passed the disease to Darleen in high school before breaking up with her. From Honey's autopsy it seems that he may have given it to her too.

"She knew something was wrong back then but was too embarrassed to go to any doctor around here for treatment. The symptoms finally went away, and she forgot about it until a few years ago when we started trying to have a baby.

"Darleen did some reading on infertility and was afraid this might be the cause. We got this report a couple of days ago, confirming it."

Skye didn't know what to say so she repeated, "I'm so sorry for you both."

"Can you take Darleen off your list of suspects now? If

she was going to kill anyone, it would be Mike Young. Besides, she was with a group of kids from her class when the murder took place. They were staking out a good spot to see the parade."

Though Skye was nodding her head, she couldn't help but think, *Then why was Honey blackmailing Darleen?*

CHAPTER 24

Photographs
and Memories

Skye entered her bedroom just as the digital display on her clock radio turned to three A.M. She swallowed some Nuprins, stuffed a handful of ice into a dish towel, and flung herself across the bed. When her alarm woke her at six-thirty, she was lying in a pool of water and her head felt as if a giant had been using it for a soccer ball. She struggled to the bathroom and took some more pills.

She decided to take a sick day and made the necessary calls. Before going back to sleep, she took the phone off the hook. When her doorbell started ringing, she tried to ignore it, but minutes later, her mother's voice jarred her awake.

"Yoo-hoo, Skye, are you here?"

Skye pushed her hair out of her face and opened one eye. May stood in the bedroom doorway.

"How did you get in?" Skye was groggy and had difficulty focusing her eyes.

"Don't you remember? You gave me a key when you moved in. Maybe you do have a concussion." May came over and perched on the edge of the bed.

Skye sank against her pillows and pulled the sheet over her head. "I knew that action was going to come back to haunt me. I told you it was only for emergencies. Like if I locked myself out or something."

"This is an emergency. You didn't answer your phone, and they said you called in sick at school."

Skye sat up reluctantly. "Okay, you're here. What's up?"

"I wanted to make sure you were all right." May looked hurt. "After all, I have one child in jail and then one almost gets burned up . . ."

Skye hugged her mother. "You're right." Knowing what would cheer May up, she added, "Want to fix me some breakfast?"

May bounced from the bed. "Sure, what would you like? French toast, waffles, bacon and eggs? You name it."

"Tea and toast would be great. I don't have the stuff to make all those other things."

"How about I go and get you some groceries?"

"No, thanks. I'll just take a nice hot shower, and you can get my tea and toast ready. Okay?" Skye headed for the bathroom.

Twenty minutes later, she emerged, wrapped in her robe, to find her mother sitting in the kitchen drinking coffee. Skye's Earl Grey was in her favorite cup, two packages of Sweet 'N Low placed beside it. A plate with toast had been set next to her tea. The butter dish and a jar of marmalade were also on the table.

"Wow, this is service. Thanks, Mom."

Her voice catching, May smiled angelically. "I could do this for you every day if you moved home."

Skye picked up her cup and drank without replying. Instead, she told May what she'd found out so far and what had happened last night, leaving out the part about finding the envelope. May was thrilled that Simon had been added to their ranks of investigators.

"Who brought you the yellow roses?" May looked at Skye as if her prize heifer had just won a blue ribbon at the county fair.

"Simon."

"Do you like him?" May started putting the breakfast things away.

"Yes," Skye admitted, taking a last sip of tea before her

mother whisked the cup from her hand. "But we've only had one date."

"When are you going to see him again?" May asked, zeroing in on the important issue.

"Probably tonight." Skye stretched and yawned. "I guess I'll get dressed."

"What do you mean, probably?" May seemed to see that blue ribbon disappearing in the breeze.

"We've got a date, but I'm not sure if I'll feel up to it."

"It would make you feel better to have some nice company, I'll bet."

"I should go see Vince again," Skye said, teasing her mother.

"Abby is going tonight, and Dad and I are going after lunch."

"Well, if I can get some rest this afternoon I'll probably feel more like seeing Simon."

May got the hint. "I'll clean up here and let myself out. Why don't you go back to bed?"

"That's a good idea, Mom. Thanks for taking care of me."

As soon as May left, Skye hopped out of bed and grabbed the envelope she'd found the night before. She carefully bent the metal clips into an upright position and eased her fingernail file under the flap.

It opened with minimal tearing. She emptied the contents on the bed. Two small reels of home movie film and a dozen negatives landed on the blanket. Skye picked up one of the negatives. Each had four or five pictures in a horizontal strip.

She switched on her bedside lamp and held the negative up to the light. After turning it several times and trying to look at it from the opposite side, she still couldn't tell who the people were, but she could see that they were definitely in the throes of some sort of passion. She examined all the negatives carefully and was pretty sure the man was the same in all the pictures. His partner appeared to be different in each one, although whenever a third person was involved she seemed to be the same person.

The reels of movie film proved even more difficult to decipher. Skye thought the film might be eight-millimeter or super eight, whatever the stuff was they used before VCRs became common.

When the phone rang, she was trying to figure out who would know about that sort of thing.

Simon's voice washed over her when she picked up the receiver. "Hi, are you okay? I just heard about your adventure last night."

"My head still hurts and I'm a little sore, but otherwise I'm fine."

"When I tried calling you at school, they said you were out sick."

Skye pushed the mess on her bed aside and curled up with her back against the pillows. "After last night I wasn't up to crazy kids and demented parents."

"Why did you go investigating without me? I thought we were a team." Simon's tone was only half kidding.

"I went to visit Vince in jail last night. After I talked to him I had a hunch."

"So, did you find anything?"

Skye took the nail file she'd discarded earlier and ran it across her thumb. "Yes. I wonder if I interrupted someone else searching the station or what?"

"What did you find?"

"I think it would be better if you saw it rather than if I tried to explain it." Skye put everything back into its envelope.

"Okay. How about if I come over now?"

"Ah, why don't you give me an hour to . . . ah . . . do a few chores?" Skye stalled, realizing her hair was a mess and she didn't have any makeup on.

"All right, but make sure your doors and windows are

locked. That person who conked you on the head and set the fire didn't just happen to be there. He must have been following you."

Skye rushed around straightening up the cottage, doing her hair and face, and finding something suitable to wear. It was a tough choice, considering what an odd second date this was.

She settled on black leggings and a white oversized tunic top and was waiting at the door when Simon arrived.

He handed her a box of Godiva chocolates.

Skye led him to the sofa. "Thanks for the truffles. They're my favorite."

"Have one."

"A little later. I haven't eaten anything but toast since lunch yesterday. I'm afraid Godivas are too rich for me right now."

"Why don't I go pick something up?" Simon started to rise.

"That would be great, but I want you to see what I've found first." Skye handed him the envelope and explained how it had come to be in her possession.

He looked through the contents. "So you had this the whole time you were hit on the head, crawled out of a burning building, and were found searching the police chief's drawers?"

"Yes, what do you think of it?"

"I agree with you. It's the same man all the way through but with different women. Although when there are three people, the second woman seems to be the same in all the pictures. Too bad we don't have any way of running this film."

"Yeah, I guess I'll have to turn it in to the police after all. I can't quite see anyone around here printing it for us." She narrowed her eyes in concentration.

Simon thought for a minute. "Mike Young is the only person I know who has a darkroom."

"That's not a good idea. Mike is one of our top suspects."

"True. How about the rest of them?"

"Okay, I'm pretty sure Darleen and Chief Boyd are in the clear. Her problem is with Mike, not Honey, plus she has an alibi. And since I only suspected him because of her . . ." Skye trailed off, having gotten lost in her own logic.

"That makes sense, although like you said earlier, I have to wonder what she was paying Honey to keep quiet about."

"Charlie has an alibi. I checked with Fayanne and she backs him up. I'll have to call him to find out what time the school board meeting ended last night. If it was after I was attacked, that would put Lloyd out of the running too."

"I drove by there at ten, and the lot was still full of cars," Simon said.

"Well, since we know it's not Vince," Skye looked hard at Simon and he nodded, "who is left?"

"Only Abby and Mike, if we're still using your original list."

"Abby is very strong and jealousy can be a powerful emotion. Or she could be the woman in these pictures, and Honey decided to start blackmailing her now that she was dating Vince again.

"On the other hand, Mike could be the man in these negatives. We know he was being blackmailed."

"Could it be Darleen in the photos?" Simon took one out of the envelope and examined it again.

"I didn't know her in high school, but unless she's changed a lot, the body type is all wrong."

They thought in silence, until Skye's stomach growled audibly.

Simon got up. "This is silly. You're hungry. Let me get us something to eat, and then I'm sure we'll both think more clearly. What do you feel like?"

"Would you mind driving over to Clay Center? I'd love some chicken from their restaurant."

"No problem. Clay Center's only ten miles away. The restaurant you mean is the Shaft, right?"

Skye nodded.

"It shouldn't take me more than forty-five minutes. Meanwhile, don't let anyone in. I talked to Wally this morning. He said that if you hadn't been hit with a cheap aluminum flashlight that broke open after the first whack, you could have been in real trouble."

"I'll lock the door as soon as you leave."

CHAPTER 25

Bridge Over
Troubled Water

Skye decided to take another look at the police report on Mike Young. She grabbed an apple from the fridge and curled up on the sofa with the pages. The police had set up surveillance at the local drive-in and caught him selling marijuana, LSD, and heroin to a high school crowd. He never did admit who his supplier was.

His original sentence was three years, but he had been a model prisoner who attended church and took vocational school courses in photography, so he was released in little more than eighteen months.

She put the report down suddenly. *What was that noise?*

Skye rose from the couch and looked out the window by the front door. The Impala was alone in her driveway. A breeze rippled through the leaves on the trees, but nothing else moved.

Sitting again, she looked at her watch. It was two-thirty in the afternoon. Simon had only been gone a few minutes.

This time the noise was louder and sounded like it came from her bedroom. Skye picked up the baseball bat Vince had given her as a housewarming gift and walked over to the half-shut bedroom door. She nudged it all the way open using her foot and, with the bat at the ready, looked into the room.

It was as she had left it. Sighing with relief, she let the bat down from her shoulder and relaxed. At that moment, someone wearing black driving gloves grabbed her arm, spun her around, and put a gun to her temple.

"You thought you were so smart, Miz Psychologist. Spying on people, searching places you had no right to be, sticking your nose where it didn't belong," Mike Young jeered as he dragged Skye through the great room, pausing only long enough to snatch the envelope containing the reels of film and the negatives from the coffee table. "Judge not, that ye be not judged."

"Mike, you sound angry," Skye responded automatically.

He slapped her across the face with the gun, and she felt the pain explode in her cheek. "Don't use that psycho-shit on me. They tried that while I was in prison. You'd better think of Matthew, chapter three, verse seven: 'Flee from the wrath to come.'"

They were in the foyer now. Mike grabbed her purse and dumped it onto the hall table. He snatched her keys and pushed her out the front door and down the steps.

He wrenched open the passenger door and shoved her into the car. "Slide all the way over. I can't be seen driving your vehicle."

Afraid that another blow to the head would make her pass out, Skye scooted over quickly. "Why are you doing this, Mike?"

She threw both hands up to ward off the impact when he raised the gun to hit her again.

Mike pushed his face into hers. "Don't ask stupid questions. You searched Honey's condo and the old train station. This is what you found." He held up the envelope containing the film and negatives.

"How do you know all that?" Skye shrank as far away from him as the seat would allow and attempted to get the keys into the ignition.

"Once the police had searched Honey's condo, I placed a surveillance camera in the hall outside. I saw you pick that lock like a pro. You and that grave digger were in there a long time, but you didn't come out carrying anything, so I had to follow you to see what you found." Mike frowned. "Now start this car, and don't forget to fasten your seat belt. We don't want the cops pulling us over." He buckled his own belt, then waved toward the road with his gun. "Drive down Stebler and take a left on Basin."

As Skye backed the car out of the driveway, she quickly scanned the area, but the road was deserted. "That's how you found me at the railroad depot."

"Yeah, I followed you from the time you left work. Until you led me there, I had forgotten about Honey using that place as a hangout. I didn't think you were going to find anything until you went back and crawled under that counter." Mike slid down in the seat until he wasn't visible from outside the car. His gun was now aimed at Skye's heart.

"Why didn't you take the envelope when you hit me on the head?" Skye turned her head to look at him, and the car swerved.

"Drive straight, or I'll kill you right here." Mike shoved the gun into her side. "I didn't take the envelope because you didn't have it in your hand. It was possible you hadn't found anything. Before I could search you, I saw the police car cruise by and slow down, so instead I figured I would burn up whatever evidence there was. Better safe than sorry."

Skye carefully made the turn onto Basin. She was looking desperately for some way to save herself, but made her voice remain calm and professional. "What exactly is the evidence?"

"You idiots are too stupid to live. I can't believe you or your boyfriend couldn't figure out what was going on in these pictures."

"How do you know we didn't figure it out? Simon's at the police station this very minute telling Chief Boyd everything."

Mike snorted. "Good try. Simple Simon has gone to get

his poor sweetums something to eat, not to tell the police anything. No, Simon is no threat to me. Only you and these damn movies."

When she had to stop at the light on Basin, Skye considered jumping out of the car, but there were few other vehicles and no pedestrians to try to signal for help. "How do you know that?"

"Turn right here."

"Where are we going?"

Mike ignored that question and answered her previous one. "I know your boyfriend hasn't got a clue because I bugged your house right after I saw the surveillance tape from Honey's condo."

Her mind frantically searched for a plan. "So, what was Honey blackmailing you over?"

"Nosy right up to the bitter end, aren't you?" Mike never took his eyes off her. "If you must know, after Honey left town she hooked up with a bunch of other young girls who had run away. They all wanted to be actresses, so she brought them down here and she and I put them in the movies. I played the male lead, and Honey made an occasional guest appearance."

Skye drove along Maryland until she got to Kinsman, where Mike told her to turn left.

He continued, "We sold those movies through ads in porno magazines. Then I was busted for drugs and went to prison. During that time Honey got a job at the Chicago TV station. She was a gofer for some local celebrity. The money wasn't the best, but she was hooked on the idea of show business.

"When I got out of prison, we both wanted to go straight, so we parted amicably. Or so I thought. A few months later, just as things started going good for me with the studio and the church, Honey called me. She demanded money, or she'd show everyone in town the dirty movies we'd made. It seems she had gone to my apartment after I was arrested and taken all the negatives and reels of film.

"The amount of money she wanted wasn't too much, so I paid."

Skye frowned. "Was she willing to expose herself? She was in those pictures too."

"Not in all of them. It would have been easy enough for her to pick out ones that only I appeared in."

"So, you were behind all the Chokeberry Days pranks. You were trying to get them to cancel the festival, so Honey wouldn't come back to town."

"You need to show how smart you are to the bitter end too, don't you?" Mike's voice was disgusted. "You never did learn your place."

Skye hardly heard his insults. She had realized they were coming up to a one-lane bridge, where Kinsman crossed over the river. *He's going to kill me when we get to wherever we're going or he wouldn't be telling me all this. I'm a good swimmer and I'd rather die trying to save myself than be shot like a helpless little girl. I'll have the element of surprise. If I drive off the bridge on his side, I can have my door open before he knows what's happening.*

"You were paying her for a long time, so why did you decide to kill her now?" Skye asked to keep him distracted.

"Because she raised the payment to fifteen hundred. She had found proof that some of those girls in the movies with me were underage."

They were approaching the bridge. Skye asked one last question, hoping to keep him talking, so he wouldn't notice her slipping out of her Keds. "Did you mean to implicate Vince by using his shears?"

"Nah. I didn't go there to kill her, but she just wouldn't back down. When I put my hand in my pocket and found the scissors I knew it was a sign from God. 'My father hath chastised you with whips, but I will chastise you with scorpions.' I had to kill her. She would have ruined me in this town. Then I searched the trailer for the film, but it wasn't there and people started pounding on the door. It was easy to slip away without anyone noticing."

As the car started over the bridge, its tires made hollow thumping sounds on the narrow planks of wood used to guide vehicles safely across. Skye had been going the legal limit of fifteen, but now she pushed the speed up to thirty-five. Taking one last look at the madness gleaming in Mike's eyes, she said as she whipped the wheel to the right, " 'Don't mess with a woman,' Helen Reddy, nineteen seventy-three."

The next few seconds seemed to tick by in slow motion as the Impala burst through the flimsy guardrail and became airborne. Skye held on to the driver's door handle with all her strength, and prayed that her seat belt would hold.

She heard Mike groan as the car lurched and he was jerked toward her. In a quick glance to her right she saw that Mike's seat belt had prevented him from sliding very far in her direction. The Impala hit the water, floated for a moment, and rapidly sank until it settled on the passenger side on the river bottom.

Skye sat for a moment, dazed by the impact and by the chaos she had put into motion with a turn of the steering wheel. Finally, she stole another peek at Mike. He had been pulled down and to the right. Cracks radiated in the passenger-side window around the place where his head had slammed into the glass. He looked dazed, but had not dropped the gun.

Skye quickly unbuckled her seat belt and struggled to wrench the door open. It was much harder than she expected. The force of the water acted as a wedge to hold the door closed. She could hear the blood pulsing in her head as she fumbled for the crank to roll down the window and relieve the pressure. Muddy water gushed into the car, and she was afraid she would drown if she didn't act quickly.

She put all her weight behind one mighty shove, and the door flew open. She quickly thrust herself through the opening. Once out, she shot to the surface, sputtering and coughing.

Immediately she began to swim for shore, worried that Mike would be coming after her. She struggled up the riverbank and turned to look.

There was no sign of Mike. Then she remembered: Jed hadn't fixed the latch on the passenger-side seat belt. Once it was buckled, there was no way to unfasten it.

CHAPTER 26

On a Clear Day

Skye sat silently in the passenger seat of the old Buick Regal as it rattled into her parents' driveway Wednesday afternoon. Although she was physically present, much of what was happening around her seemed to be playing on a movie screen rather than in real life. She watched May hurry out of the kitchen and Jed appear from the garage. She saw an unspoken signal go between her parents, broadcasting that neither recognized the car or the heavily tattooed man who got out of it.

As Jed stepped forward, the boy in the backseat bounced out and opened the front passenger door. He reached in and grabbed Skye's hand, pulling her out of the car like a stuffed toy.

He was the first to speak. "This here is Miz Denison. She's from my school. I found her by the river. You her folks?"

Hurrying forward, May put her arm around Skye, who was still soaked despite the heat's rapid drying power. "Yes, she's our daughter. What happened to you, honey?"

Skye didn't answer, and the boy chimed in, "She ain't said much since I found her."

Jed walked over to the tattooed man and stuck out his hand. "Jed Denison."

"Earl Doozier, and this here's Junior." He shook hands with Jed.

"Thanks for bringing her home. What happened?" Jed gestured to Skye, who stood dripping onto the gravel.

Junior spoke up. "I was playin' near the river when this car started across the old bridge. Sudden like, it sped up, and then just drove offa the bridge—exactly like on TV. In a few minutes I seen Miz Denison swimmin' to shore. Then I run home and got Daddy."

Jed swore under his breath.

May exclaimed, "Oh, my God! Oh, my God!"

"She wanted Daddy to jump in the river to see if this here Mike guy was still livin', but Daddy don't know how to swim. When she found that out she made us drive lickety-split to the police station, and she went in and came out right quick. Then we brung her here. Think she was tryin' to kill herself?"

Skye spoke up for the first time. "Junior, I wasn't trying to kill myself, but someone was trying to kill me."

May, who had been herding them all toward porch chairs, halted abruptly. "Everyone, sit down," she ordered. "Skye, tell us what happened."

Her audience sat listening intently as Skye relayed the events prior to her trip off the bridge.

"What happened when you stopped at the police station?" May jumped up from her perch on the table edge and began to pace back and forth.

Sighing, Skye closed her eyes. "I didn't want to find myself in the backseat of Chief Boyd's squad car again, so I told Thea the story and asked her to send the rescue squad. I probably should have gone back to show them the exact spot, but I just couldn't."

Junior had seated himself at her feet and was leaning against her leg like a puppy. "Don't you worry, Miz Denison, they'll find it right off. You can see the car from the bridge. I looked when we drove over."

Skye turned to her father. "Well, that's it for the Impala." A slight smile hovered at the edge of her lips. "Guess I'll finally have to get a new car."

*   *   *

Skye woke up with a start. *Where am I?* She slowly scanned the walls and realized she was back in her old room at her parents' house. Memories of the last few days were nudging their way through the sleep-induced haze when May popped her head into the room.

"Come in. I'm awake," Skye said.

"How are you feeling?" May sat on the edge of the bed and smoothed Skye's hair from her forehead.

"Okay. What day is this?"

"It's Friday. Doc Zello gave you a sedative and you've slept for almost two days."

"So, the thing with Mike and the car wasn't a dream?" Skye sat up and rubbed her face.

"No, I'm afraid not."

"What's been going on while I've been sleeping? Is Vince out of jail?"

May took the pillows and arranged them so Skye could lean back. "Vince has been home since yesterday. He's staying here until things calm down a little. He insisted on opening the shop for his eight o'clock appointment today, so your father drove him to work. Jed's cutting the grass at the shop for him."

"Now I know I'm dreaming," Skye said. "I can't believe Dad has given in."

May frowned. "I wouldn't say that to your father."

"No, of course not. What else has happened?"

"I'd better start at the beginning or we'll be here all day. Let's see. On Wednesday, right after Doc Zello started examining you, Simon and Wally arrived. Both had heard the news on their scanners. They both wanted to talk to you, but Doc Zello said absolutely not."

"I'll bet the chief was ticked."

"Neither was a happy camper. They recovered Mike Young's body and the negatives late Wednesday afternoon. I had already called your friend Loretta. That is one tough lady lawyer. She really got them moving to release Vince.

Boy, was she mad when they wouldn't let him go Wednesday night. She's talking about a wrongful imprisonment suit."

"Wow. Anything else?"

"Oh my, yes. The police searched Mike Young's studio and found the gloves he wore when he stabbed Honey. They'd been washed, but blood always lingers." May got up from the bed. "They also found the surveillance camera he had rigged at Honey's condo and the listening device he had planted at your cottage."

Skye closed her eyes and wondered exactly what Mike could hear. She certainly hoped it didn't pick up sounds in the bathroom. "It must have been pretty busy around here."

"You don't know the half of it. Everyone we know has stopped by to see how you and Vince are, and they all brought food. I can't get another thing in the freezer."

"Wow." Skye shook her head. "Gee, I'd love to take a shower and get into some fresh clothes. Could you go get me something to wear from my cottage?"

"Already done." May grinned. "I got you a couple of outfits and your cosmetics. I knew you'd never willingly face the world without some makeup. I'll bet you were the only Peace Corps volunteer in Dominica who wore mascara."

Simon and Charlie were sitting at the kitchen table when Skye emerged from the bathroom. Jed and Vince arrived shortly after that. Chief Boyd pulled in seconds later.

He strolled into the kitchen, nodded at its occupants and said, "Could I speak to you alone, Skye?"

Simon, Charlie, Vince, and Jed said no, but Skye spoke over their objections, "Sure, let's go into the den."

The den was really a fourth bedroom that had been equipped with a sofa, chair, and TV.

Before the door was fully closed, Wally whirled on Skye and ground the words out between his teeth, "What in heaven's name possessed you to drive your car over the side of that bridge? You could have been killed. Are you crazy or just plain stupid?"

Skye took a step forward so that they were nearly nose to nose. "What should I have done? Waited for you to rescue me? I'd be dead now, and you'd still be trying to pin the whole thing on my brother."

"You could have . . . ah . . . you could have signaled someone for help." His tone lacked conviction.

"Right. There are so many people hanging out on Cattail Path."

"Well, you should have done something else."

"That's the point, Wally—there was nothing else to do. I would have rather died trying to get away than be shot like a helpless child."

Wally shrugged and eased himself into the La-Z-Boy. "Okay, tell me everything that happened from the time Mike appeared at your house." He clicked on a tape recorder. "All right if I use this?"

"Yes." Skye sat on the sofa and explained the events leading up to her kidnapping and Mike's death.

He nodded. "That's what we figured. We found all kinds of stuff that Mike must have stolen from his friends and customers. There must have been a hundred ashtrays alone. Why would he do that?"

She shrugged. "Must be something in his background. Some need he was trying to fill."

"Well, he didn't have an easy time of it with his father that's for sure. His dad was an alcoholic and liked to knock his family around when he was drunk."

"I never knew that. Is that common knowledge in town?"

"Might be. Hard to keep secrets in Scumble River. But it's one of those things everybody knows but no one talks about. Because if you admit to knowing it you'd have to do something about it. I only found out yesterday by looking at old police records and questioning some of the older dispatchers."

Skye stretched and got up. "At least we don't have to put everyone through the misery of a trial. You have enough to wrap things up, don't you?"

The chief grudgingly agreed that the people being blackmailed had suffered enough, so he would let the matter drop. Skye was sure his wife's involvement helped him make that decision.

Wally turned down May's invitation to lunch and left.

The rest of them sat around the table and discussed the past few days as May began serving the food. First she placed a ham on the table and handed Jed the carving set. While he was occupied, she put out bowls of scalloped potatoes, Waldorf salad, creamed peas, pearl onions, and glazed carrots. Grandma Denison had sent over a batch of her rolls, served hot with butter. May poured iced tea and they dug in.

No one spoke until Skye finished her first helping and wiped her mouth with a napkin. "Charlie, I forgot all about the board meeting Tuesday night. What happened with Lloyd?"

Charlie snickered. "Oh, we fixed his wagon. The district is now accepting applications for a new junior high principal."

"How did you manage that?" Skye reached past Vince for a roll.

Leaning back, Charlie took a generous swallow of his iced tea. "You remember when my house was broken into, right?"

"That was Mike, wasn't it?" Skye nabbed the butter as it was being passed.

"Nope, Lloyd did it. He was looking for Honey's yearbook. I must have mentioned looking for it in front of him, and he got nervous about what he wrote by his name." Charlie sipped his drink.

"What made you realize that it was Lloyd?" Simon questioned.

"I didn't, but I took the opportunity when everyone was so involved in the murder to break into his office."

"Oh, Uncle Charlie, how could you?" Skye's knife hovered above the half-buttered roll.

"I knew there was something fishy about that guy. It turns out he and Mike Young had a scheme going with the school pictures. Say someone bought a package worth twenty-five dollars. Lloyd and Mike would take half the money and the records would show a payment of only twelve-fifty. The school board always wondered why the junior high's profit on that fund-raising activity was so much less than the other two schools." Charlie folded his hands over his stomach and grinned.

Vince wondered out loud, "So, Lloyd broke into your house and you broke into Lloyd's office. Where was Mike Young in all of this?"

"Getting ready for his date with me, no doubt." Skye shot Vince a look.

Simon added, "Don't forget he was also searching Honey's condo, rigging the surveillance camera, and bugging Skye's cottage. I'd say he was pretty busy."

"I want to know how he got hold of my shears," Vince said.

Skye answered, "Chief Boyd explained that. Turns out, in addition to his other nasty habits, Mike took things."

"What do you mean, took things? He was a thief, too?" Vince reached for his glass.

"Yeah. I'm never letting you set me up with a blind date again."

Simon took Skye's hand. "That's good to hear."

They were interrupted by a knock on the door and a voice calling out, "It's Darleen Boyd. Can I come in?"

Jumping out of her seat, May rushed to the door. "You come on in. You're just in time for dessert."

Darleen tried to say no, but before she knew it, she was seated between Skye and Charlie. As if by magic, a piece of apple-slice pastry appeared in front of her.

May finally allowed Darleen to speak after everyone was served their sweet. "This is kind of hard to say in front of you all, but I know that you already know most of the story. When Wally stopped by the school and told me about the record of my being blackmailed, I decided to start fresh. I took half a personal day and came over here to explain."

Skye turned to her. "You don't owe any of us an explanation. I'm just sorry your personal problems got dragged into the open as much as they have been."

"But I want to tell you," Darleen insisted.

Charlie patted her arm. "We're all ears."

"Well, Wally and I decided to try and have a baby about three years ago. At first we weren't concerned when I didn't get pregnant right away, but then I started to worry. About a year went by and we started talking about getting tested. Before we decided, I got a letter in the mail. I still can't figure out how Honey found out about this, but we weren't keeping our attempts to conceive a secret.

"Anyway, the letter revealed that back in high school Mike had a sexually transmitted disease that he gave to Honey, which made her sterile. She figured I must have the same thing and that was why I wasn't getting pregnant. So she threatened to tell Wally if I didn't pay her to keep quiet.

"I quit telling Wally I wanted us to be tested and paid up. A month ago Wally insisted that we get examined. When I got the results, I finally came clean with him and stopped paying Honey."

Skye poured her a glass of iced tea and said sympathetically, "We're all so sorry."

Darleen got up and made her way to the door. "You know, I do feel much better now that I've talked about it. Since this nightmare started, I haven't been able to eat much, but now I think I'm actually hungry."

Those were the magic words that May lived to hear. She packed a lunch and had it in Darleen's hand before anyone else could bat an eyelash.

Skye's curiosity was still not satisfied. "I wonder why Honey raised the blackmail amounts so suddenly?"

"I can explain that," Charlie said. "When I talked to her agent, she said her show had been canceled. She was going to be out of a job come September."

"This time I have a question for Simon." Skye pinned him to his seat with her gaze. "How did you find out my favorite flower and brand of chocolates?"

He looked guiltily at May. "I asked your mother."

There is no such thing as privacy in a small town. Haven't I just watched a bunch of people learn that the hard way? Skye straightened. "Let's get back to Vince's questions about Mike's stealing. He never took valuable items, just bits and pieces. People mostly thought they'd misplaced things. When the police searched his place they found boxes of sunglasses, pens, ashtrays, key rings . . . you name it. A lot of the stuff had people's names on it."

"Why would he do something like that?" Jed asked.

They all looked at him in surprise, as he rarely contributed to conversations.

"Well, Dad," Skye replied, "Mike's family wasn't anything like ours. His father was an alcoholic and abusive. He must have always felt like an outcast."

May asked, "How do you know all this?"

"Wally told me about Mike's dysfunctional family. I'm guessing the rest from my experience as a psychologist," Skye said.

May frowned. "Seems that people are always just telling you something."

"After all this," Simon said, "maybe next time someone tries to confide in you, you'd better not listen."

Hey, Diddle, Diddle, the Cat and the Riddle

Skye Denison warily studied the hostile faces of Gus Yoder's parents. As a school psychologist, she often attended uncomfortable meetings, but this one was murder.

Scumble River High School Principal Homer Knapik was seated to her right, and every time she glanced his way, her attention was drawn to the hair growing out of his ears. The long wiry strands quivered like the curb feelers on a car's wheels. Skye had heard the students call him Mr. Knitpick behind his back, and she was beginning to understand why. The man could not make a decision to save his life . . . or hers.

Across the table Leroy Yoder raged, threatening the school with everything from a law suit to an atomic bomb. He and his wife, Charlene, had come in demanding that their son be allowed to graduate with his class, and nothing either the principal or Skye said seemed to penetrate their anger.

Homer and the parents had been posturing and snarling for over an hour, with no sign that they would stop anytime soon.

Skye watched in hypnotized fascination as a drop of sweat danced on the tip of Leroy's off-center nose. In Illinois, even the first day of June could have temperatures reaching into the nineties. The underarms of her own blouse were soaked and she squirmed uncomfortably in the plastic chair's too-small seat.

Tucking a loose chestnut-colored curl behind her ear, she narrowed her green eyes and tried once more to intervene, rephrasing what she had been saying over and over again since they had first sat down. "Mr. Yoder, Mr. Knapik and I have told you that whether or not your son graduates is not up to us. It is a matter you must bring up to the school board. Since we have only a week of school left, you need to request a special hearing so you have a decision before graduation night."

Homer glared in Skye's direction and Charlene Yoder hunched farther down in her chair, looking as if she would like to cover her head with her arms.

Leroy Yoder swung his massive head toward Skye and pinned her with his frenetic stare. "I want my son to graduate. Gus passed all his courses. You got no right to keep him from getting his diploma with everyone else."

She felt sorry for these parents. Like many others, they couldn't let themselves believe that their child could do the awful things of which he was accused. "As Mr. Knapik and I have explained, our handbook states that a student who is in the process of an expulsion is not eligible to participate in any school activities, including graduation. This is a school board policy. We have no choice in the matter."

"You people should never've started this whole thing. Gus didn't do nothing wrong," Leroy shouted.

"He tried to rape a girl at knife point, and was found with drugs in his possession," Skye stated calmly.

Charlene Yoder started to speak, but was interrupted by her husband, who sprang out of his chair and lunged across the table, bringing his face to within inches of Skye's. His breath was like a furnace belching rotting eggs, and she unconsciously moved back.

He grabbed her upper arms and dragged her halfway across the conference table. "My son didn't touch that girl." Yoder gave Skye a shake as if to emphasize his point. "The boy didn't have no weapon." He shook her again. "And Gus don't use no drugs."

Skye tried desperately to free herself from his grasp. Her breath was coming in shallow gasps and she felt lightheaded. She couldn't get her voice to work.

Homer seemed paralyzed. Nothing moved, including his eyes.

After a final shake, she was abruptly dropped back into her chair as Leroy Yoder continued, "The whole business will be thrown out as soon as we get ourselves a hearing." Ignoring his wife, he stomped out of the room, his words trailing behind him: "Let me make myself clear. Either Gus graduates with the rest of his class or you two don't see another school year."

It was a relief for Skye to return to her office at Scumble River Junior High. She slid down in the chair until she could rest her head on its back. From this angle, all she could see was the stained white ceiling. The odor of ammonia was strong today, brought out by the humidity, but at least she was spared the sight of the battered, mismatched furniture in the claustrophobic six-by-six-foot room.

Skye didn't dare complain about the conditions. It had taken a minor miracle to get what she had. In the elementary and high schools, she had to scrounge for any open space each time she needed to work with a student. That meant she had to lug any equipment she needed from school to school like a door-to-door salesman. Still, she counted her blessings. She knew of many psychologists who had it worse.

It was nearly one, but she didn't want lunch. She was still too upset from the morning's events at the high school to consider eating. Skye was accustomed to parents whose walls of denial went up like the force field on the Starship *Enterprise*, but the Yoders had no clue that their son was hooked on something, and it wasn't phonics.

Even though she'd been gone from Scumble River for many years before her recent return, Skye remembered that the townspeople liked to handle their problems by themselves. Still, she was upset that Homer had refused to call the police on Mr. Yoder, and had forbidden Skye from contacting them. She rubbed her bruised upper arms and shivered. Yoder had clearly assaulted her and threatened them both.

After brooding for a bit, Skye remembered the emergency chocolate bar she had stashed away for just such an occasion. In one smooth motion she snatched her key ring, turned toward the file cabinet, and retrieved the candy.

She was just peeling back the silver wrapper of a Kit Kat when the PA blared. "Ms. Denison, please report to the office. Ms. Denison, please report to the office."

Skye reluctantly rewrapped the bar and tucked it into her skirt pocket. Why did everything always have to happen on a Monday?

* * *

The junior high's new principal, Neva Llewellyn, paced outside her door. She had held the job only since September, having been promoted from high school guidance counselor when the previous principal was forced to leave unexpectedly. For some reason, the Scumble River School District had great difficulty holding on to its employees.

"What's up?" Skye asked as she stopped in front of Neva.

"It's Cletus Doozier."

"Junior's brother?"

"Cousin. His father, Hap, and Junior's father, Earl, are brothers."

"I got to know Earl and Junior pretty well last fall. They really helped me out." Skye smiled wryly. "That's quite a family."

Neva wrinkled her nose. "Wait until you meet Hap. The cheese slid off his cracker long ago."

"Wonderful. Is that his real name?"

"Far as we know."

Sighing, Skye asked, "So, what's up with Cletus?"

"He's got a black eye and bruises all along the side of his face."

Skye drew a sharp breath and winced. "Did he say what happened?"

Neva put her hands on the knob. "Says his father beat him up."

Skye closed her eyes for a moment and shook her head sadly, then gestured for Neva to open the door. She entered the office and looked at the eleven-year-old sitting at the table, coloring. He was small for his age, and his feet dangled above the floor. The left side of his face was entirely black and blue.

She pulled up the other chair. "Hi, Cletus, my name's Ms. Denison. My job is to talk to kids who need help or have something bothering them. Would you tell me what happened to you?"

"Dad beat on me again last night." Cletus didn't raise his head from his drawing.

She knew better than to try to touch him. Abused children didn't like to be handled. "Has this happened before?"

"Yeah, usually when he's drunk. But this time I thought he was gonna kill me." Cletus stared at her with dead eyes.

Skye kept her face expressionless with great effort. Pity was the last thing this child would accept. "Cletus, I have to call and report this. Then someone else will want to talk to you. In the meantime, I'm going to get the nurse to look at you. Okay?"

He nodded without emotion and went back to his coloring.

After closing the door, Skye asked Neva to locate the school nurse and fill her in. Then she found Cletus's cumulative folder and sat down to call the Department of Children and Family Services to report the abuse.

She was surprised when DCFS said they would have a case worker at the school within the hour and would talk to the parent immediately afterward. It was usually the next day before they sent someone. Skye shrugged. They must be under investigation again.

After Skye completed her call, Neva came over and sat on the edge of the desk. "Be prepared. Hap is not going to take this peacefully."

Skye reached into her pocket and retrieved the Kit Kat bar. Its smooth chocolate surface felt soothing under her fingertips. She broke it down the middle and handed Neva half. Both women took bites. The afternoon was shaping up to be as bad as the morning had been.

The three o'clock sun beat down hotly as Skye walked toward the parking lot, thinking about buying a new car. She had to make a decision. She'd been borrowing her grandmother's for nine months and that wasn't right, even if Antonia couldn't use it anymore. Skye's Impala had been totaled last fall. Luckily, she had walked away without a scratch.

A voice interrupted her thoughts: "Skye! Skye Denison, is that you?"

Skye looked to the left and spotted a woman hurrying across the grassy area that separated the senior from the junior high school. *Oh, no, it's someone else I should remember but don't.* She hated hurting people's feelings by admitting she didn't recognize them. It was tough to be back in her hometown after having been gone for twelve years.

As the woman got closer, the breeze ruffled her short

brown hair from its smooth caplike style and played with the hem of her simple gray knit dress. Everything about her seemed familiar, but it was her expression that finally struck a spark of recognition in Skye. Her open features bore a look of good humor and high spirits.

"Oh my God, Trixie Bensen! What are you doing in Scumble River?" Skye grabbed her old friend and gave her a big hug. Trixie and her family had moved away during the girls' sophomore year.

Hugging Skye back, Trixie said, "My husband bought the old Cherry farm a few months ago. I'm interviewing for a job at the high school." She took both of Skye's hands and stepped back to look at her. "How about you? Don't tell me you live in town. You vowed never to settle down here."

By unspoken agreement the women moved to a concrete bench along the sidewalk.

Skye sat with one leg tucked beneath her and said, "Well, I did manage to escape for quite a while. I went to the University of Illinois, then spent several years in Dominica serving in the Peace Corps. After that I attended graduate school and did my internship in Louisiana, and spent a year working in New Orleans."

"Wow! So how did you get back here?"

"Oh, last year I had a little trouble with my supervisor and ended up breaking up with my fiancé, so I needed a place to recoup. I'll look for another job in a year or so, once I get a good evaluation."

Trixie patted her hand. "I'm so sorry for all the bad stuff." She grinned. "But this is too cool. We're together again."

"Tell me what happened since you moved. Why didn't you write me back?" Skye frowned, remembering how hurt she had been when she never received a reply to her letters.

"When we moved to Rockford, my parents had a misguided idea that I would adjust better if I didn't have any reminders of Scumble River, so they never gave me any mail. They never told me until I was getting ready to move back here."

"Well, that explains a lot."

Trixie screwed up her face and shook her head. "Parents."

"So tell me the rest."

"Okay, it's not very exciting. I finished high school in Rockford. Went to Illinois State for my B.A. and then got my master's in library science from the University of Illinois. I married Owen Frayne right out of college and we've been renting a farm in Sterling until we could save enough to buy our own. And voilà, here we are." Trixie beamed.

"You might be just in time. A lot of farmland is being purchased by developers who are gambling that Scumble River will become the next satellite suburb of Chicago."

"Boy, I'll bet people around here are hot on that subject."

"Lots of fighting going on between neighbors, and even between fathers and sons."

Trixie frowned. "That's a shame. Is your family thinking of selling?"

"No. Grandma Leofanti would rather die than sell an inch of her land."

"That's good. Does she still make those fantastic apple slices?"

A look of sadness crossed Skye's face. "No, I'm afraid not. She's still strong as an ox physically, but her mind's not too good for recent stuff, and she forgets to take care of herself sometimes. Around Christmas the family hired someone to live in and make sure she's okay."

"That's too bad. She was such a fun person. So outspoken. And a real feminist. She always seemed ahead of her time. More modern than your aunts." Trixie was silent for a moment. "Did you have trouble finding someone to take care of her? We sure did when Owen's mother was sick."

Skye nodded. "Yeah, we finally had to hire someone from an agency in Chicago. They supply women fresh off the boat from Poland. Mrs. Jankowski, the one we have now, seems okay, but she speaks very little English and that can't be good for Grandma. Plus, she doesn't drive, so she and Grandma are both stuck on the farm unless someone picks them up."

"It makes you scared to get old. Maybe that's why people stop going to visit the elderly. They see their own future and can't stand it." Trixie shuddered.

"At first I sort of felt that way," Skye admitted. "But then Grandma started telling me the family history. She'd never talk about the past before, so I'm finding out a lot about my family. We're up to her first year of marriage. Grandpa was not her only fiancé. The first guy got killed in an auto accident. Sounds to me like she married Grandpa on the rebound. I stop by almost every day after school. Actually, that's where I'm heading when I leave here."

Trixie jumped up. "You'd better get going then. She'll be looking for you." She rummaged in her purse, finally locating a scrap of paper and stubby pencil. "Here, write your number down."

After Skye complied, Trixie tore the slip in two and wrote her number on the other piece. They hugged and Trixie scurried back the way she had come.

Skye climbed into her borrowed car and turned the air conditioner on max. After pulling her hair into a ponytail, she peeled off her pantyhose, slid on a pair of blue chambray shorts, and removed her skirt.

The fuel gauge showed less than a quarter of a tank. She'd better stop for gas on her way back from seeing Grandma. Her visit with Trixie had put her behind schedule and she didn't want to arrive just as her grandmother was sitting down to eat.

Grandma Leofanti lived halfway between Scumble River and the neighboring town of Brooklyn. Skye's Uncle Dante, her parents, and her Aunt Mona all lived along the same road—separated only by acres of corn and beans. They could all see one another's houses when the crops weren't mature.

Heading north, then turning east, she spotted the remains of the original Leofanti farmhouse, which had been leveled in the tornado of 1921. The only thing left was the building's chimney, which rose out of the field like the stack of a ship sailing on a sea of corn. A few minutes later she passed her relatives' farms. No one was in the front yards and all the garage doors were closed.

As Skye pulled into her grandmother's driveway, she noticed a large group of hawks circling the isolated farmhouse, braiding the breeze with their feathered wings. She frowned. That was weird. She didn't remember ever seeing more than a single hawk at a time before. A shiver ran down her spine and she was glad to emerge from the car's icy interior into the heat of the June afternoon.

The white clapboard house was situated about a quarter of a mile back from the road, surrounded on three sides by fields. It was small by modern standards and Skye often wondered how her mother, two younger sisters, and a brother had managed to live there without killing each other.

She parked in her usual spot beside the garage, and as she crossed the concrete apron, her grandmother's cat, Bingo, paced anxiously near the front door of the house. Bingo was a beautiful blue-cream tabby.

Skye bent and scooped him into her arms. "What are you doing here? You know you aren't allowed outside. Did you get away from Mrs. Jankowski?"

Bingo blinked his golden eyes and yawned. Hoisting the cat up to her shoulder with her left hand, Skye grabbed the knob and pulled with her right, only to stumble backward when the door wouldn't open. That was odd. First Bingo was outside, and now the door was locked. Grandma hadn't locked her doors since she'd stopped leaving the house.

The key was kept on a nail hanging on a nearby window frame. Skye used it to open the door and replaced it before going inside. The entryway was painted a dark green, with worn gray linoleum. Its dankness reminded Skye of a cave. Straight ahead, five stairs led up to the rest of the house.

She called out as she climbed the steps into the kitchen, "Mrs. Jankowski, it's Skye."

There was no answer. The kitchen light was off and the stove empty. She set Bingo down. He immediately ran to his water bowl and hunched down for a long drink.

What in the heck was going on? Her grandmother liked to eat at four and it was already ten to. And where was Mrs. Jankowski?

The dining room was empty and the door to the bathroom was open, so she could see that no one was inside. Skye peeked into Mrs. Jankowski's room. The bed was made and the dresser top was clear.

"Yoo hoo, anyone here?" Skye's voice quavered. Had something happened to her grandmother? The only reason she left the house was to go to the doctor. Where was Mrs. Jankowski?

The living room was empty. Grandma's chair was placed against the wall, squared with the empty eye of the television set. Beside it, her knitting bag was partially open with needles sticking out the top. Pink, blue, and yellow yarn seeped over the edges, indicating that Grandma was working on another baby afghan.

Taking a deep breath, Skye forced herself to walk toward

her grandmother's bedroom. Other than the screened front porch, it was the only place she hadn't looked.

The door was closed. She knocked. "Grandma, are you okay? It's Skye."

No answer. The knob turned easily under her hand, but the door squeaked loudly as she pushed it open. At first she couldn't see because the blinds were drawn and the room was completely dark. Skye fumbled for the light switch.

Grandma Leofanti lay unmoving in the bed, the white chenille spread pulled over her face. The only thing visible was a cloud of snow white curls. At five feet tall and ninety pounds, she didn't take up much space on the double bed.

"Grandma!" Frightened, Skye stepped closer and pulled the counterpane down to her grandmother's chest. Who had put the cover over her head? Antonia Leofanti was claustrophobic and couldn't abide anything covering her face. She wouldn't even wear a dress that had to be put on over her head.

Skye's sense of fear grew. Putting her hand on the old woman's shoulder, she gently shook her.

Antonia was unresponsive. Skye felt for a pulse, and when she couldn't feel one, laid her head on her grandmother's chest, searching for a heartbeat. Nothing. Throwing the bedclothes all the way back she started CPR, ignoring the fact that her grandmother's body felt cold and stiff.

Oh, please Grandma, it's not your time. You haven't told me the rest of your story yet.

She paused. The CPR wasn't having any effect, but she bent to try again. *The doctor just told us that there was nothing wrong with you physically, that you could live to a hundred. Come on, he gave you twenty more years.*

There still was no response and drawing a ragged breath, Skye conceded defeat. She sat on the floor, laid her head on the bed, and sobbed.